PAT
CADIGAN: DERVISH
IS DIGITAL

Also by Pat Cadigan

Novels

Synners

Fools

Mindplayers

Tea from an Empty Cup

Short Story Collections

Patterns

Home by the Sea

Dirty Work

Letters from Home
(with Karen Jay Fowler and Pat Murphy)

Non-Fiction

The Making of Lost in Space

The Resurrection of the Mummy

Young Adult

Avatars

PAT CADIGAN: DERVISH IS DIGITAL

TOR®

A TOM DOHERTY ASSOCIATES BOOK
NEW YORK

DERVISH IS DIGITAL

Copyright © 2000 by Pat Cadigan

This book is printed on acid-free paper.

First published in Great Britain by Macmillan, an imprint of Macmillan Publishers Ltd.

A Tor Book
Published by Tom Doherty Associates, LLC
175 Fifth Avenue
New York, NY 10010

www.tor.com

Tor® is a registered trademark of Tom Doherty Associates, LLC.

ISBN 0-312-85377-7 (hc)
ISBN 0-312-87656-4 (pbk)

First Tor Hardcover Edition: July 2001
First Tor Trade Paperback Edition: July 2002

Printed in the United States of America

0 9 8 7 6 5 4 3 2 1

For Mic Cheetham,

Konstantin's best friend

Human being *extraordinaire*,

Role model, defender of the faith

Not to mention timeless beauty

With admiration and love.

Thank You:

Ellen Datlow, Gardner Dozois and Susan Casper, Merrilee Heifetz (tomorrow's agent today), John and Judith Clute, Oisin Murphy-Lawless, Sweet Potato Queen Jeannie Hund, Lisa Tallarico-Robertson, and Kathy Griffin (I still can't believe it was *twins*), Pawel Frelik, and the Indispensable Friday Lunch Gang, including but not necessarily limited to Paul McAuley, Kim Newman, Russ Schechter, Jon Courtney Grimwood, not to mention the occasional Barry Forshaw.

A round of applause to gamesmaster and debonair man about town Bob Fenner, whom I would like a lot even if he weren't the son I love, and bouquets to my mother Helen S. Kearney for her encouragement, patience, and understanding. And cooking.

Big thanks to inhouse good guy Jael Denny, for making our home an even more pleasant place to be.

Beth Meacham and Peter Lavery are two of the best editors on the planet—boy, did I get lucky.

A very special thank you to our good friend Kypros, and to all our friends at Haringey Cars, for looking after my mother so well, and taking us everywhere we need to go.

And big thanks to Chris Fowler, muse, confidant, soulmate, other half, and the love of my life. (You know, I always did like you.)

1

Sitting on the fake leather chair in the cheesy hotel room, Konstantin thought, *This will be a* very *serious weapon.*

"Now, *this*," said the slim, angular woman sitting on the bed, "*this* is a *very* serious weapon." Konstantin could see that she was a very serious arms dealer, meticulously well dressed, the tasteful, classic lines of her jacket and pleated skirt suggesting a high-ranking officer of a yacht club that would not, for one moment, consider admitting Konstantin or anyone like her. Especially not in *those* leggings with *that* tunic. The one detail that said otherwise, the detail you had to watch for so you could tell the difference between the president of the yacht club membership committee and a very serious arms dealer, was the little finger on her left hand. It was artificial, stainless steel with a brushed surface and a rectangular-cut sapphire where the nail would have been. That was as close as she came to wearing jewelry—no earrings, necklaces, bracelets, rings, studs, or pins. The stainless-steel finger seemed to impart even more grace to her gestures as she caressed the weapon lying across her thighs in a way that made Konstantin think of game-show prizes you couldn't possibly win.

The weapon itself looked like a cross between a micro-missile launcher with onboard laser targeting and a giant hypodermic syringe, also with onboard laser targeting, but designed by some fetishist psycho who insisted every line on the thing have a curve so full as to be practically lascivious. No question that it was deadlier than average—you could tell by the shine as well as the curves. The deadlier the weapon, the higher the shine, and this one could have been made out of blue-black chrome. As if it had been produced for a specific catalog entry: *This year's look is all full curves and hot shine— and don't forget that ammo!* Probably the only way it could have been more lethal would have been if it had simultaneously killed both shooter and target. Doré Konstantin had seen stranger things. "What's it do?" she asked.

"What's it *do*?" The woman tilted her head, letting the shoulder-length blue-black hair fall to one side like a curtain. The cool light blue of her eyes matched the blue tones in both her hair and the weapon, Konstantin realized. *Don't just arm yourself—accessorize!* Konstantin swallowed hard, ordering herself not to corpse unless she wanted to be one. Weapons dealers weren't renowned for their great sense of humor. "It looks good and it kills shit."

"What kind of shit?"

"*All* kinds of shit." The woman's face was so narrow that her smile was almost V-shaped. "Your choice. Your weapon, your shit. Any shit you want to shoot, you shoot." She lifted the weapon up and held it out to Konstantin. "Go ahead. Touch it. You know you want to. It's light but solid."

"I can see that," Konstantin said, keeping her hands to herself.

"Light. But *solid*," the woman repeated carefully, as if she thought Konstantin might find this hard to remember. "If you want to carry something heavy, pick up a brick. You want to get the job done—" She balanced the weapon on two fingers. "Get real."

Konstantin felt her amusement souring to boredom. Did they all go to some kind of school, these people, that taught them the same kind of sales patter, facial expressions, mannerisms? All the arms dealers she'd seen this week seemed to have been stamped from the same mold. If she got any more bored, she would start confusing them with each other. Maybe they had to take a seminar before they were allowed to deal weapons. *Angularity and Specularity: Twin Keys to Success in the Arms Trade.*

Her ex would have told her she was doing *it* again, although exactly which *it* that would be—oversimplifying, ridiculing, avoidance, or something else she couldn't remember at the moment—it was hard to say. Maybe, Konstantin thought, she could take her pick and be glad of the choice.

"I'm not keeping you awake, am I?" The dealer's amused tone had a sharpness to it and Konstantin knew she'd have to straighten up and keep her focus or plead a migraine and flash on out of there, queering the deal for good. Arms dealers weren't much for the old not-now-I've-got-a-killer-migraine routine. She was about to say something neutral when the woman suddenly grinned and launched the weapon at her as if she were playing volleyball.

Konstantin caught the weapon in mid-air. It was like catching an unexpectedly sturdy soap bubble. *People are always throwing things at me,* she thought. *Why are people always throwing things at me?*

"Nice and light, right?" the woman said. "But substantial. Go ahead. Handle it. Feel it. Feel it all over."

Konstantin went ahead and did just that, fingering the weapon as thoroughly as any weapons fetishist would have, focusing her gaze on the shiny, lethal lines and curves. She wanted to hurry, to get it over with so she could flash out of this highly seedy hotel room. But fetishists generally *liked* highly seedy hotel rooms, and they *didn't* like hurrying. The worst part, she thought as she watched her fingers move along the trigger before going onto the stock, was that she was beginning to understand the fetishist point of view.

"Hot, isn't it?" the dealer purred. "Hot as I told you."

"The very furnace of cool," said Konstantin, and winced inwardly, wondering where the hell *that* had come from. On the edge of her vision, she saw the dealer frown for a moment as she tried to figure it out.

"Well, obviously you're a connoisseur," she said at last.

"Thank you," Konstantin answered, dismayed by the purr in her own voice. *Caught between the absurd and the banal,* she thought. *Behold, I am the epitome of the human condition.* Before she could come out with any more conversational gems, she found the thing she had actually been searching for, etched into the outside flat of the stock, near the end. "Well, well, well." She tapped the stock with one finger.

"Put it to your shoulder," said the dealer. "It'll feel like it grew there. I'm telling you, a weapon like that can get you on TV."

"For what?" Konstantin said. "Shopping at the same hyper-mart as Wile E. Coyote?"

Now the dealer was offended. "That does *not* say Acme."

"Might as well," Konstantin told her loftily. "Next, I suppose you're going to try to sell me a drop-box address in a town called Springfield and sign me up with an answering service on the 555 exchange." Konstantin tapped the logo with an impatient finger again. "Even a *virgin* would know this is pure fiction. 'LockNLoad, RockNRoll'? You can say that with a straight face? Only some slave-waged, tin-eared, moonlighting greeting-card copywriter would come up with something like that. Looks good, kills shit—what else is new? *Everything* looks good and kills shit." She tossed the weapon back at the woman and made as if to gather herself up and leave.

"Come on, pal," the woman said, hefting the weapon and caressing it. "Where do you think you are, Malaysia? This weapon looks *better* than good. You know it. I know you know it. You want to quibble about a *trademark*? What are you really after, a superior weapon or a brand name?"

Konstantin did her best to look inscrutable. "Do you really have to ask?"

The woman put the weapon aside, folded her arms and stared hard at Konstantin. They sat like that for a while, Konstantin knowing that the woman was as aware of the time clicking away as she was. *This is my life*, Konstantin thought, *watching other people being conscious of their time passing*.

"You think you can wait me out, do you?" the woman said finally.

"I know I can," Konstantin told her, "but only for so long. I have to compensate for the time like anyone else would, though, so the price goes down as the clock goes 'round. When we get to zero, I flash outa here and leave you to it."

"But then it was all for nothing. What good does that do you or anyone else?"

"It's not *my* nothing, it's *your* nothing."

The woman's wary expression made her face look even narrower. "You've got a key to the city? Is that it? Or someone else's key to the city?"

Konstantin made a movement that could have been taken for yes, no, or anything in between.

"Of course, everybody lies about that," the woman added, confidence creeping back into her voice.

"Everybody lies about everything," said Konstantin carelessly. "Even when they're telling the truth."

The woman laughed at her. "Just get your degree in media studies, did you? Semi-idiotics, maybe?"

Konstantin got up. "I don't bother waiting out anyone who

bores me." She moved toward the door, slowly enough so that the woman could reach out and grab her forearm. The thing was, Konstantin thought, feeling the hand close on her, the woman knew she was moving slowly enough to be stopped, and she could see by the woman's expression that the woman knew that *she* knew. Nonetheless, neither of them would drop the charade, under any circumstances. *Violate not the kayfabe, shall be the whole of the law.*

"Nice muscles," the woman said, giving Konstantin's arm a squeeze. "You must work out a lot. *Do* you have a key to the city? Yes or no."

Konstantin disengaged the woman's hand with a practiced easy twist. "If I say yes, I'm lying. If I say no, I'm lying. What can you do?"

"I can ask to see it."

"You can. And I can say no."

The woman nodded, her hair swinging back and forth flirtatiously. "Well, I'm open to suggestions."

"And I've made my suggestions. If the best you can do is a second-rate Acme trademark—"

"All right, all right, all right." The woman picked up the weapon, showed the stock where the brand name was, and peeled it off. Underneath, it said Smith & Wesson. She flipped the weapon around expertly, made several more adjustments too quickly for Konstantin's eye to follow, and then offered it again. Konstantin took it from her, impressed. It looked different now. Konstantin's silent pop-up reference verified the authenticity.

"You got one of these inside every Acme, like a prize?" Konstantin asked.

The woman smiled back at her. "If you have the right source-codes, you can put anything inside of anything else. Like a prize. Or a booby-trap. So now you got a weapon four times as expensive as it was, and not quite as good. Happy?"

"You *bet*," Konstantin said, shocked at the intensity of the lascivious note in her voice. Her hands traveled over the weapon again. It was indeed a pure S&W product, a perfect reproduction of a prototype built under a military contract and still in development. And, according to the pop-up, supposedly still classified. Somebody, either S&W or the military, had sprung a leak.

Konstantin raised the weapon to her shoulder and aimed at a stain high on the far wall. "This feels like it grew into my shoulder, too. Why didn't you show me this right off?"

The woman leaned back on her hands and crossed her long legs, still flirting. "Because the design you had first is superior."

"You really think so?"

"I *know* so. Because it was *my* design." The woman nodded, her smile turning sour. "Yeah, that's right, I'm the 'slave-waged, tin-eared, moonlighting greeting-card copywriter' who thought up 'LockNLoad, RockNRoll.' Maybe I got a tin ear for brand names, but I'm the best damned weapons designer there is. You give me fifteen minutes with any weapon, any weapon you can think of, and I can make you a better one."

Konstantin shrugged. "*I* wouldn't know, *I'm* not an expert. I just want the right brand of weapon that looks good and kills shit."

"What if I put the S&W trademark on the better weapon?" suggested the woman. "It'll still cost you, since you want to buy the logo, not the real thing."

"No," Konstantin said firmly. "I pay for S&W, I *get* S&W."

"Crap. What the *fuck* do you want S&W for when I just showed you a superior weapon? What is it with them, no matter how shitty they are, people got this brand-loyalty dogma. The up-and-coming armourer these days is just fucked over before you even get out to the drawing board."

"That's what you are—an armourer?"

"Yeah, that's exactly what I am," the woman said, sitting up straight and forgetting to flirt. "I spent a *hell* of a lot of time paying my dues on target ranges and in themelands. So, then I *finally* get an appointment with a really big supplier, and they decide they'll go with the goliath just because S&W can churn the stuff out with cookie-cutters." Her hands had balled into white-knuckled fists. "Because they say individual craftsmanship is just too slow. You believe *that? Too slow.* So there's a hot flash for artisans everywhere—doesn't matter how brilliant you are, in the end you're just *too slow.*" She stood up and snatched the weapon away form Konstantin. "I'd tell you how fucking lousy that is, but it wouldn't mean shit to you."

Looking into that fierce, narrow face, Konstantin had the sudden sensation of seeing all the way through the woman to the angry real person manipulating the image from someplace far removed from sleazy hotel rooms and the intrigues of glamorous arms dealers or anything exotic, exciting or significant. A weapons designer for jaded gamesters, who had thought the high demand for hot weaponry among the aficionados would mean work that was not just steady but demanding as well, something that would call for imagination, for innovation, for an inventiveness that would surpass the mere need to kill. And instead, the jaded gamesters and cloyed chimeras took a quick look at her offering and turned up their virtual noses, saying *Is that all?* and *That the best you got?* and *Where's the designer label?*

"I can see it makes you upset," Konstantin said, "for real."

"Oh, yeah. Damn *right* for real. This shit gets real real, real fast." The woman began to take the weapon apart, thrusting the pieces into a padded container shaped like a violin case.

Konstantin had to suppress a smile at the *hommage*. It was unlikely that a real customer would catch the reference to old gangster dramas. "I might as well go back to making broadswords and battle-axes for the sad bastards at Renaissance Festivals."

"I *like* Renaissance Festivals," Konstantin said, telling the truth with impunity.

"You *would*. Maybe that's where you oughta be, in somebody's lower forty, talkin' trash to varlets."

"You're not gonna do business with me?"

"Can't sneak one past you, can I?" The woman slammed the lid of the violin case down and latched it. "I'm goin' home, see what's on TV. There's gotta be something better than this."

"A second ago, you were fussing about it all being for nothing. Now you don't even want to see if I have anything you want," said Konstantin in her most innocently reasonable voice. "I'm just having trouble keeping up with the way the wind's blowing around here is all."

The woman paused and looked at her tiredly. "Do you or do you not have a key to the city?"

Konstantin produced a thick portfolio about the size of a box of her ex's favorite chocolates. "This is my life's savings. You could probably make a key out of what I've got here, or damn near. Or trade it for something almost as good."

The woman straightened up, the light blue eyes cloudy with skepticism. "Even a virgin would know you weren't offering me the whole thing." Pause. "Right?"

"Well." Konstantin looked sheepish. "I thought we could talk about what you might be interested in for the S&W. I got all kinds of stuff. *All* kinds."

The woman's gaze traveled from the violin case on the bed to the portfolio. It was a gorgeous portfolio, deep blood-colored leather with feathery designs hand-tooled all over it. Konstantin had created it herself. "And now we come to that old billion Euro, all-singing, all-dancing, all-season question," she said, hands on her hips. "Are you a cop?"

Konstantin sighed. "If I say yes, I'm lying. If I say no, I'm lying. It's so hard to give anyone a straight answer in this joint. But I'll tell you what—you, I will cut a break. Yes, I'm a cop."

The woman looked genuinely taken aback by Konstantin's admission. It was probably the only answer she hadn't been expecting. "Yeah, well. What I thought all along." She sounded both superior and nervous at the same time. "Nobody, but *nobody* saves up *that* much."

"You're right," Konstantin said. "Most of this stuff I strong-armed off people in shakedowns, or in return for favors. Bribes, in other worlds. I mean, words." She grinned and the woman allowed her a smile. "All works just like it's supposed to. In the words of the prophet, 'It doesn't matter where it comes from, just as long as it comes.'"

They both laughed as the woman sat down again on the bed. "So," she said, one hand on the violin case. "What now? We fight? I gotta kill you to get out of here, or do you still want to deal?"

"I'm crooked, so we deal, of course." Konstantin shrugged. "Unless *you* want to die. You don't, do you?"

The woman shook her head. "I'm having too much fun. You?"

"Likewise," Konstantin said. "Too much fun."

"OK, we deal." The woman's smile was satisfied. "And then what? And before you answer, you should know that I'm speaking strictly hypothetical here. It's not a done deal us dealing. Not yet."

"We can talk about it."

The woman's expression went flat again. "We've already

done a *shitload* of talking, my sister. What kind of deal are you wanting to make? One weapon? Several stashes? Regular upgrades, personal service? I do it all."

"How about a partner?"

The flat expression held for a moment longer before the woman burst out laughing. "I don't do partners. There's matchmaking bureaus for that shit."

"I was thinking of you and me," Konstantin said. "Business. Nothing personal."

"Yeah? Well, nothing personal here, either, but I'm not allowed to take on partners."

"Not allowed? I thought you were self-employed."

"You catch on quick."

Konstantin pouted. "So then how does somebody who wants to be in the business go about getting a toehold?"

"Dunno," the woman said brightly. "You could try watching more TV." She picked up the violin case. "And now I really am outa time. So . . ." Her voice died away as her gaze fell on Konstantin's portfolio.

Konstantin held it out to her. "Not the sort of riches you can just flash away from, is it?"

"I must be in decline." The dealer sighed and put the violin case down. "What's the best stuff you got?"

"The *best* stuff?" Konstantin turned a page. "You think *one* S&W is worth my *best* stuff?"

"All right, show me the best stuff you could give me for it," the woman snapped. "And don't waste any more of my valuable time, either."

"You mean your overpriced time," said Konstantin, leafing through the portfolio to one of her more prominent bookmarks. "How about this?" she said, peeling a season pass for global rapid transit off a page. "Look good?"

"Looks like a *start*." The woman accepted it so that it dangled by a corner from her stainless-steel finger. "Got anything that looks good with it?"

"Like what?" asked Konstantin. "A year's supply of turtle wax?"

"My turtle is shiny enough. I was thinking of some passwords good for fuel, coin of the realm, something like that. Maybe a step-up converter."

"A step-up converter? *I* should be asking *you* for that," Konstantin laughed. "Here, this is as good as it's gonna get today." She peeled a half-price coupon off another page and held it out. "Half-price online anywhere."

The woman frowned over it for a few moments and then looked up at Konstantin. "Only three months?"

"Three *subjective* months," Konstantin corrected her. "Runs on *your* clock, not theirs."

"*Shit*," the woman exclaimed in admiration. "How'd you get the coding for that?"

"Custom job," Konstantin said carelessly, buffing the cover of the portfolio with her sleeve. "There's no code I can't renoodle."

"Well, ain't *you* a caution." The woman gave her a long, considering stare. "That kind of talent, seems to me you don't have to bother being a cop. Even a crooked one."

"Crooked cops get all the best codes to renoodle. Does this mean you're taking it?"

"You see? I never could put one over on you." The woman tapped the violin case. "Want me to reassemble it?"

"Are there instructions?"

"Sure. Nothing a crooked cop qualified in code would have trouble understanding. I just thought I'd save you some time."

"Considerate of you, but I want to get acquainted with it before I go out lookin' good and killin' shit." Konstantin watched as the woman stuck the pass and the coupon to a couple of empty spaces in a folding wallet. Her pop-up assured her that the extra codes in the pass and the coupon were digging in undetected. "Bye now."

"Yeah," said the woman, looking troubled and making no move to leave.

"What's the matter?" Konstantin asked uneasily. "You got a bad itch or something?"

The woman sighed. "I really *must* be in decline. Where's my brain? I should have held out for a personal transit stop."

Konstantin just managed not to sigh with relief. "I heard about this one blowfish put up one of those in a room like this," she said. "You know what happened?"

"What?" asked the woman warily.

"Great big old eagle flies in the window, plucks our hero up in its claws, flies out again. But the code's faulty and the bird lets go too soon." Konstantin nodded solemnly at the dealer's distressed expression. AR was a wealth of scare stories. "Another one where the code was faulty, a subway car pulls up out of nowhere. The blowfish gets in, subway car turns into a giant boa constrictor. The blowfish goes nuts with the claustrophobia. Waste of time, valuable, overpriced or any other kind." Konstantin laughed a little. "If you really want to wish for something, wish for a decoy time sink."

"Now, that's *gotta* be an urban legend, the decoy time sink," said the woman, tucking away her wallet. "Because if it was real, one of us woulda come across it by now." Pause. "Right?"

Konstantin made a vague gesture. "If I ever do, I'll look you up."

Another pause, just long enough for Konstantin to know she didn't believe that for a moment. "Likewise."

Konstantin watched her fade out, and then opened the violin case. All the pieces were still tucked away neatly inside, no shell-game today. The S&W logo was still on the stock. Her pop-up went into a frenzy, confirming the authenticity of each part.

"Item acquired and verified," she said, closing it up and sending it into her inventory. "Next case."

"Down these mean casino aisles," said the cyborg to Konstantin as they walked through the gambling palace, "something, something go. Or is it go something something?" He was a patch-work cyborg, very leading-bleeding edge these days. His name was Darwin. Konstantin had traded her street-life outfit for shiny pastel plastic and a nondescript painted-lady face. She might have stood out among the far more ornamented crowds in the glitter and sparkle of the casino, except she was sure that she was invisible in the shine.

Konstantin paused at a roulette table where everything was so jeweled she couldn't tell the wagers from the wagering board they rested on. She wondered if any of the equally bedizened blowfish clustered around the table could. The croupier was an even more bejeweled demon of a kind she hadn't seen before, but that didn't mean anything. The Hong Kong mound added a multitude of demons and kicked out others every day. It would have been impossible for even a scholar in the classics to keep up with, and Konstantin's knowledge was more on the mahjong level. This was one of the lower-middle layers of the HK mound, where the climate was controlled as strictly as the gambling and there was never any raw skyspace to interfere with the permanent evening sky simulation.

That wasn't as hard on the nerves as the casino sprawl itself, where one gaming joint melted into another without either a mark or a pause. *The revel without a pause*, Konstantin thought. She'd heard that hardened Vegas veterans had been found, within an hour of arrival, curled up in the foetal position under craps tables, shaking and crying and hemorrhaging money from every orifice. It was the sort of story Konstantin had been tempted to dismiss as clever PR disguised as an urban legend. Now, besieged by glitter—blitzed by the glitz, so to speak—the idea of someone melting down under the onslaught didn't seem so far-fetched. Withstanding this kind of sensory overload took either nerves of stainless steel or really good drugs, and the former seldom came without the help of the latter.

She turned to Darwin and waited for him to offer her a dose. Instead, he tugged at her arm, pulling her away from the roulette table, toward something bright. Not that it wasn't all bright, everything around her, but this was even brighter. Probably just some game of chance trying to get their attention, Konstantin thought, feeling the first touches of ennui at the edge of her mind.

Abruptly, the brightness flared into a blinding explosion of light, soundless but so intense that Konstantin's ears rang and she lost her balance. Some moments later she found herself blinking up at Darwin's face; she was bent backwards in the crook of his arm as if they'd been dancing.

"All right now?" Darwin asked cheerfully.

"Paparazzi?" guessed Konstantin, righting herself clumsily and pushing away his hands. They didn't feel as metallic as they looked. She didn't like that; the trainer had told her that illusions you couldn't trust implied more serious treachery to come, but Konstantin's objections were based on a dislike of literally mixed literal metaphors.

The brightness had died down to a more tolerable level and she saw they were standing on a promontory overlooking a lake of fire. Automatically, she took two steps back, raising a hand to shield her face, but there was no heat at all.

A sort of demarcation between this casino and another just

beyond? Konstantin adjusted the shading feature in her vision and the lake of fire became a shimmering pool of opals.

"Doesn't this ever become a feast too far?" Konstantin asked the cyborg. As if in response to a keyword (probably *feast*, Konstantin thought), two people in chef drag passed in front of them, walking over the lake in midair on a bridge that appeared under their feet at each step and disappeared behind. They were carrying a platter with the most enormous roast duck she had ever seen. Their puffy white hats and aprons advised her where she could enjoy a similar treat, in any of several branches worldwide.

"What do you mean?" Darwin asked her, looking longingly after the duck. She wouldn't have thought anyone with a lower jaw made of platinum would be all that interested in eating. Maybe it had just been a long time since breakfast.

"I mean, don't you get *just* a wee bit tired of jewel-bedecked this-and-that?"

"I hear the Vatican makes this place look poverty-stricken, but they won't let any civilians in, so I can't say for sure—"

"A big strong cyborg like you can't hack into the Vatican?" Konstantin was surprised. "I'd have thought you'd have done that so often by now that the idea bored you."

The right hemisphere of Darwin's brain, visible through the transparent half of his skull, showed a pinker undertone in the grey matter. "I didn't say I *couldn't*, I'm just not posing for mugshots this year. Besides, I'm not Catholic. I don't even bother to watch it on TV. What we got here, this is the *big* leagues. Mean aisles in mean casinos. Beggars, trash, dirt, it's all been abolished. They got a very serious dictatorship running things here."

"In the whole mound, or just this level?"

Darwin spread his mismatched fingers. "A few levels both ways. And I never knew any dictatorship that wasn't dying to expand its horizons. They brainwash people. It's easy in a place like this. After a few hours here, you'd believe anything, anyway."

"But if people do it voluntarily—" Konstantin shrugged, watching as creatures who might have been humans crossbred with jeweled dolphins swam through the opal lake, cheered on by groups now gathered at either side. It didn't seem to be a race but Konstantin was sure they were betting on something. "And you know it's gotta be voluntary, so it isn't against the law."

"Who says it's *always* voluntary?"

"Look, they come here knowing what kind of place it is. It'd be hard not to know. It's advertised heavily enough and you can't turn around without seeing a warning sticker on your way in. People put themselves through it so they can say they survived it. It sounds cool to have done it, and you're the envy of everyone. My Mom got brainwashed in lowdown Hong Kong and all I got was this lousy Mickey Mao holo."

Darwin eyed her as if from a great height—one brown, organic eye, one glowing green LED that briefly flashed the local time at her. It was later than she'd realized, but there was no way she'd be able to hurry Darwin. "They *don't* know," he insisted. "They *think* they know, just because they can see it on TV. They *think* it's like an amusement park ride or something, but they're wrong. The after-effects linger a lot longer than Hong Kong says. Some of them may never disappear."

"Never?" said Konstantin skeptically. "Look, I know it's hard to figure out why anyone would willingly live, even temporarily, under a totalitarian regime that would brainwash them. But it's a big world and there's no explaining what some people want. In the words of the prophet, the joint is jumping. If enough people weren't coming here, and watching it on TV besides, this place would be gone, turned into something else—

sex playground, sewing circle, you name it. Hey, can we walk over this on one of those visible/invisible bridges, like the chefs?"

Darwin nodded and she strode out from the promontory into the space above the pool of opals, enjoying the feel of the step-bridge coming into existence under her feet as she went. The steps gave a little as she put each foot on them, with a bouncy sensation that wasn't at all unpleasant. The cyborg stumbled after her gracelessly. "So you think it's all right to lure people to a place like this, get them all worked up—"

"No," Konstantin said, letting the steps lead her away from the lake of opals and up to another level. Darwin nearly fell trying to keep pace with her. She was only too happy to leave the opals behind; she'd begun to feel slightly hypnotized. Now she was walking down a wide aisle/boulevard lined with card games.

The tables, all at different heights, were shaped like calla lilies or lotuses. She wasn't sure how the players climbed up to their seats on the higher ones. Maybe they were airlifted.

"Truthfully, I don't. In the perfect world defined by what would be the Great and Powerful Me, places like this don't exist. But we're not on that planet, and it's not my job to close down legal businesses just because I don't approve." She shrugged. "If the ratings fall off, it'll get cancelled."

"But don't you *care*?" Darwin said melodramatically.

Konstantin winced. Not that one again. She moved a little faster.

"Come on, now, you care or you don't," Darwin said, chasing alongside her. "It doesn't have to be a perfect world for you to *care*."

You care or you don't. Where had she heard *that* one before? Don't answer that, she told herself. "OK, I'll admit it," she said wearily. "I don't care. I don't care about anything or anyone.

Not only do I *not* care, I loathe and despise anyone who does. I also hate the helpless and the innocent. Especially children. I think all children should be sold into slavery. I detest whales and seals. I spit on rhinos and white tigers. And that's nothing compared to how I feel about the world in general and everything in it. It's all one big abomination as far as I'm concerned. The biggest favor anyone could do us would be to perfect a doomsday device that would blow this ball of low-grade mud we live on into a billion, trillion—"

Four golden uniforms materialized around her and Darwin amid the tables. Everyone, those at the tables and those cruising along the aisle, ignored them. The golden uniforms were unadorned and unmarked, and something about the way the surfaces looked suggested to Konstantin that they were closer to liquid than solid. The heads were as featureless as the bodies, each one vaguely helmet-shaped, but without any visible openings for sight or speech. She couldn't see where they had come from; for all she knew, they had congealed from the glitter in the air.

"Papers," said the one directly in front of Konstantin. Something might have moved behind the featureless gold expanse at face level, or not. Konstantin thought of an antique photograph she'd seen in a museum, of a police officer from the previous century wearing mirrored glasses that reflected the scene directly in front of him, including the photographer. Who'd have thought that sort of thing would have caught on in Hong Kong, she thought as she produced a visitor's pass. She was not surprised to see it disappear into the flexible scoop that served as the thing's hand.

While the officer, or whatever it was supposed to be, considered her pass, she looked the mechanism over, careful to keep her posture unaggressive. All the major joints were perfect ball-and-socket arrangements, meant to allow movement in any direction. Good for law enforcement—in the event of physical confrontation, there would be no dislocations. Pity they couldn't manage that where she came from, she thought. Her own shoulders, never great, were giving her more trouble with every year.

It stretched its hand-scoop toward Darwin, who obligingly produced his own pass. She took a chance and looked at the other uniforms, feigning innocent curiosity. They were probably scanning her and Darwin as thoroughly as any ultra-expensive hospital scanner could. Most likely, they were just an extension of the one in front of her, and she doubted they had passed any information to it yet.

"What are you doing here?" the gold uniform in front of her asked.

"Playing?" Konstantin asked, hoping she had guessed right at what he wanted to hear. She sneaked a glance at Darwin. The problem with a cyborg was that the face wasn't meant to be especially expressive. No cues forthcoming.

"You have played nothing," the golden uniform said.

"We couldn't make our minds up," Konstantin said uneasily. "We were trying to decide."

"Your behavior does not conform to normal activity patterns," the uniform told her.

Konstantin wondered if it had been talking to her ex. Darwin nudged her. Finally, a reaction, she thought. Now, if only she knew what he was expecting her to do.

"Your conversation indicates that you are antisocial, and so could be intending to act in antisocial and disruptive ways," the golden uniform went on impassively. "This gives us due cause to take you into custody and decide if it will be necessary to regularize you, which is our right under global guidelines for local peacekeeping, crowd control, and law enforcement."

Konstantin looked at Darwin again. The time readout in his

digital eye had changed from numerals to *EEEE*. Big help, that boy. "And how would that be accomplished, this being regularized?" she asked, turning back to the uniform. Darwin nudged her again and she grabbed his wrist before he could pull away.

"We have a complete program of conditioning and behavior phasing, which will last as long as your stay within our borders. It is non-toxic, with no lasting side-effects, and will not interfere with any other activity in any other location."

The people at the gambling tables and the traffic in the aisles seemed to become more colorful and ornate, the jewels larger, stranger, more exotic, the movements stronger and the music more intense, but still everyone ignored them. More than that, Konstantin decided; it was more like they were no longer visible to anyone else.

The idea gave her a faint preview of panic and she looked around quickly, wondering if she could catch anyone in the act of sneaking a look at them, or even ignoring them intensely.

High up on one of the leaf perches around a calla lily gaming table, an Oriental guy in a painfully authentic tuxedo glanced briefly past the cards fanned out in his left hand, and met her gaze for a fraction of a fraction of a second.

Or had he? Suddenly, she wasn't so sure. He wasn't seeing her now, even though he hadn't turned all the way back to the dealer in the center of the flower-shaped table. Either that or he had especially fierce control over what he allowed to draw his gaze.

"Will this treatment have to be repeated if we decide to come back?" Konstantin asked smoothly. "Or does it kick in again automatically every time we hit this part of the mound?"

"There are no lasting side-effects," repeated the uniform.

"That doesn't answer my question," Konstantin said.

"Yes, it does," said the uniform, still without any emotion or expression whatsoever.

"No, it doesn't," Konstantin insisted, in spite of Darwin stepping on her foot. "I want to know if this is brainwashing that wears off out of context, or not. I think it's important."

"Brainwashing is too inexact a term, leading to misunderstanding and misrepresentation," the uniform said. Konstantin wasn't sure whether she was imagining that some smug had finally crept into its tone.

"We'll decline the regularization, thanks just the same," she said. "Just point us at the nearest exit—"

"Normally this would be the procedure," the uniform said. "But you have expressed negative and destructive emotions towards entities unable to defend themselves effectively against aggression. You may constitute a danger to those whom we are bound by law to protect."

"Not if we leave," said Darwin nervously.

"If we allow you to leave, we may be held responsible for any harm you may do in any neighboring sovereignty, state, city, or territory within easy access of this location. Records would show that monitoring had revealed you as an antisocial, aggressive, and potentially dangerous individual. Our failure to act could make us partially liable for any harm you may cause."

"But how will your regularizing us make the world a safer place?" Konstantin asked. "I thought you said there were no lasting side-effects."

"They didn't say anything about *after-effects*," Darwin whispered harshly.

"Our monitors can pick up whatever you say, at whatever volume," the uniform told Darwin. "We can also detect and decode pop-ups."

Darwin's befuddlement was obvious, in spite of his partly machine-made face.

"This is simply informational, for your benefit," the uniform went on, "meant to save you any wasted effort if you were thinking of trying to communicate covertly with each other."

Something began to take shape in the air around them, shimmering into existence like a reflection reappearing on the surface of a body of water as it calmed after a disturbance. Konstantin looked up again at the guy who might have made eye contact with her, but she could no longer see him through the thickening barrier coming into existence around her and Darwin. *Only* her and Darwin, she noticed; somehow the uniforms had either stepped away from them or simply been excluded. The stealth port-o-paddy-wagon, probably the latest thing in crowd control and regularization here in the ever evolving and still inscrutable Far East; perpetrators and would-be perpetrators would never see it coming. Binds invisibly with dust motes until turned loose by law enforcement—

Something caught her in the back of the knees and she sat down suddenly. Darwin was sitting on a bench across from her, titanium-hinged elbows on his organic thighs. Konstantin winced.

"Happy now?" Darwin asked her.

"At least they left the lights on," she said lamely. They both jerked as the box they were in accelerated forward.

"So, are you ready to have your brain washed, dried, and martinized?" Darwin asked her.

"Snap out of it," Konstantin told him. "We aren't even handcuffed. This wouldn't even raise a blip on a bondage meter, let alone false arrest—"

"Yeah?" Darwin sat back and folded his arms. "Try to get up."

Konstantin obeyed and discovered that someone had super-glued her butt to the bench. "OK," she said, "*now* we're getting somewhere." She moved her eyes in the requisite pattern and

PAT CADIGAN

the exit pop-up appeared on the right side of her visual field. "The exit pop-up's working."

"You mean, you can *see* it," Darwin said ominously. "Just try to use it."

She felt an uneasy chill as she blinked at the pop-up. It was followed by annoyance as she found herself standing in the first-stage exit lobby, amid the usual multitude of regular users entering or leaving AR.

"You *really* looking for the exit?" said a smooth voice close to her ear. "Or is what you *really* want the *way out*?"

Konstantin winced, drawing away from the voice. A disembodied mouth, several times larger than life-size, smiled oozily at her with exaggerated, lush lips. She made a gun out of her left hand and aimed at the mouth; it dodged the bright blue lightning bolt that leaped from her fingertip and blew her a string of heart-shaped bubble kisses. "Missed me, missed me, now you'll have to kiss me," it jeered. She fired again and, to her surprise, hit it this time, just at the extreme left-hand corner. The mouth zoomed away with a sound like a scalded weasel.

Stupid spam, she thought poisonously, and blinked her filter on so she would be invisible to any others, for the rest of this session at least. They were getting better at slipping through the filters, masquerading as personal or business communications or even legitimate sponsor ads. Annoying but not yet illegal. She looked around for Darwin, but no solid image of the cyborg appeared among the multitude of semi-ghosts moving around her. She whistled for him, first on the police-witness frequency and, when there was no answer, she started on the ten private ones he'd given her.

A message came back via pop-up on the seventh. *Callee is currently unable to answer your whistle personally, and left the following message for you: "You may never see the REAL me again."*

That assumes I saw the real you to begin with, Konstantin thought, amused. *Highly doubt that I did.* Nonetheless, she zapped him a get-out-free pass and waited to see if he'd use it to join her, not really expecting him to. She'd written him off as a crank (likely) or a disgruntled gambler (far more probable) who'd lost all his *stuff* in a game he'd known all along was crooked and was trying to swindle it back again. Konstantin had a filter for those, too, but a canny few always managed to bob and weave enough to get through to her. Most of them needed therapy than anything else and, for the thousandth time, she thanked the random forces in the universe that she was not a therapist.

Her pop-up gave her a polite reminder of how long she'd been in, and suggested she withdraw soon to avoid a headache or, in extreme cases, a seizure. Supremely annoyed now, Konstantin grabbed the pop-up and whited out the seizure bit. The commissioner's scare tactics bothered her a hell of a lot more than anything AR hot dogs like Darwin might.

"*You* have defaced official law-enforcement equipment," said a businesslike contralto.

"Really? My hand slipped." Konstantin was about to request departure when, through the speedy blur of the semi-ghosts transiting to and fro, she saw someone perfectly recognizable approaching her, which meant he had requested her frequency. It took her a moment to place him.

"Well, *you* look different on eye level than you do ten to twelve feet in the air playing blackjack," she said.

The man was Japanese-occidental and very, very annoyed. "What the hell did you think you were doing back there?"

"Back where?" she asked.

He shifted position, slipping one hand into his jacket pocket and coming out with a silver case. He clicked it open one-handed, selected a pure-white cigarette without offering her one, and put the case away. The cigarette lit itself; he drew on it and blew a stream of smoke over her head.

"Impressive," said Konstantin, meaning it. "Where'd you get it?"

He didn't answer. On impulse, Konstantin grabbed his face, pushing his cheeks together to purse his lips. He batted her arm away angrily and took a step back.

"That's not an animation," Konstantin said admiringly. "That's a real simulation. That is really, *really* good. It *really* is. *Really.*"

"You didn't answer my question," he snapped. "What the *hell* did you think you were doing back there?"

"Well, who the *hell* wants to know?" Konstantin asked pleasantly.

"You intruded into an investigation of practices in the lower Hong Kong mound."

Konstantin crossed her arms. "Excuse me if I interrupted the rhythm of your investigation. Sure it isn't more like a master's thesis or a news-porn feature story?"

"You fuckin' *American.*"

"Pardon?"

"Yeah, I thought so. It just figures. Only a fuckin' *American* goes stomping into any place, any time, anywhere, without a second thought as to who else might be at work." He blew another stream of smoke over her head. "I've been stationed in that casino for two Hong Kong months, gathering evidence as part of a major police investigation. Maybe the first of its kind in AR. For sure the largest."

Konstantin gestured to the semi-ghosts shifting and blurring around them. "I'd believe you, except for the obvious impediment. We're still in AR, and there's no truth in AR."

He took another drag on his cigarette and, to her surprise and revulsion, blew the smoke in her face this time. "After you decrypt that, give me a call."

She had felt nothing, of course, when the smoke had surrounded her head, but she could sense it sorting itself into an encrypted chunk in her inbox. "You guys watch too many old James Bond revivals on TV," she said.

The man paused with the cigarette halfway to his mouth. It hadn't shrunk at all. "What gives you that special insight?"

"Because Bruce Lee and Jackie Chan didn't smoke." She waved a hand in front of her face. "Officer ready to depart."

2

Konstantin was reclining fully in the hotchair, both hands holding onto her headmounted monitor. The lock had already disengaged and she wasted no time pulling the front open, letting in the sight of the acoustic ceiling squares in the large closet the department called her investigation booth. She braced herself for the moment when the ceiling would seem to rush toward her. Perceptions always warped under the influence of AR. Taliaferro had suggested this was because AR induced a serious rift between mind and body. Of course, Taliaferro had always been overly credible when it came to scare stories about AR. His initial response to the news of her reassignment had been to promise her a novena—whatever that was. But either she was getting really good at this or she was just having a better day than usual, because the ceiling appeared to come only half the usual distance before snapping back. If that was progress, she'd take it.

She worked the headmount off and sat up carefully before giving it a thorough inspection. *Your eyes may water excessively and you may find yourself drooling as well as sweating heavily,* the trainer had told her during her orientation sessions. *It's as if the body is protesting the simulation of activity by producing as much real activity as possible.* Konstantin had thought it was probably more like stress, but nobody liked stress any more as an explanation for anything—too one-size-fits-all so as to be uselessly vague for insurance forms.

The trainer was a hefty young guy named Tonic who had never called what he was doing providing shortcuts, hints, and cheat-codes for a fee. Konstantin had been given to understand that no one in Tonic's line of work called it anything but orientation, as few people who used the service wanted to admit, even to themselves, that they needed hints and cheat-codes. No cheat-codes, no stress? OK, *no habla*, as the kids were saying these days. She would use the things that weren't cheat-codes and afterwards wipe the non-stress sweat out of the headmount to prevent corrosion damage. If that happened, they'd stick her for repairs, and she couldn't afford that—this particular model of headmount cost the department more than she did. The front opening had jacked up the expense even more, but she had insisted on it, along with the panic-button program that would release the lock and allow her to bypass the protocols and open the headmount instantly. She hadn't really wanted the job as Chief Officer in charge of Techno-Crime, AR Division, but if she had to do it—and they'd made that part clear enough—she'd do it *her* way.

She peeled the hotsuit off herself by rolling it down from her neck, something that always reminded her of some old-fashioned stage drama that her ex had dragged her to, where an actress playing a nineteenth-century prostitute had removed her stockings by rolling them down the length of her legs. The playfully erotic qualities with which the actress had imbued that bit of business escaped Konstantin completely at the moment. But then, nineteenth-century stockings hadn't been lined with wires and sensors.

According to the advertisers, hotsuit wires and sensors were getting thinner and lighter all the time. Could have been, but Konstantin found they still left their mark on her. She examined her skin, debossed with patterns that had become so familiar she thought she could probably draw them in her sleep.

Her sore muscles impressed her more. She felt as if she'd overdone it at the gym after a long period of inactivity; it was the way she always felt after a session in AR. Tonic had given her an involved explanation having to do with tension, stimulation, involuntary movements, sense memory, and how some people's bodies took situations at face value.

Or, to make a long diagnosis short, he'd added, *you're what we in the profession call 'body credible.' It's all in your head, but your body won't accept that. Eventually, you'll build up a tolerance. You have to—everybody else does. Try stretching exercises. Better yet, take up yoga.*

Body credible—the body believing what the mind knew was false. No doubt next year, they would discover the kayfabe chromosome. But it would seem that her body wasn't *that* credible, she thought as she eased into one of the few yoga postures that didn't bring tears to her eyes, because so far there was no sign of this fabled tolerance that everybody else built up. Maybe her body had a mind of its own; maybe it figured that it was being cheated out of something, so it insisted on cramping her muscles.

As if in confirmation, her left foot seized up and she fell over onto the carpet, rubbing her instep and pushing her toes back hard. The cramp ebbed, renewed, ebbed again. She got up and limped around the room, trying to coax her foot back to normalcy.

So what had that been about, she wondered, dressing slowly and carefully, in case some other muscle decided to mutiny. What was that message—don't mess with the flesh? Muscular convulsions are transplanted headaches? If we are the sum of our parts, why don't they add up?

Or was that last thought something she'd seen spray-painted in glitter on the side of the diet clinic that Bruce

Ogada had urged everyone in the department to join? Everyone, but especially those whose movements tended to occur more often in AR than in whatever they were calling the real world these days—*common reality* and *consensual reality* were two other terms Konstantin was steadfastly refusing. Others included *mainstream reality, ground floor, home base,* and *purgatory.*

She managed one more yoga-style stretch and then finished dressing. The navy-blue uniform tunic felt a bit tighter across the shoulder blades, and the stretch waistband of her trousers seemed close to the limit. Great, she thought, stepping into her shoes and pausing while the inner soles remembered the contours of each foot. Maybe she could convince Ogada that her credible body was getting muscle-bound. *All that transcutaneous muscle stimulation, chief—it's making me bigger than Man-Mountain Gentian.* Ogada had dedicated himself to a crusade against preventable health problems in the work force, and obesity-related ailments were at the top of his list. Konstantin had been tempted to put on ten pounds just to test his patience. Taliaferro had suggested kiddingly that she hire herself out as a professional irritant, unaware that her ex had made the same suggestion a few days before moving out.

"Well? And? Yes?" Bruce Ogada rubbed his hands together as if he were trying to start a fire in midair over his desk.

Konstantin nodded. "Got the arms dealer dead to rights. She whipped it out and showed it to me, you can see it plain as anything on the archive footage. Blatant piracy, industrial espionage, theft of credit, aggravated mopery, and dopery."

Ogada stared at her, mystified.

"Sorry, private terms," she said. "I have to keep reminding

myself I'm doing important work, chasing down these brazen infringers of copyright and scuttling patent pirates on the high seas."

Ogada didn't take offense; Konstantin didn't think he could. "For years they couldn't get Scarface on criminal charges or racketeering. You know, Capone? Always gave the authorities the slip. But then they had an accountant go after him, and *then* they got him good. Clamped him for cheating on his taxes." He smiled as if he had just related one of his own personal triumphs. Konstantin had lost count of the number of times he'd told her this one. On the other hand, he wasn't playing Guess Your Weight with her, either.

"I know—criminal heirs of Scarface."

"If I've told you once, I've told you seven hundred times," Ogada said, nodding.

"Seven hundred and one, I think," Konstantin told him. "But really, who's counting?"

Ogada frowned at her like a disapproving father. "You're getting that unreal feeling again, aren't you?"

"'Fraid so," said Konstantin, feeling sheepish.

"Too bad. Shake it off. Go have a workout at the gym— personally, I think you could use it—or take a walk, talk to the shrink on call, whatever you need to do to feel real again. Take all the time you need. Up to an hour. Then clean up your archive footage and have it in my inbox so we can go over it with the DA."

Konstantin unrolled the slender cushioned mat she had been issued last year along with everyone else, during the mercifully brief transcendental-meditation revival. She slid it as far under her desk as it would go and stretched out. The ambient noise in the office worked for her the way ocean surf or rain worked for other people; she was out in a matter of moments.

It was generally understood that, if anyone asked, she was meditating.

She hadn't always slept so brazenly or, for that matter, so easily. In her youth, it was as if her motor had always been running with the idle set on high; *Insomnia*, she would say, *is my middle name*. Eventually, the buzz of excess energy began to fade as she grew older, but her best sleep had not started until after her ex had moved out.

No . . . no, that wasn't quite right, and she knew it. She was even admitting it to herself these days. She hadn't slept so well until her ex had moved out *and* she had made her first truly extended foray into Artificial Reality. AR. Known to the more credible, the stubbornly optimistic, and the socially doomed as *Alternative Reality*, a term she was avoiding as doggedly as *ground floor*.

The strange part for Konstantin was that there was no real connection between the two events. It had been nothing more than coincidence that her ex had chosen to move out on the day she had caught the call on the murdered kid in the AR parlor. Perhaps it had been knowing that there wouldn't be anyone at home from then on that had made her feel a little more dedicated to the job and, at the same time, a little more reckless than she would have been otherwise. Or maybe she'd have elected to investigate the crime by hunting the killer in AR, no matter what had happened that morning. She had no insight on that, even now that the case had been closed and the loose ends had been tied up or tucked away, and she couldn't think of anyone who would.

Meanwhile, time passed, life went on, and that strange Japanese woman continued in her bizarre non-sleep/non-coma/non-braindead state. Would she ever wake up or would she remain ... inert? Perhaps the exotic Joy Flower, currently resident in a correction facility that neither corrected nor facilitated much of anything, could have answered that. Or maybe not. The point was moot, since Joy Flower never said anything at all. Probably the wisest course, considering the cocktail of drugs that Flower had had visited on her via her Boyz. If the world continued without justice—and why not—Konstantin could foresee the time when Flower would eventually walk free, while poor Yuki Something-Or-Other persisted in the non-conscious state that the neurologists insisted wasn't exactly a coma. As the feeding and waste conduits performed their functions, her body continued to age and breathe on its own, the foetal curling that was typical of the comatose nowhere near as pronounced as it should have been. Brain activity was strange as well; something was happening in there, the doctors said, but it wasn't the sort of thing that manifested as the usual waves measured by an EEG.

Technically, Konstantin's only concern was how this affected the charges to be filed against Joy Flower; personally, she was completely bewildered, a condition she was becoming all too familiar with. Sometimes she thought the only thing in the world that she *could* understand was the graph Taliaferro had once drawn for her of a parabola approaching zero. *This,* he said, pointing to the line, *is our understanding. Of anything. Or, what the hell, everything. It approaches zero constantly without ever getting there, thus enabling us to understand less and less all the time. If it ever actually reached zero, there would be nothing left not to understand and the universe would be annihilated.* The fact that they had both been pretty annihilated themselves on some old-style, non-technical but very high-powered gin had probably contributed to Taliaferro's erudition and her ability to comprehend it. Nonetheless, comprehension had remained, even after she'd slept off everything else.

Ogada had said the biggest favor the non-coma woman could do any of them, including herself, was to die, if for no other reason than to allow them finally to clamp Flower to her murder. Konstantin would have agreed, but only if the murderer's sentence could have been the same period of time in the same inert state. This new streak of eye-for-eye-ism in Konstantin surprised her, though sometimes she thought she would have been surprised if she hadn't developed it after nearly a decade on the job.

And now the job had changed on her, right under feet while she'd thought she'd been standing on solid ground. Techno-Crime—what the *hell* was TechnoCrime?

Crime with a techno prefix, Celestine had suggested, smirking. Brilliant, yes—thank you so much. Celestine along with her partner DiPietro had been assigned to Konstantin's authority on an as-needed basis. Konstantin loaned them to auto-theft as often as possible.

Privately, however, she had to admit Celestine had had more of a point than she would ever openly acknowledge. Crime out here = crime in there, QED, you're welcome, next case. As near as Konstantin could tell, however, almost all the crime in question seemed to be copyright infringement, product piracy, industrial espionage, or what had once been called bunco—fraud and confidence games. The last of these was nearly impossible to prosecute, given the standing rule that nothing in AR constituted what the lawyers liked to call a legitimate contract.

Or, as the screens were obliged by law to remind you before each and every session in AR, nothing was true, everything was a lie, and all of it in billable time.

But—thank heaven—not *her* billable time. Your tax dollars at work, brothers and sisters and netizens of every shade between and among. They all expected a lot for their money, too, just like they always had. *Après VR, le déluge*—the complaints poured in until finally a portion of those precious tax dollars had had to be allocated for some administrative layers to filter real complaints from the chaff. Konstantin didn't know anything about the chaff and didn't want to.

Meanwhile, her request for a full crew had remained in a special sort of limbo where it looked as if it were being acted on, while its due date expired, requiring her to refile. As an administrative strategy, she had to admit it was brilliant—she was responsible for keeping an eye on the due date and refiling. After a while, most people gave up, figuring it was better to take a hint than press the point. To Konstantin's surprise, however, her request had been allowed a period much longer than usual before she would have to refile in order to ensure the request didn't lose its place and get shuffled to the bottom of the pile. It almost made her believe that Ogada, or the powers above him, actually took her seriously, even if experience told her it was more likely that they were hoping she'd get busy and forget all about it.

After all, giving her a full-time, fully trained crew would, in effect, be giving her a subdivision to lead, and that, in turn, would be a promotion. Not just any promotion but a very serious promotion, into the ranks of the decision-makers. At the lowest level, of course, but still—her parabola would start to approach Ogada's zero, so to speak, and *that* would mean he could no longer exercise his ability to be oblivious to her.

Or maybe she was being too hard on Ogada. God only knew what *his* parabola was approaching, or what it would annihilate if it got there.

Her thoughts turned, slowly and without any urgency, to

what the rest of the day might hold. Apart from going over the report with Ogada, she would probably review whatever complaints made it through to her desktop. For the millionth time, she wished Taliaferro could have been reassigned with her, but his claustrophobia had made him no-go. Arguing that he could function as her outside back-up cut no ice with Ogada. *You can't have someone who never goes in,* he'd said. *That would be like having a street cop who never went out. What kind of police work is that?*

It had been like resisting the straight line from God, but somehow she had managed to keep herself from giving him an answer. As it was, she already got away with plenty on the grounds of feeling unreal after a session in AR—unreal in the sense that she was unable to take anything very seriously for a certain period of time after coming out, until she could decompress. Early on, even she herself had thought it was a convenient excuse for undisciplined behavior bordering on insubordination. She could even hear how it might play out in court: *Your Honor, this officer was suffering from diminished capacity due to a case of the psychic bends.*

But the surprise had come when the police psychiatrist had produced a report confirming it as an actual syndrome, and recommending recovery time immediately after all sessions in AR. *Just as you would for any other undercover assignment,* the doctor had added, sealing the argument so airtight that even Ogada couldn't find a hole in it. So she got all the time she needed. Up to an hour.

The alarm on her watch was chiming politely when she felt a soft tap on the sole of her left foot, which immediately threatened to cramp again. "I know, I know," she said, using the sides of her desk to slide herself out from under, mat and all. DiPietro was standing over her looking amused, but then DiPietro didn't seem to have any other expressions. As if to counter his partner's excessively wide muttonchops, he had recently gone completely hairless, eyebrows and eyelashes included.

"I was meditating," Konstantin said, sitting up. "You're supposed to know that."

"I do know it," DiPietro said. "And when you lie on your back, we all know it. Ogada sent me down here to get you *immediamento*."

"He's supposed to know I'm meditating, too," said Konstantin as she pushed herself slowly to her feet. Maybe she *could* stand to lose a few kilos, she thought grumpily.

"He does," said the officer, offering her a hand she ignored. "But the DA's schedule doesn't know it. Oh, and by the way, the action's come through on your request for a crew."

Konstantin grunted. "Don't tell me—he woke me early so he can tell me they said no."

"No, they said yes. Actually, what they said was, they'd *already* said yes to begin with," DiPietro added. "You've got me and Celestine. When you're not loaning us to auto-theft. That's as good as it's going to get. Unquote."

Konstantin nodded, resigned. She should have known.

3

The DA was a hardbody named Harlowe Featherstonehaugh. Konstantin had met her before. She was very young and very tall, slightly over six feet, with a smooth short cap of hair the color of a thundercloud and the biggest biceps Konstantin had ever seen outside of a bodybuilding convention. And she'd really only seen that on television. Featherstonehaugh was another oddity of pronunciation like Taliaferro, who insisted on spelling his name one way and pronouncing it another—Featherstonehaugh came out as "fanshaw," for reasons only Featherstonehaugh and possibly God knew. Private joke, maybe—the DA's personal equivalent of mopery and dopery.

She found Featherstonehaugh appealing for the way she tended to loom over Ogada without realizing it. Today, Ogada had decided to handle that simply by giving the DA his chair while she looked at the footage of the weapons dealer Konstantin had taken. He was trying to loom over her, but the best he could manage was breathing down her neck.

"Solid work," Featherstonehaugh said approvingly, smiling at Konstantin cheerfully. "No trouble indicting on this. What else have you got?"

Konstantin frowned and looked at Ogada, who was gazing at her expectantly, and maybe a little evenly. "What else?" she said after a moment. "What else would there be?"

The DA sat back, ignoring the way Ogada's chair groaned

as she did. "Weren't you investigating some kind of brainwashing complaint in lowdown Hong Kong today, or was I misinformed?"

Konstantin shifted position, wishing she too could make a chair groan, or at least this one. "Well. How reliable do you think your informant is?"

Featherstonehaugh turned to look at Ogada as if he knew something, and then turned back to Konstantin, her friendly smile cooling on her broad, dark-brown face. "I only mention it because there was some talk on the grapevine about a Japanese law-enforcement officer being somewhat put out about an American technocrime investigator barging into an ongoing operation in one of the lowdown casinos."

"I can't admit to anything like that," Konstantin said, smiling back at her, "because you can't admit to anything in AR."

The DA stood up, transferring the copy of the footage into her briefcase office. "Well, be smart, detective, and don't admit to anything outside of AR either."

Konstantin had been planning to ring Taliaferro so she could tell him about the interlude in Ogada's office and ask him what he thought the DA had meant by her parting remark, but a freshly decrypted message was waiting in the inbox on her desktop. Probably a transcript from Ogada of what had just transpired—Ogada's insistence on backing up all forms of information made him a one-man data tsunami. But when she opened it, a multitude of calla lilies blossomed on the screen, turned into fireworks, and then into a shower of flower-petal confetti. Of course; her Japanese friend with the bad cigarette habit.

Greetings from low-down Hong Kong! If you can read this, you have been officially tagged by East/West Precinct! We don't know who you are yet, but we will the next time you enter our jurisdiction, so be sure to say hello!

"East/West tagged you?"

Konstantin jumped. Celestine was reading over her right shoulder while DiPietro was pretending not to read over her left. "You know them?"

"Only by reputation," Celestine said. "I'd probably know more if you didn't keep loaning us to auto-theft. More time for research."

"Then go do some research right now," Konstantin snapped at her. Celestine marched off obediently.

"This here," said DiPietro, tapping the lower left-hand corner of the screen, where a series of ideograms were flashing through a sequence Konstantin was barely able to discern as repetitive, "this here is a trawler."

"Wonderful," Konstantin said. "How do you turn it off?"

"You don't. Instead, we give it what it's asking for—information. We fill it full of junk mail. Hits capacity in half the time it would take if it was getting real information. Blows up real good."

Konstantin was impressed. "How real good?"

"Chain reaction follows a line back to the source via the trawler return path, burns up like a fuse. Hits the source like a thunderbolt from God. They'll be picking porn out of every blank space between bits from now till their next pay raise. I like to call it 'Tits for Bits.'"

"You sent *porn* to a Japanese law-enforcement agency?"

"Oh, not *just* porn. Feature-length videos on the complete range of life-insurance policies in the early twentieth century, Italian cooking for beginners, excerpts from *The Communist Manifesto*, plus any other ads we had lying around in the buffers. *This* time. We try to vary it so that they can't fingerprint us by our junk mail." DiPietro looked pleased with himself.

"There's never a shortage of porn to send out, but the *Manifesto* was my idea."

"You do this often?" Konstantin asked, several times looking from the screen to DiPietro and back again, wondering if she'd be able to tell when something blew up real good.

"Oh, yeah, all the time. People are always tagging each other, hoping they'll hit someone important or famous. Or maybe a cop. That'd be the Big Casino, tagging someone and having them turn out to be the cops. But I got the junk-mail idea from my grandmother. She used to tell me stories about this guy she knew, worked for one of those old oil companies— what was the name? Something like Shoal. The whole world was always trying to tag them, and this guy's job was, I swear to God, just to make up messages, encrypt them, and send them out steadily, all the time, without stopping. So anyone keeping track of the traffic patterns of going in and coming out would only see there was this constant buzz, like ambient noise. Guy went quietly nuts sitting at his desk there in Shoal Oil, or whatever it was. Sent out his entire autobiography, wrote complete novels that disappeared into the air." DiPietro let out a breath, looking nostalgic. "In her later years, Grandma came to believe that it had all just been floating around in the atmosphere, waiting for the right kind of receiver, which she also believed was her artificial heart. But that's another story."

Konstantin nodded. "Is that how your grandmother knew about him in the first place?"

"Oh, no," DiPietro said cheerfully. "He was one of her ex-husbands before she married my grandfather."

"Oh. Well, just don't tell me about *him* right now. I'm busy."

DiPietro looked surprised. "Who, Grandpa? God, why would I?"

*

TechnoCrime: What It Is, Why It's Different From Ordinary Crime, and Who's Going to Do Something About It.
   An Overview of Online Crime From the Beginning.
   Metaphysics, Mindgames, and Multiverses.

Konstantin paged through the screens of dense text at what she hoped was a plausible speed. The info dump had come from Ogada—research he thought she'd find useful in the good fight (unquote)—and he always attached a page-rate meter to make sure she read the stuff rather than skimming it at the speed of light and flushing it. Most of the stuff seemed to have come from seminars held at conferences she'd never heard of, probably for lawyers rather than law enforcement. In which case, she figured she could be excused for not understanding more than two words in five.

Abruptly, the text was replaced by the slightly sneering features of her recent Japanese acquaintance, making her jump. For a moment, she thought it was a real-time break-in but then the definition on the screen fuzzed in spots and she realized she was looking at a snip out of some surveillance footage. And not a very long snip at that—perhaps five seconds of a sneer about to happen, looping over and over to the point of absurdity.

The frame shrank on the screen then, and three stills appeared below it—a very old man, a sulky youth who might have been the man's grandson, and a boy about nine with the unmistakable grime and facial gang tattoos of a long-term street rat. All of them were Japanese; no doubt they were all her Japanese friend as well.

"This is the guy that tagged you," DiPietro said from behind her. "The only name we can get on him is Goku, and only for the main face there. Any of him look familiar?"

"I'd say we'd met," Konstantin said, smiling grimly at the screen with half her mouth, "but I'm not supposed to admit to anything today."

"OK, tomorrow, next week. No rush."

She flicked a finger at the street kid's image. "I don't like that."

DiPietro leaned in closer to the screen, frowning. "You don't like kids?"

"I don't like people who *pretend* to be kids. They're sneaky."

"*Everybody's* sneaky in AR," said DiPietro, sounding surprised.

Konstantin flicked the kid's picture again. "Yeah, but this is *too* sneaky. Shows a mind that's already too devious for its own good. Or anyone else's."

Now DiPietro was amused. "You know, not *everyone* who runs as a kid is looking to lure someone into a red-lust lounge for blackmail."

"Prove it," Konstantin said flatly.

"What, *now*?"

"Tomorrow, next week. No rush."

"Keep me off auto-theft and it could happen," DiPietro told her evenly, and walked away.

She enlarged the kid face and studied it, trying to remember if she'd ever seen it, even just in passing. Silly or not, she knew she'd never shake the feeling that there was something wrong with someone who affected a child's appearance in AR, even for purposes of undercover police work. Maybe especially for that.

No, make that definitely, she thought, contemplating the cherry tattoo on the kid's left temple. Three cherries attached at the stems: the old jackpot symbol, supposedly the antique gambling-machine symbol of a potential jackpot. *If* you got a certain number of them in a row, of course. How many had there been—three? Five? More?

So could that have meant the street gang would be arranged in cells of three? Or five, or however many? The number wasn't as important to Konstantin at the moment as simply knowing that at least one of the guy's aspects was literally networked up. She could send Celestine and DiPietro in to do the donkey work of finding at least one of his faces.

She wrote up a duty memo for them and then buzzed Taliaferro.

"I'm surprised they let you get away with this," she said, looking around the empty expanse of rooftop. "I thought you had medication."

"I do," said the big man sitting on the overstuffed cushion under the large patio umbrella. "But it's one of those periods when the condition isn't paying attention." Konstantin found she couldn't shake the impression of Alice's caterpillar on the mushroom with a hookah, in spite of the fact that the cushion didn't look like a mushroom, Taliaferro didn't look like a caterpillar, and he wasn't smoking anything.

He moved over and patted the space beside him. There was plenty of room; otherwise, she knew, her ex-partner wouldn't have made the gesture. Taliaferro's claustrophobia waxed and waned, responding well to medication at some times and almost not at all at others. Over the five years of their work partnership, Konstantin had become so accustomed to his headbugs that she hadn't noticed how much she'd been working around them until her reassignment. Under the circumstances, she supposed she could have been excused for feeling nostalgic.

"So how did you persuade them to let you have a rooftop office?" she asked him.

Taliaferro spread his hands over the souped-up archiver

resting on his knees. "Don't ask, don't tell. Remember that one?"

"Not firsthand."

"Well, it's an uneasy truce. They don't ask me any questions, I don't volunteer any lies. They said be on the premises, I'm *on* the premises. Anyway, it's easier to think up here, even when my medication isn't crapping out."

"I can believe that," Konstantin said, looking around at the jagged profile of the cityscape all around them. It was a profile that, outwardly, had changed very little in the last seventy years. The changes took place on the inside now, the space rearranged, refitted, revised, having little if any effect on the exteriors. As if, Konstantin thought suddenly, there was some hostile, omniscient observer that humans were trying to fool into believing that absolutely nothing was happening, nothing at all, nothing going on here but the status quo, boss. Maybe this was the standard learned behavior of a society that had put itself under permanent surveillance. Disturbed by the thought, she shook it away.

"You're getting that unreal feeling again, aren't you?" Taliaferro said, watching her with an expression that wasn't quite amused.

"No, I think it might actually be hyper-real," she said honestly. "Or maybe I'm just getting agoraphobic."

Taliaferro actually paled with alarm. "I hope *not*. That would be some very serious warp in your woof."

Konstantin's other eyebrow went up. "Unlike claustrophobia, which is more normal?"

"As a matter of fact, it is," Taliaferro told her seriously. She gave him a look. "Well, it is. We come from a small, tight space out into a world larger by a gazillion magnitudes. It's the natural progression of human life. But agoraphobia—that's backwards. Agoraphobia is regressing, wanting to go from the large place back to the small one. Except that place will always be too small for a functioning human being. Definitely unnatural, if you see what I mean."

Konstantin found herself at a loss for words. "You know," she said after a bit, "that puts a whole new stripe on it that I find, frankly, unsavory. *And* disgusting. The world dodged a bullet the size of a cannonball when *you* passed up psychiatry for police work."

Taliaferro was unoffended. "Told you, I'm a big Italian mama's boy. Nothing new there. What's new with you?"

"If you look in your inbox, you'll see," she said.

"Oh, you mean him?" The Japanese guy's faces appeared on the archiver's screen.

"Goku Somebody, or Somebody Goku."

"Goku Mura, of the infamous East/West Precinct," Taliaferro said smoothly. "He's what I believe is known in the trade as a 'barefaced liar.'"

"No shit," Konstantin said admiringly. "How'd you turn that up?"

"Well, much as I would like to promote this as a work of intuitive genius on my part, the *I Ching* warned against massaging the truth this week. So I have to admit that this is apparently a common practice among the East/West gang. Or more specifically, among the Japanese members. Which, when you think about it, only makes sense."

Konstantin frowned at the screen, saying nothing. "Is this practice getting more widespread?"

"Among the Japanese, or in general?"

"Either."

"Representations of real people have been on the increase," Taliaferro told her, dividing the archiver screen so he could put some kind of chart next to Goku Mura's face. "At present, the dumb-brute book-keeping data indicates that within most formally organized metropolitan areas, real-person representations run from a low of thirty percent to a high of fifty percent."

"Where do they get that kind of information?" Konstantin asked.

"Dumb-brute," said Taliaferro, "hotsuit survey software. It doesn't match the real-person to the real-person in any traceable way, it just sends a yes-or-no."

"Sends it where?"

"City census. They use the demographics to place advertising more effectively."

Konstantin burst out laughing. "I keep forgetting about advertising. Product placement. I swear, if we knew half of what advertising knows about people—" She sobered suddenly. "Jesus."

"Yeah, even a lot of cops wouldn't want to live in that kind of police state," Taliaferro said.

The solemn tone in his voice made Konstantin wince. "That's why it's giving me a good old-fashioned case of the creeps to ask you what I'm about to ask you."

Taliaferro lifted an eyebrow at her. "And that would be?"

"Tag me, in real-time. Can you do that?"

He stared at her for a moment and then laughed. "Can I tag her, she wants to know. Pal, when I tag you, you'll be so tagged that even death will not release you."

Konstantin wasn't smiling. "I'll be holding you to that."

"You do realize, though," Taliaferro said, sobering, "that I can't go in and pull you out if you get into trouble or anything like that."

"Where I'll actually *be* is in a little room in a hotsuit."

"I know. And I'm not going in any little rooms to get you out."

"Fine. Pull a fire alarm, then, I don't care. I just want an independent back-up monitoring everything I do online."

"Any particular reason?"

"One of this Goku Mura's online faces is a child. You know how I feel about that. And why."

Taliaferro nodded. "Yeah. I guess there are some things that make it worth the invasion of privacy."

"'Privacy.'" Konstantin frowned more deeply and made a show of scratching her head in exaggerated confusion. "What's 'privacy'?"

Taliaferro lifted the other eyebrow. "You're soaking in it."

4

By the time she would have been finishing up the lunch she had forgotten to eat, Konstantin was 'suited up and watching the TV wall in her virtual office.

Konstantin thought the virtual office was probably the best feature of the whole TechnoCrime-fighter-in-AR thing. Its television wall could show many different small flatscreens, or one very large, very detailed, high-res scene. She could switch it from one mode to another with a shrug, while keeping an eye on the dataline and sorting her inbox.

This afternoon she was rotating the one hundred most popular ARs on the wall, more for the company of the sound than for any useful purpose. *Noisy wallpaper*, Taliaferro called it, *resorted to by the inept, the alienated, and the doomed.* But then, Konstantin reasoned, Taliaferro hated walls to begin with, so there was no use trying to sell him on wallpaper. On the other hand, she thought, scanning the screens with a little bit of a lost feeling, it might have been more constructive to try to articulate, at least to herself, exactly what she thought she was doing in trying to watch so many different ARs at once. Maybe nothing more than appear busy in case Ogada ever decided to look in on her.

She was about to open her inbox when she heard a soft chime. It took her a moment to remember it was a request for access. Ogada, already? Taliaferro, letting her know he was on the job via a puppet? Or maybe her Japanese friend, the one who part-timed as a kid for no good reason?

"Anybody home?" came Celestine's voice after a few moments.

"Sorry, access granted. Or come in, whatever works." Konstantin was amused to find she was slightly disappointed that it wasn't the Japanese guy. She'd been waiting for a chance to tell him what she thought of fake children.

Celestine materialized in the chair on the other side of her desk. Konstantin's amusement faded; the officer had opted for a cyborg appearance. Most of it—the transparent diamond-crystal skull, an LED eyeball mismatched with an organic, the translucent skin stretched over chrome structure—was the stock model from central stores, a kind used mostly by scavengers who liked to collect limbs and organs and then trade among themselves. Celestine's torso was mostly biological, with a fancy torque meter built into the waist; one artificial hand, two combination-flesh-and-artificial legs with partially exposed cording but, to Konstantin's relief, no exposed chrome buttocks. The metal-fiber muttonchops had to be Celestine's bit of customization. They didn't look any better to Konstantin in AR than they did outside of it.

"Don't tell me," Konstantin said after a moment, "you've always wanted to experience metal in a personal way."

"Oh, so you've been there, too," Celestine enthused. "What did you think of the templates?"

Konstantin hit another mental speed bump. "Been where?"

"Personal Metal. Best cyborg outfitter I've ever seen in AR. It's in the Little Tokyo area of post-Apocalyptic Noo Yawk Sitty. I swear, the Sitty will never die. Just when you think it's finally had its day, it buds out another borough."

"Little Tokyo in post-Apocalyptic Noo Yawk Sitty," Konstantin said, shaking her head. "Did post-Apocalyptic Tokyo have a fire sale?"

Celestine's metal-thread eyebrows went up. "More like a

sponsorship deal, actually. They're thinking about reorganizing all the post-Apocalyptic areas under one umbrella and making them all boroughs of a single post-Apocalyptic section, instead of having them all separate from each other like now. So they want to see how it goes with each place having a sort of a part of another place contained in it, if you see what I mean."

"Does post-Apocalyptic Tokyo have a Little Noo Yawk Sitty inside it?" Konstantin asked.

"I don't think it's open for general access yet," Celestine said. "Want me to check?"

"No." Konstantin turned on her inbox.

"Well, I'm on the mailing list. I'll know as soon as it's operational."

You expect it to get weird, Konstantin thought, pulling the monitor up out of her desktop and setting it so she could swivel it toward Celestine if she needed to. *You even expect it to get really weird, but the weirdest thing is that it gets weird in such a matter-of-fact way. Post-Apocalyptic Noo Yawk Sitty? Sure, check the ad rate, send out the newsletter. Who's this week's sponsor, who bought ad space? What's the share, what's the rating? Better open a Little Tokyo so we can cover off anyone who can't cope with the genuine Japanese stuff. Have everyone speak English, serve sushi, and dress like the Seven Samurai are in town. Whoever they are.*

"Any more brainwashing complaints from lowdown Hong Kong? Or anywhere else?" Konstantin asked, tapping the monitor. It lit up and immediately showed her a screensaver. She got rid of it and tapped for the day's reports.

"Complaints from two different families of older users, unconnected to each other as far as we can tell, having to do with said users changing their wills to cut out their nearest and dearest and leave all their real property to purely digital AR entities. I think that makes half a dozen for the month." Celestine chuckled; it sounded like several pieces of metal colliding in her throat, which, to Konstantin's surprise, was rather musical. "Good audio, isn't it?" Celestine added pleasantly. "Custom voice box. The two latest disinheriting parties each follow the pattern of the rest of them—refusing to believe that the entity isn't in some way real unto itself."

Konstantin found the cases and paged through them on the monitor. "This is beginning to sound more like a psychiatric problem to me, one of those mass hysteria things. That's assuming there's really no direct connection between any of the cases."

"DiPietro and I aren't really sure of that," Celestine said. "Right now we're trying to run down a possible dotted line between one of the early complainants and an AR entity not involved in any of the complaints but connected to one of the entities that *is* involved, except with a different complainant. Follow?"

Konstantin frowned. "Put a diagram in your report. What else?"

"A stalker with a twist."

"Uh-huh. And the twist is, the stalker isn't human, right?"

"Right—*but*," added Celestine, holding up a brushed metal forefinger, "the stalker *used* to be human. According to the complainant."

"Definitely twisty," Konstantin said, impressed in spite of herself. "Somebody's cast-off persona revamped for animation?"

"Nope." Celestine's smile was enhanced, though not improved, by the muttonchops. "Try again."

"This isn't a game show, for chrissakes."

Unperturbed, Celestine pointed at the monitor. "Well, if it were, you'd never get this one."

Konstantin tilted the screen and started reading. After rereading the same four paragraphs several times, she turned back to Celestine. "*Changeling?*"

"Complainant's term, not ours," the officer said serenely. "Sounds a bit more intelligent than 'bodysnatcher,' don't you think? More poetic, anyway. I mean, you'd have to have some education to know what a changeling is. Besides, our complainant states that she doesn't know if the stalker in question was swapped completely, or whether the entity had taken over and revamped the existing person. Which would be the person in question. Or the person *we* question." Celestine shrugged, smiling. "Question authority."

"Oh? Says *who*?" Konstantin paged over to the complainant's particulars. "Stalking online is harder to prove than most people think. Especially those people who file the complaints. I'd like to interview this one, see if this"—she squinted at the screen with watery eyes—"Susannah Ell is one of those people who thinks aliens are invading from AR."

"Ell didn't mention aliens, but we have another report on someone who does. It makes exciting reading."

"Any connection to Ell, or anyone else we've heard from?" Konstantin asked, suspicious.

"Don't know yet. DiPietro's hunting up any possible dotted lines. Should know soon, unless someone steals a vehicle in the next few hours."

"OK, OK, you've made your point," Konstantin said. "You can tell auto-theft I said you're permanently busy. Now let's go visit Susannah Ell."

Susannah Ell was in her own online workshop where, according to preliminary information, she designed a line of clothing for a small catalog house. The catalog house itself was virtual, although the clothing was both real *and* virtual. Nothing better than a product that would place itself, Konstantin supposed.

Ell's workshop would seem to have been a placed product as well, executed by someone with a serious retro-fetish. It was a recreation of a loft from sometime in the previous century, cluttered with bolts of cloth, dressmaker dummies, feathers, sequins, beads, shoes, hats, and assistants. The assistants seemed to have all been stamped from the same mold—young males, or possibly neuters with a male bias, small, thin, and eager to be of service to Ms. Ell, who was about two feet taller than they were, though perhaps not quite as heavy.

"What do you think?" Celestine murmured as they paused on the other side of the access threshold in spectator mode. "Seven feet tall, maybe eighty-five pounds?"

Konstantin made a hushing motion at Celestine, even though she was probably right. Ten of those pounds might have been the rich, thick coils of streaky reddish-blonde hair. Anorexic, domineering, almost certainly a proud member of the Sisters of Rapunzel/Daughters of Medusa—probably exactly how this particular neighborhood expected its design geniuses to look. Konstantin stepped across the threshold from gallery to access, pulling Celestine after her.

One of the assistants was in front of them immediately, appraising them over the tops of his trifocals, which, given the height difference, wasn't easy. Konstantin found herself wanting to bend down to him.

"Do you have an appointment with Madame?" he asked.

"Do we need one?"

"It would be very good if you had one."

Konstantin looked pointedly around the loft-space. "Is there anyone else waiting to see Madame?"

"No one without an appointment," the assistant said smoothly.

"How about anyone *with* an appointment?" Konstantin asked, just as smoothly.

"Well . . ." He looked sheepish as he brushed a hank of black hair back from his forehead. He reminded Konstantin of a leprechaun, albeit a leprechaun in a bright white shirt starched to within an inch of its life and slightly baggy black trousers that pooled a bit around his ankles. Two yellow measuring tapes hung around his neck and the points of his open collar were serving as pincushions. "Look," he said, leaning forward a bit and lowering his voice confidentially, "we get a lot of spectator traffic. We don't want to give anybody the wrong idea about how valuable Madame's time is. Especially when she's in the middle of designing the new line, you know—she can't have people just popping in on a whim. It's not like she's *prêt-à-porter*."

"Your accent is flawless," Celestine said.

"Madame made a complaint about a stalker," said Konstantin, while the assistant was still beaming over Celestine's compliment. "We've been sent to investigate this. We're from the technocrime unit."

The assistant's expression shifted to wary. "And how does Madame verify this?"

Celestine produced a small card from a slot in the palm of her left hand. "You can call the precinct. It's a free call. Including the time *for* the call."

"*Ah.*" The assistant made a show of scrutinizing the card carefully. "I shall show this to Madame so she can verify that you are who you say you are. If there is an effect on the billable time, Madame will see you post-haste." He zipped away to push through the crowd of other assistants around the terribly busy Susannah Ell, who was shaking her head vigorously as she ripped ragged bits of cloth from an hour-glass-shaped dummy and tossed it away in disgust.

Konstantin saw her reddish head dip toward the assistant she and Celestine had just been talking to. Moments later, time came to an abrupt stop.

"Ah-ha!" said Susannah Ell, looking around the suddenly silent workshop, over the heads of the now-frozen assistants. A feather sat in midair as if it belonged there, the tiny fronds still graceful, though completely rigid and immobile.

"I take it you're satisfied," Konstantin said.

Ell turned to her and Celestine, startled. She probably hadn't realized that the stoppage of billable time wouldn't freeze her visitors, too.

"I'm just not used to being put on hold like this," she said, brandishing a pair of scissors that doubled as a telephone. "You cops have such ingenious ways of telling the truth in AR, when all the rest of us can do is keep on telling the same lies. Too bad it can't last all day."

"Since it stops billable time, there's really no such thing as 'all day,'" Konstantin said. "But it's not indefinite, if that's what you were thinking of. But even if it could—well, try doing anything."

Susannah Ell poked a swatch of cloth she had started to reattach to the dummy's impossible bosom. It might have been made of stone.

"Frozen solid," Celestine confirmed, as if she were supplying the technical definition.

"So." Susannah Ell tried pushing at the heads of the assistants surrounding her; they too might have been stone. "How do I get out of this?"

"Climb over them," Celestine told her. "They'll never know the difference."

Ell put each hand on top of an assistant's head and boosted herself up, swinging her legs high over the frozen group and managing to touch ground without setting foot on anyone. She straightened her black shirt and trousers and stood back to survey the tableau her assistants made without her. "Aren't they darling. They really *are* as attentive and devoted as the program promised they'd be." She turned to Celestine and Konstantin. "Supposedly, it's a dog AI running them."

"Did your changeling get into any of them?" Celestine asked her.

"This group? No. The last group, though, I had to have them all purged because they'd gotten infected."

"How?" asked Konstantin.

"*I* don't know the technical details. I design clothes, not changelings. How does anything get infected with anything else?"

"I mean, was it just one of them, or was it in all of them?" Konstantin clarified.

"Oh, I'm not sure whether it was in all of them simultaneously, or hopping from one to another very fast." Ell stroked her impossibly long, lush red hair; it coiled around her wrist like a living thing while another section caressed her shoulder. "Sh," the woman told her hair, and gave the coil braceleting her wrist a tender nuzzle with her lips. "Not now. Wait." Konstantin was unsure whether she should avert her gaze. "It was unacceptable, this possession, but so thorough. At the molecular level, in the virtual sense."

"I'm not sure what you mean," Konstantin said.

"I mean, it's like he's left a stain or a smell behind that I can't get out of my infrastructure. Sometimes I can sense he's using it to hide in and watch me from somewhere very close— in the walls of this building, or the floors. Maybe the color of the walls, or the dirt on the color of the walls. Or the dirt on the windows."

Konstantin glanced at Celestine, who only nodded at the

woman. "That would take a lot more processing power than most end-users could—"

"We're not talking about most end-users, are we?" Ell snapped. Her eyebrows became two very pointed arches. The hair bristled and rearranged itself around her protectively. "We're talking about Hastings Dervish, race traitor."

"What did you say?" Konstantin asked. If her own hair had been able to move, it would have been standing on end, hissing.

"I said race traitor, and I meant it," Ell said feverishly. "He's betraying us, his own race."

"What race would that be?" Konstantin asked stiffly.

"The *human* race. What other race *is* there?" Ell looked annoyed and bewildered. "Don't tell me you're a couple of those believers in the Living Pixel. Are you?"

"Church of the Living Pixel," Celestine said to Konstantin. "Of course not," she added to Ell. "We're strictly law enforcement, here to investigate your complaint. Our personal beliefs don't apply."

Ell's suspicious expression disappeared. "OK. If you were Church of the LP, you couldn't say that."

Celestine nodded reassuringly. "That's right. We're lucky that they're one of those groups that feels a greater need to advertise than to encrypt."

"So to speak," Konstantin murmured.

Ell didn't hear her; she was beaming at Celestine. "Ah. I see you're familiar with W. J. Williams' First Law of Free Speech— 'Assholes always advertise.'" Her smile faded. "Unfortunately, stalkers are something worse than assholes. Now that Dervish is in the infrastructure, he can be anywhere any time he wants. He could be right under my feet right now, *or* yours. *Or* watching from the ceiling." She looked up. "If you're up there today, Dervish, I *swear*—"

"No user, even one with top-line tech, has the capacity or power for that kind of interactive self-encryption," Konstantin said, trying not to sound overly patronizing or put out. "Anyone can observe you from open gallery space, and some of the more skilled peepers can open a window where you don't want one."

"I suppose now you're going to tell me how important it is not to let anyone find out my password," Ell said sourly.

Konstantin shrugged apologetically. "Is all of this space your own?"

"My private domain," Ell nodded. "Every pixel."

"Then any intruders, no matter how well encrypted within this environment, would still be running on their own billable time. Which means that the free police time we're currently running on wouldn't freeze them, which would register immediately. We'd know if there were an intruder—"

"Dervish is *not* an *intruder*," Ell said impatiently. "Dervish is *digital*."

"Is what?" Konstantin blinked.

"*Digital*, dammit. *Digital*." She paused, looking from Konstantin to Celestine and back several times, as if she were waiting for them to catch on to something they should have known all along.

"And how did that happen?" Celestine asked calmly.

"The old switch-ola."

Celestine's voice was a miracle of neutrality; Konstantin thought that made her sound even more skeptical. "You believe in the old switch-ola, do you?"

"Hey, there are things you believe, and then there are things you *know*. One of the things I know is Hastings Dervish. I mean, I *really* know him. He's my ex-partner. Not just business, but ex-friend, ex-lover, ex-husband, ex-spare brain, ex-everything. There's a way you get close enough to someone that you could recognize them by the way the air moves around them? The way the floor feels when you're both standing on it. The way they bend light and reflect it back, in here, out there, anywhere there *is* a where." She looked from Konstantin to Celestine and back again. "Does any of this sound even a little familiar to either of you?"

"So," Konstantin said, taking a breath, "you're saying that you know when Hastings Dervish is present just from certain clues perceptible to anyone familiar enough with his habits?"

"*That's* a remarkably antiseptic way to put it." Disapproval was gravelly in Ell's voice. "Look, I know it's supposed to be so clean and tidy in here that you can wade through anything without ever actually getting any on you, yackety-yackety and so forth. But I'm not in here *playing* at being a tortured artist. All this you see? This is my life. I mean, I design clothes for a living, and I do it in here because it's cheaper than a real room full of real fabrics and real assistants whom you couldn't get with this much dedication in the first place. I have what I want. I'm not frustrated, I'm not looking for the Out door, I'm content without a partner, I'm minding my own business, and my ex is stalking me. Stalking is still illegal, isn't it?"

"I can't argue with any of that," Konstantin said. "But only because I'm stuck back on 'Dervish is digital' and 'the old switch-ola.'"

Ell rolled her eyes. "Hastings is *not* happy. He is *not* content. He *didn't* get what he wanted, he *is* frustrated. He *was* looking for the Out door but he couldn't find it. So he took the next best thing."

"And that's the old switch-ola," Konstantin guessed.

"That's the old switch-ola. He managed to make contact with an AI looking to swap. Leave it to Hastings to sell his soul to the devil. Metaphorically speaking," she added quickly. "I don't want you to get the idea that I'm some kind of weird satanist. Anyway, the AI is out there, somewhere out on the ground floor, walking around making plans for world conquest, and Hastings is in here working on his own version of world conquest."

"Sounds like a full schedule," said Celestine. "When does he get time to stalk you?"

"I don't appreciate your sarcasm," Ell said mildly.

"I wouldn't, either," Celestine admitted, "but this is very difficult and you have to understand our position. We're paid to be suspicious and skeptical. That's what *we* do. Maybe it would be easier for us to be less suspicious and skeptical if you told us how Hastings Dervish accomplished the old switch-ola, what his version of world conquest is, and how you think an AI could go about the equivalent of world conquest out here."

"Well, *I* don't know how they did the old switch-ola," Ell fumed. "The mind is a strange and terrible thing. Dervish's mind is, anyway. And, now that he's digital, he doesn't need to worry about having enough processing power. He doesn't just *have* processing power, he *is* processing power. He morphs, he torques, he crawls on his belly like a reptile. He's only limited by the power within the system itself. He's a self-initializing program with consciousness and intent. Getting any clearer for you?"

Konstantin wavered and then decided to treat the question as rhetorical. "Do you have an address for Hastings Dervish? Out there, I mean, in the more usual reality?"

"I just *told* you—he's *not out there* any more," Ell said, throwing up her hands. The back of her left hand hit the feather frozen in mid-air and she winced.

"Last known address for him out there, then," Konstantin said. "Just because the AI with which he did the old switch-ola will probably be living at his residence as well as using his body. If you see what I mean."

"Oh, sure." Ell nodded slowly, her voice grave. "I know what happens next. You go see that creature you think is Hastings Dervish, and tell him about his crazy ex-wife. 'Oh, yeah, her,' he'll say. 'Never got over the break-up. Thinks I'm following her around with sinister intent.' That will satisfy your need for the continuation of the mundane, no matter how you have to twist and distort reason just so you can explain everything away. Even if you two were somehow to come across some undeniable visual, physical proof, you'd probably turn yourselves in at the nearest locked ward for a cure rather than believe."

Celestine's smile was compassionate, which was just about miraculous, considering. No doubt she had a better program for facial expressions than Darwin had had. "On the other hand," Celestine said, patient, "you wouldn't *really* expect us to buy your whole spring line, so to speak, without at least getting a good look at Dervish and seeing what he has to say."

Ell allowed herself a momentary pout. "This is the *summer* line. But, yes, you're right. Have a look at him. Have a good, long look and then come back here and tell me that's not one of your more ambitious AIs walking around loose and making plans." She turned and went back to the huddle of assistants, still frozen in attitudes of aid and supplication around the space where she had been. She started to climb up over them again and then paused, looking over her shoulder at Konstantin and Celestine as she balanced with one hand on an assistant's head and her knee on another assistant's shoulder. "I really hope this wasn't a waste of time. But if it was, I'm glad it wasn't billable time."

"Hastings Dervish lives on Key West," DiPietro told her as she sat down. "That's one of the islands just off the—"

63

"I know where Key West is," Konstantin said, not unkindly, pulling open a drawer and then forgetting what she wanted in it. "Not exactly in our neighborhood, much less in our jurisdiction. But I guess we could phone him through the local authority. Or maybe I should just fly out there and hook up with the Key West precinct."

"You can hop and drop both ways in most of a working day if you have to," Celestine said. "I made open reservations, just in case."

Konstantin raised her eyebrows at this outburst of efficiency. Celestine's smile, framed in muttonchops and seeming twice as wide as it actually was, would still take some getting used to, but that wasn't impossible. "Well, before I go hopping and dropping, I'll speak to Key West first, see if they have any information on him in the criminal department, and then see about chatting with the entity himself." She started to punch up a Florida exchange. "DiPietro, put out a national search enquiry for any complaints similar to Susanna Ell's. Let's see if it *is* some kind of mass hysteria or one of those ailment fads or something. And you"—she nodded at Celestine—"look into the old switch-ola. I want to know how old it actually is."

DiPietro started to ask a question.

"We're off stolen vehicles indefinitely," Celestine told him, "maybe forever. Come on." They left Konstantin alone at her desk and she watched them head off through the room, with a small but growing feeling of competence. *All I need now*, she thought, *is someone to dial Florida for me.*

"Got Key West PD on hold for you if you want them," came Taliaferro's voice from the monitor speakers, making her jump.

"Thanks. How did you know I wanted you to keep tapping me?"

"I didn't," Taliaferro told her, sounding amused. "I just

left it on, figuring that eventually you'd say, one way or the other."

"Oh." She paused, her finger over the hold-call button. "Is there any place you *can't* tap me?" she asked.

"Don't know. You haven't been everywhere. Yet."

"Yet," she echoed, and took Key West off hold.

5

"Hastings Dervish inherited residency rights on Key West," said the officer on the monitor. Her name was Dolores Rojas and there was something about her features that reminded Konstantin of the arms dealer with the pirated Smith & Wesson. "We have a full file on that crew going back several decades."

"What about Dervish himself?"

Rojas' expression was slightly apologetic. "That's a lot sketchier. There's almost no information on him at all, since he didn't actually reside on Key West until he inherited the property last year."

"Well, he must have lived *somewhere* before last year," Konstantin said. "Just give me his previous known address."

Rojas' expression became pained. "You don't know anything about Key West, do you?"

Konstantin sighed. "No, I guess not. But I have a feeling I'm going to and I won't like it."

"Nobody does, not even me," Rojas commiserated. "It's quite a long story, involving decades of legal gymnastics funded by people who patronize legal gymnasts for very good reasons of their own. The short version goes like this: Key West is a legal event horizon."

This time, Konstantin felt the speed bump rattle her teeth, even the fake ones. "Gymnastics and black holes. That's a combination I haven't met before. Is it unique to Key West?"

"Practically. There are only a couple of other places like it in the world. What it means—short form again—is that all Key West residents have the right, under law, to seal any and all records of their lives prior to taking up legal residence on Key West, unless they should happen to be convicted of a felony as a Key West resident. *On* Key West," Rojas added quickly, before Konstantin could say anything. "Only then can any records dating from before the time they took up residence on Key West be opened—*unless* extenuating circumstances can be demonstrated. If those extenuating circumstances apply, then the records can*not* be opened."

Konstantin nodded glumly. "That must have been some Olympic-class gymnastic event."

"It was a series of events, really, some happening together, some separately." Rojas made a small shrug. "It all had to do with privacy. That's Key West's key word, you might say. Every part of the island is privately owned, including the nature reserves. The reserves are subject to government inspection, but that's limited strictly to determining compliance with government standards for nature reserves. All of Key West's nature reserves exceed those standards by several magnitudes."

"And who could expect anything less, really," said Konstantin.

"Well, not *this* strictly-by-the-book law-enforcement officer," replied Rojas with a half-smile. The resemblance to the arms dealer became even more striking. Konstantin had the fleeting thought that they could be one and the same—another barefaced liar, perhaps?—and then thought it was more likely to be either an extraordinary coincidence or another case of stolen faces, a prank popular among the adolescent as well as the adolescent-at-heart. "The flamingoes have never had it so good. A lot of the rulings came at a time when privacy was the cause of the moment, and Key West decided to go the distance. There's no news-reporting media of any kind on the island itself—all news is imported, and any news about the Key or its residents is essentially a pr release. Due to the adjective shortage."

Konstantin blinked. "The adjective shortage?"

"Yeah, it's a real problem. On Key West it's illegal to describe someone in a public statement or news story as, say—and this is just for the sake of example, it's *strictly* hypothetical—um, Houston Drabbish, owner of parcel four on the Sunshore Beach Reserve who was convicted twenty years ago of conspiracy to subvert justice and for trafficking in human organs on the black market. Unless the news story in question concerns Houston Drabbish being newly convicted of an equally grievous felony, this description of Mr. Drabbish is considered highly defamatory and legally actionable."

Billable, Konstantin thought.

"After all," Rojas went on, "that was twenty years ago. But even if it had happened last year or last week, how the *hell* is poor Mr. Drabbish supposed to see the error of his ways, turn over a new leaf, and cleave to the straight and narrow when the media insists on presenting him to the world as a criminal?"

Konstantin nodded slowly. "The scary part is, I can see the point."

"Me, too. Who wouldn't, when you put it that way?"

"But suppose a Key West resident—say, your Mr., uh, Drabbish again—is convicted of a felony elsewhere?"

"In that case, it gets complicated."

Konstantin gave a short laugh. "Oh no, not that."

"Unless anything directly connected to the person's Key West property is central to the crime, no records from Key West are available for legal purposes, and no records pertaining to the crime are available in Key West, for any reason. Anything else is . . ." Rojas thought for a moment. "Expensive."

Konstantin laughed again. "So what is it you do there, if you don't mind my asking?"

Rojas' own smile was knowing. "I enforce the no-trespassing laws. Admission to Key West is by invitation only, as you might have figured out by now. It being the world's most exclusive community, we get a fair number of trespassers. Some of them actually try to sneak onto the island in the middle of the night, carrying all sorts of contraband to try to bribe an invitation out of our residents or even us law-enforcement officers. Amazing, the stuff they get hold of: stolen software, hardware, even organs—kidneys, hearts, skin, corneas. Then there are the bootlegged VR modules, and some of the more primitive kinds of guilty pleasures, like tobacco and happy pills. We always confiscate and prosecute, though, of course, the legal residents are completely untouchable in those cases. How can they be held responsible for the actions of some desperate blowfish who'll do anything to get into what they think is the hottest, most exclusive club in the hemisphere?" There was a pause while Rojas rubbed one side of her smile. "You're getting it now, aren't you."

"I was getting it all along," Konstantin said. "I just don't really understand how it all went from defamatory statements to unavailable criminal records."

"You want to know the truth, I don't either. Legal precedents can be cumulative in a way that nobody foresees in the beginning. All I really know is, it started out with privacy, people wanting to keep their personal records from being accessed and made public. Eventually..." Rojas spread her hands. "Personally, I look at it this way." She leaned half out of the frame of Konstantin's monitor and picked something up. "You see this?"

Konstantin jumped. Rojas seemed to be holding a smaller

and less complicated version of the Smith & Wesson she'd bought from the arms dealer. Had that only happened this morning? Or had there been a day in between? Suddenly, she couldn't remember. "Is that a—a Smith & Wesson?"

Rojas aimed the barrel straight up and pulled the trigger. A stream of water sprayed out. "Not really."

"A squirt gun." Konstantin thought she should have felt relieved, but for some reason, she didn't.

"Not just *any* squirt gun," Rojas chuckled. "This is an *illegal* squirt gun."

Konstantin didn't dare shake her head, in case it made her dizzy. "How can a squirt gun be illegal? Pirated design?"

Rojas frowned in bewilderment, took a closer look at it, and then shrugged. "Possibly, but that's not the problem. Not the problem of record, anyway. It's illegal because it's so realistic, a well-meaning officer of the law—myself for example—could mistake it for the real thing when found in the hands of a well-meaning if playful citizen, and shoot said citizen dead. So I, well-meaning officer of the law, can always be sure that if I see something like this in the hands of a would-be well-meaning citizen, I'll know that the citizen is, in fact, licensed to carry a weapon, since the real thing *is* legal on Key West. That trespassing problem we've got, it's a monster. Some of those trespassers can be dangerous. Our residents demanded, and got, the right to defend against home invasion."

"I can't decide whether I'd find your job interesting or not," Konstantin told her.

"That's because you've never seen Key West," said Rojas. "Have you?"

"No."

"Island life here is something you either have a taste for or you don't. I do, and I doubt I'll ever inherit property here.

However, as an employee, I'm granted the privilege of living in rented accommodations for the sake of my job. The Key West consortium can extend that privilege into my retirement, provided I work a certain number of years."

Konstantin leaned closer to the monitor. "You're not Florida law enforcement, are you?"

Rojas had the decency to look slightly embarrassed. "I am an *agent* of Florida law enforcement, answerable directly to them and directly under their command—"

"But independently contracted and paid by the Key West consortium."

Rojas dipped her head in what might have been a nod or a shrug.

"The uniform had me completely fooled," Konstantin said. "It looks just like a real one. Which outfit—Fargo–Pinkertons?"

"Phase 3 Interpol," Rojas said evenly. "And the uniform *is* real. It's the official uniform of Key West law enforcement, as determined by the Key West consortium. They have that right, too." Rojas leaned forward on her elbows. "Come on, I know what everybody thinks of P3I. But I'm on *your* side. Nothing else should matter. If it really bothers you, though, I'll give you the contact information for the Florida legislature. They passed P3I through for this job."

"Same legislature that made squirt guns illegal, right?" Konstantin said.

Rojas shrugged. "Funny old world, isn't it?"

"Isn't it just." Konstantin sighed. "But getting back to our original subject—"

"Hastings Dervish, yes. Of Clan Dervish."

"*Clan* Dervish?"

"It's the social structure of Key West, which is also a form unto itself," Rojas said cheerfully.

Oh, God, Konstantin thought, *here comes another info dump. Why can't I ever get briefed in advance? Why doesn't someone warn me?*

Something must have showed on her face because Rojas suddenly gave a small, sympathetic laugh. "Look at it this way—a day in which you learn something isn't a total loss, is it? In Clan Dervish, as in the others, the members may or may not be related biologically. Some are, some aren't. We have records on any of them actually born on Key West; Hastings Dervish isn't one of those. So I can't tell you if his relationship to the rest of the clan is biological, clannish, or simply as a placeholder."

"And what's that?" Konstantin asked.

"A placeholder makes sure none of the clan property ends up as part of someone's contested estate—or, worse, as part of the holdings of an intestate."

"I'd have thought dying intestate would be illegal on Key West," Konstantin said sourly.

"In a way, it is," Rojas said. "Considered bad form, at the very least."

"In the absence of qualified inheritors, wouldn't the property just go to the consortium?"

"Right. And no one would want to see that happen. The internecine conflicts here are no joke." Rojas' face had turned solemn. "Any clan that lost a piece of property to the joint ownership of the consortium would experience quite a fall in status. It sounds like one of those silly social things, but they all take it very seriously here. No one wants their family members to have to face class prejudice, everyone else on the island thinking they can just pick on them. The clan's karma would get so bad, they'd even find themselves preyed on with greater frequency by trespassers. Predators have an innate sense for picking out prey."

"Amazing," Konstantin said. "An area that moneyed and

protected and there aren't any social programs in place to teach people that prejudice in the community isn't nice."

Rojas shook her head with exaggerated sadness. "The tragedy is, those programs are mainly for poorer areas, where a good many of the citizens may have other problems such as illiteracy, and don't know better. Key West doesn't qualify for a program like that because it would be government-subsidized, and Key West obviously has too much money. But also all of the residents are well educated, which means they aren't prejudiced because they don't know any better. They simply choose to exercise their constitutional right to the pursuit of happiness. In this case what makes them happy is being prejudiced against clans of lower standing." There was a drawn-out pause. "Still with me, or did my *Weltanschauung* eat a hole in the fiber optics?"

"Job pays well, does it?" Konstantin said.

"The pay is almost as good as the scenery. The flamingoes and I have never had it so good."

"Is there any way I can talk to Hastings Dervish himself?"

Konstantin could almost hear the click as the woman went into official mode. "Is there a complaint against Hastings Dervish for anything he may have done either in Key West or elsewhere while a Key West resident?"

"A former life/business partner claims that Dervish has been stalking her online, invading her VR. Virtual trespassing, I guess you'd call it on Key West."

"The only thing Dervish has been involved in while resident here is the contesting of his inheritance in a divorce action. A Susannah Ell claimed half-ownership." Rojas' smile was amused. "That your complainant?"

"Ms. Ell has made some other statements as well," Konstantin said.

"I wouldn't be surprised," said Rojas good-naturedly.

"Dervish initiated the divorce action from here, after his inheritance was disclosed to him. He doesn't have my vote for Nicest Guy In The World. But, then, if he did, he probably wouldn't have inherited property on Key West."

"But can I talk to him?"

"As a matter of fact, you can. Not only that, Dervish *has* to talk to you by law. All of Key West's law-abiding citizens believe in full cooperation with law enforcement—wherever it doesn't compromise their rights, of course. I can forward your call in about fifteen minutes—thirty if he hasn't made a will yet."

"What a relief," said Konstantin.

Rojas smiled. "Isn't it?"

Hastings Dervish fanned his cards out over his lower face and blinked coyly at Konstantin over the tops of them. Above the cards, he seemed to be a golden beach-bauble with a taste for gambling. "The intrepid Rojas tells me I must talk with you," he said with exaggerated boredom. "Does it have to be *now*? When I'm in the middle of a *game*?"

"You folks in Clan Dervish have all the comforts of home mixed with the luxuries of far away," Konstantin said, forcing herself to keep a neutral tone and expression. "I didn't know you could also have gambling casinos in Key West."

The eyes above the fan of playing cards widened; he was wearing copper eyeliner. "There are no casinos in Key West. A friendly game for bingo buttons once in a while at someone's home, yes, but nothing that would involve our having to ask the Florida State Gaming and Software Commission to inspect and approve. That graft is too rich even for our blood. I mean, we've got it, but the fossils on the gaming commission aren't what we like spending our millions on."

"So how friendly is the game you're playing right now?" asked Konstantin.

"Completely unfriendly. Not a friendly face in the house. I'm coming to you live from lowdown Hong Kong."

Konstantin felt a sharp surge irritation. "I see. If you don't mind, sir, I'd like you to log out and talk to me outside of AR."

Dervish winked at her as if they were both in on a joke. "*No.*"

"'No?'" She sighed. "'No' as in 'No, you don't mind'?"

"No. That's No as in No. What part of No isn't clear?"

"Just the refusal part," Konstantin answered, making herself sound as cheerful as he did.

"OK, it's really very simple. I'm refusing to come out of AR to talk to you. Key West law says I don't have to log out to talk to you, only that I have to talk to you."

Even when I think someone's warned me, nobody's really warned me, she thought, feeling desperate. *Why?*

"I see nobody mentioned that part to you," Dervish went on. "They never do. They figure everyone knows, I guess." Dervish turned his gaze to his cards and then he tilted them sharply toward his chest, glaring at her with mock suspicion. "You weren't looking at my cards, were you?"

"I understand you've been having some trouble with your ex, Susannah Ell."

"Nowhere near as much as I had when we were together." Another face moved into the frame of the monitor, a mutant lizard-bird with human blue eyes. Dervish tilted his own head so that it was touching the lizard-bird's. "She is a *very* disordered individual—almost as much as I am. You see, she's having hallucinations in AR: she thinks I'm stalking her. The fact that she would think I'd want to is reason enough to have her placed under observation for seventy-two hours, wouldn't you say?"

"What about you?"

"Oh, I'm under observation twenty-four hours a day, *every* day," Dervish said carelessly. "I just stay here and go from casino to casino, party to party, level to level, city to city, and any place I hang my hat is home."

"You *never* come out?"

"Don't have to. I'm a wealthy man. I have household help to look after anything that needs looking after out there. All perfectly legal on Key West, you know."

"Oh, I figured," Konstantin said, leaning back and folding her arms across her chest. "A law-abiding citizen like you wouldn't do anything that wasn't perfectly legal on Key West. So who's observing you the clock round?"

"Anybody who cares to look." Dervish swiveled sideways, toward the mutant, which made a clacking and hissing noise.

"Among all these observers, is there anyone who has seen you *not* harassing Susanna Ell when she says you were?"

Dervish snapped the fan of cards shut against his index finger and gestured vaguely around. "It's a big universe. Must be someone."

"Any guesses as to who they might be?"

"Of course not. Burden of proof's on the accuser, if I remember right. Right? Right. So until you can show me some solid proof that I've been stalking Susanna, I'm not going to bother myself about naming any names myself. They're probably all liars, anyway." He put one arm around the lizard tenderly and gave the creature a deeply passionate kiss. Konstantin put her chin on her fist and waited. Dervish finally broke the embrace, turned toward her, and pretended to be surprised. "Still here, detective? You must have nerves of steel. That display usually drives even my closest outdoor friends away in seconds." He leaned toward the monitor. "But maybe you're as kinky as I am. Kinkier even? Or do you just like to watch?"

"I don't *like* to watch," Konstantin said calmly, "but I will, if that's what it takes."

Dervish wiggled his eyebrows. "Think you can keep up with me?"

"You may never know."

The man's eyes widened. "Why, detective, are you going to stalk *me*?"

Konstantin chuckled and hung up on him. She made a note to send Susanna Ell information on how to put herself under surveillance so as to catch any intruders in her private area. It was the best she could do for now.

6

"Mercenary police in a place like Key West doesn't surprise me," Taliaferro said. "I think I'd be more surprised if the place were overrun with genuine civil servants."

The night wind blew Konstantin's hair back from her face. They had changed rooftops, from headquarters to the building where Taliaferro maintained an apartment. His concession to shelter from the elements was an airy, transparent pavilion of the type you found at overdone weddings. For all Konstantin knew, that was probably where he'd gotten it, a secondhand bargain. Whenever he wanted something other than the few items of furniture he kept under the marquee, one of the building's freelance gofers brought it up from the apartment he maintained indoors. Apparently, Taliaferro's landlord didn't care if he squatted on the roof, as long as he paid his rent plus the service charge for the gofers. Konstantin thought he was taking the no-meds approach to life much too far.

"Mercenaries are much better in the situation, when you think about it," Taliaferro said. "They're well paid, so you don't have that enormous economic gulf. Cuts the potential for bribery and corruption, especially with those perks. The officers feel more like members of the community, less like hired help—and that's just from the perspective of the people who live there. The rich are different, but the rich of the magnitude of the Key West clans are off the different meter. They don't respect it unless they pay too much for it. This private police force is the only solution for them."

"I don't know if *I* buy that," Konstantin said grumpily. "In fact, I can't tell you what I *do* buy. About *anything.*"

"Parabola approaching zero," Taliaferro said, his voice serene and wise.

Konstantin yawned.

"That, and the fresh-air effect," he added. "Exhilarating, and then it knocks you right out. I'll tell you, I get the best night's sleep after a day on the roof. Why don't you spend the night?"

Konstantin blinked at him.

"I mean in the actual apartment, downstairs." He produced a key-card. "Nobody there but you chickens. Unless I send a gofer in for something, that is, but none of them would bother you."

She meant to give him some excuse and get up and leave. Instead, to her surprise, she found herself accepting the key-card from him. "Thanks. I bet you've got a really big bed, too."

"Probably the biggest you'll ever have slept in," Taliaferro told her. "It's a good one, too, not a thing wrong with it. Except the walls, the ceiling, and the floor around it."

Taliaferro had dispensed with interior walls completely; his apartment was now one enormous room, with a ceiling twice the normal height for a place like this. This was a corner unit as well, which put big cathedral-style windows along two walls instead of just one. His claustrophobia had to be pretty bad these days to keep him out of this place, Konstantin reflected as she picked up a remote control from one of the low window-sills. She aimed it at the big fat couch squarely in the center of this space; it unfolded into what looked like an acre of bed. She plumped down on it to test its firmness. As she did, one of the big windows opaqued and showed her a menu of home entertainment as well as an up-to-date inventory of the contents of the refrigerator, which looked to be half a mile away in the kitchenette behind her, as well as the liquor cabinet a half mile in the opposite direction. Overwhelmed, she used the speed dialer on the back of the remote to ring Taliaferro on the roof.

"I know, I know," Taliaferro said cheerfully before she could get a word out. "If I can afford all this, what am I doing grunting for the police? Well, I *can't* afford it. I inherited every bit of it, apartment, couch, home-entertainment center, liquor cabinet and everything inside it. Yes, really."

"OK," said Konstantin. "I was just curious."

"Who wouldn't be?" said Taliaferro. "I'll tell you about it sometime when I don't want to go to sleep."

"Amen." Konstantin disconnected and turned to the menu on the window. Selecting the random-formations screensaver, she stretched out, intending to let the shifting patterns hypnotize her to sleep. She should take off her clothes first, though, she thought lazily, and save herself the trouble and expense of getting another tunic and slacks out of the vending machine in the locker room. She knew damned well she didn't like the built-in underwear in the vending-machine stock.

Random formations blossomed and morphed into other random formations as her eyes closed. Taliaferro's big bed was really comfortable. She felt as if she were sinking into a weightless state. No, make that dissolving, she thought luxuriously. This had to be a lot more restful than his ridiculous chaise longue on the roof, no matter how good the fresh air made him feel.

"We interrupt this screensaver for the following communication."

For once, she wasn't having the dream where she had confused an AR scenario with a real-life situation and appeared in public all but nude. It wasn't always the same dream—her ex had once told her that she was nowhere near obsessive enough to repeat a dream detail for detail—but recurring circumstances, usually involving some dangerous criminals, innocent bystanders and witnesses, along with media coverage and Ogada. This time, however, she was dreaming that she was lying sideways on Taliaferro's great plain of a mattress and watching the screensaver, which was showing her a series of faces among the configurations: faces she knew, faces she thought she might know, and faces she had never seen before. They were scrolling up from the bottom to the top, where they would funnel into the pointed arch and disappear, moving in a steady stream at about the speed of cumulus clouds on a windy day.

"I said, we interrupt this screensaver for the following communication."

Konstantin rolled over and put her back to the window.

"I know you're there," said the voice, "even if I can't see you."

"You have me confused with someone else," she mumbled comfortably.

"Come on, Dory, wake up."

Konstantin's eyes snapped open and she rolled back, alert and not happy about it. Instead of random formations, the window was displaying—at several times larger than life-size—the head and shoulders of her Japanese friend in his child aspect.

"Doré," she said firmly. "It's Doré, not Dory, and I'm off the clock. Go back to lowdown Hong Kong and wait till after 10 a.m. my time. And while you're waiting, grow up. I'm not in Juvie."

"I thought you Westerners were big on that child inside and becoming like little children to enter the kingdom of heaven—all that."

"You're ruining the best sleep I've had in months."

"Serves you right for overloading my mailbox with *The Communist Manifesto*. Not to mention *The Consumer Manifesto*, *The Commensalist Manifesto*, and *The Cyberpunk Manifesto*."

"The *what*? Oh." Konstantin couldn't help laughing a little. "Well, then, next time, don't tag me with a trawler. Just ask, I'll tell you whatever you want to know." Her laughter faded. "How did you find me—at all, let alone here?"

"The trawler's really just a regular phone call. Traced the line, looked up the duty roster. Your laws make duty rosters a matter of public record. You were listed as being on duty at the right time for you to have been in AR."

"And how'd you find me *here*?"

"Surveillance cams. Put in a search and your trail ended at this address. I picked you up in the corridor, unlocking the door to this apartment. Don't ever let anyone tell you that it's impossible to trace anyone from AR to the outside. It just takes a hell of a lot more processing power and patience than most civilians have."

Konstantin gave up hope that he'd go away and let her sleep. She used the remote to turn the bed back into a big fat couch, and made herself comfortable on that. "And what's so important that you felt you had to go to all that processing power and trouble to ruin my sleep?"

"What does American law enforcement think is so important in lowdown Hong Kong that they send people stomping through without even bothering to find out if there's an operation already in place?"

"Why do you care?" Konstantin asked, suspicion waking her up a little more. "And why are you acting as if lowdown

Hong Kong were a real place within an actual precinct? Which, even if it were, would hardly be in a Japanese jurisdiction?"

"Why the hell are you so paranoid, when we could probably help each other out?"

"Because *you're* not volunteering any information. You just keep demanding answers from me without letting me in on anything." Konstantin paused to take a breath. "And I told you—I don't talk to kids."

The giant image on the window took on a typical street-kid pout/sneer. "Don' shit you-seff ovah nothin', lady-lady. 'Sa' mattah, you gotta bad boy back home?"

Konstantin picked up the remote and clicked the window off. The image melted away as the connection broke, showing her the predawn indigo sky, given a jagged edge by the city skyline. She closed her eyes with relief and curled up on the couch without bothering to turn it back into a bed.

"It's my precinct that wants to know."

She opened her eyes again; the Japanese guy she had met in the exit phase looked blindly out at her from the window. Her gaze flicked to the remote, still within easy reach.

"Mainly because, if you're onto the same operation we're onto, there's no point in the duplication of effort, if you see what I mean. I told them I thought you were just some ham-handed American heat with two left feet, sweating some small stuff on behalf of some tourist who only got what he deserved. Am I right?"

She knew he was waiting for her to answer, and she kept silent.

"Because if I am, I can just go back and tell my superiors that. That I'm right, I mean."

Konstantin sighed. "And what operation would that be?"

"I just told you why we're so interested in you. You answer, and we're even."

Underneath her need to be spiteful over the street-kid aspect, and her ruined sleep, something blipped on her radar. Or maybe that was her parabola. But he still had yet to tell her anything real, she thought—and, as the prophet would have said, had there been a prophet: In case of ignorance, shut the hell up. Besides, Featherstonehaugh had warned her not to admit to anything.

"Sorry," she said, "but I can say no more."

He didn't bother with so much as a parting vulgarity. Abruptly, she was looking at the predawn skyline again. The remote control buzzed and she picked it up.

"Don't you think you were kind of hard on that guy?" Taliaferro asked her.

She laughed in amazement. "Don't you ever sleep?"

"All night. Now it's time for breakfast. Come on up and we'll have blueberry pancakes."

"Gimme about twenty." She put the remote down and walked what seemed like half a block to the bathroom.

Pancakes of any kind, Taliaferro told her, amounted to the finest serotonin re-uptake inhibitors in the finest kind of delivery system known to civilization. Konstantin didn't argue; there wasn't time. Taliaferro's regular ride in to the stationhouse arrived only a moment after they finished. The fact that it was a surveillance helicopter they had to climb up to via twenty feet of flexible ladder while it hovered in whisper-mode would have given her pause, but Taliaferro had her on her way up before she could think about it. Except for the wind snatching her breath out of her mouth, it wasn't really so hard, not any more effortful than anything she did in AR form day to day. Even her muscles *sans* hotsuit didn't feel all that different. Or maybe that was just the high level of blueberry serotonin in her chemistry this morning, she thought, looking down between her feet at Taliaferro. He reached up and pushed the bottom of her foot, mouthing, *Get going.*

She looked up and saw someone leaning out over her, stretching out a hand to help her in. Beyond, the helicopter blades whuffed and whispered in many-imaged circles. Taliaferro gave her a boost and a strong hand on her wrist pulled her up and in. She found herself lying on the floor with her legs hanging out for a moment before Taliaferro climbed in and dragged the rest of her in with him.

Someone slid a pair of headphones with a mike attachment down on her head. She winced and adjusted them.

"You got to be Konstantin," said a crackly voice in the headphones.

Konstantin looked to Taliaferro, who was sitting as close to the open door as possible without actually hanging out of it, and then at the person who had spoken to her, a wiry brown woman with a full head of thick, glossy black hair hacked off in the artfully artless style of the moment.

"Rosita," the woman said, shaking Konstantin's hand. "Taliaferro told me about you. You used to be partners. I remember picking the two of you up on outdoor close-up surveillance sometimes. God knows why, they got satellites that can read over your shoulder and kibbitz on crossword puzzles, but hey, it's a living. Right?" She gave Konstantin a companionable slap on the arm and moved from the cabin to the cockpit, taking the co-pilot's seat.

"Taliaferro?" Konstantin said.

He waved a hand at her without turning away from the open door. "I'll be fine, just don't make me turn around and look at you in here." His voice was strong but nervous, though she wasn't sure if that wasn't a headphones distortion. Sound quality was better in AR, better than in life.

Abruptly she ran her hands over her face, tracing her eye sockets with her fingers, rubbing her cheeks hard with her palms, just to remind herself of where she was. You couldn't do that in AR, not quite in the same way anyhow. There was a special attachment you could put in the headmount so you could kiss or be kissed, but Konstantin had not been able to bring herself even to try it out. The idea of a mechanism for kissing mere centimeters from her mouth, waiting for a cue, was perverse to her in a way that she couldn't begin to describe.

She kept rubbing one side of her face until her skin was tingling. Beyond Taliaferro in the doorway, the city jittered past.

It hit her as soon as she sat down at her desk. A simple action, occurring simultaneously with a simple idea, so simple she might not have thought of it at all except that, for half a second, she had been thinking of nothing in particular besides not bumping her knees. Every so often, she marveled, she *did* manage to get out of her own way.

"Sealed records," she muttered. "Sealed from who? Or whom?" She waited; nothing. "*Taliaferro*," she said, laughing a little. "I don't talk to myself as a matter of course. I know you're listening."

"Yes, but not *intently*," he replied, his voice coming from the speaker in her desktop. "I just had a sort of half an ear half-cocked in your direction."

"Dervish's records are sealed," she said, "but Susannah Ell's aren't. According to the information Celestine dumped in my inbox, she's got no criminal record. All that means is, tracking her footprints is going to be boring."

"You could put a gofer on it," Taliaferro suggested.

"I could. But gofers only fetch. They don't evaluate or interpret as they go."

"That sounds lethally boring, all right."

"Depends on how much I have to dig for. I can probably get Susannah Ell to hand most of it to me. Even just a few things to serve as keywords would help." Two desks away, Celestine jerked a thumb at her AR chamber and looked at her questioningly. Konstantin put up a hand and turned away, lowering her voice a little. "After that climb into the helicopter this morning, I've decided *boring* isn't all that bad."

"You want me to dial up the lady Ell for you now?" Taliaferro asked cheerfully.

"Why not." In her peripheral vision, she could see Celestine and DiPietro making signs at each other. She turned her back to them and picked up the telephone as soon as she heard the click of the connection in the speaker.

"I can't work with all these interruptions," Ell's voice said, managing to purr complainingly. "So I hope this is good news. *Really* good news."

"A request, actually," Konstantin told her. "I'd like to get as many of your records dating from the time you and Hastings Dervish were together as you can possibly come up with."

There was a long pause. Konstantin knew they hadn't been cut off only because Ell's breathing had a deep, put-upon sigh on both inhale and exhale.

"Did you get that?" Konstantin asked finally. "I said that I'd like to—"

"I heard you just fine, detective." No purring now at all. "For fuck's sake, *why?*"

"For the sake of piecing together information on Hastings Dervish," Konstantin said, too surprised at the woman's reaction to sound apologetic. "Since he's moved to Key West, his records have been sealed. But yours haven't. If we can track down any information on him tied in with someone else as a matter of public record—"

"I am being *stalked*," Ell said angrily, "and you're asking me to strip naked for the world?"

"Well, just for me, really. I know it's a gross violation of privacy—"

"You don't know any such of a thing!" hollered Ell. Konstantin winced and held the receiver away from her ear. "You don't need *records* to catch someone stalking me! All you have to do is post someone in a likely place and have them stay alert! It doesn't even have to be *someone*, it can be a gofer! I *told* you what he does: he gets in the infrastructure. Put the *infrastructure* under surveillance, have someone watch the numbers and the coordinates on the energy, and when it doesn't match up, *he's there*! You go in and get him, case closed. What's so damn hard about *that*?"

"It's not hard," Konstantin said patiently. "It's a commitment of labor, equipment, and expense that an allegation of non-violent harassment in AR can't justify."

"I am the victim of a *crime*—"

"You're the accuser," said Konstantin heavily. "The burden of proving guilt is on the accuser. The department's participation in proving guilt is discretionary, which means that sometimes they say they'll do all that and sometimes they say they won't. I guarantee you that, in this case, they'll say no. I can, however, give you our complete self-surveillance program—"

"*Self*-surveillance?" The purr had gone completely shrill. "What in fuck's *name* is *self*-surveillance?"

"You put yourself and your surroundings under surveillance by—"

"I don't *do* surveillance. *I am a clothing designer!*" Ell shrieked. There was a pause. "I'm sorry. I don't shout in here. It's just not me." Her voice was quieter. "But I know now what I have to do."

"I can upload the self-surveillance pro—"

"Don't bother," Ell said. "I'm calling Phase 3 Interpol. They'll have everything I need." The sound of the disconnect was only slightly too loud.

"Tomorrow's law enforcement today," Taliaferro said. "They've got the warm bodies and the equipment. The new solution to the problem of the old switch-ola."

Konstantin sighed. "I'm still stuck on the Out door."

"The Out door is still among the beloved legends of our time." Taliaferro sounded amused. "It's just a matter of which you find more plausible."

"More plausible than what—the guy who died from an AR cobra bite, or the blowfish who claimed he was kidnapped by aliens who strayed into our AR from their own?"

"Well, I've already put in a search for all of Ell's matters of public record for you," Taliaferro told her soothingly. "By this afternoon, it'll all be sitting in your inbox, organized chronologically, geographically, and alphabetically."

"If I let any more stuff go in there today, the damn thing'll explode," said Konstantin.

"So empty it once in a while."

"That's a day's worth of work by itself."

"I said empty it, not work on it. Plead overloaded circuits and blanket erasure. Mail will supply you with back-up copies in a couple of days."

"Pragmatist," Konstantin said.

"Ah, so's your old man."

7

The thing about lowdown Hong Kong, Konstantin thought, was that it never, ever seemed to change. At least, not this particular lowdown level of the mound.

She sat with her feet up on her virtual desk, feeling decadent and indolent, and watched the activity on the virtual wall-screen. Watching television in AR was a joke that, except for Taliaferro, no one else seemed to get. Celestine and DiPietro only looked at her blankly when she tried to explain the humor to them. After all, how else were you supposed to carry out any sort of surveillance, even in AR?

Taliaferro, on the other hand, got it right away. *Figured*, she thought as she browsed the casino, occasionally dividing the screen so she could come at an area with different angles.

Wouldn't it be really funny, she thought suddenly, for no reason, *if Taliaferro were deliberately exacerbating his claustrophobia because he secretly knew that he was an AR addict-in-waiting, and if he ever did go into Artificial Reality, he would be even tougher to get out than Hastings Dervish?*

Probably not funny to Taliaferro. But it sounded just crazy enough to make a perverse kind of sense. Which was just about the only kind of sense she could make out of life in the real world lately. And, speaking of perverse, she wondered if her Japanese friend would turn up in one of his guises. Now that he knew she was likely to be sniffing around, and how she felt about child personas, she'd probably never see him over the age-of-consent again.

Prick.

The Lounge Lizard that Hastings Dervish had been tongue-kissing—or one identical to it—emerged slowly from the fiery pool of opals, its ridiculous naked body a mix of reptilian and mammalian features—which was to say, jeweled patterned snakeskin stretched over ridiculous large breasts, a wasp waist, lush hips, and perfect thighs. The sight reminded Konstantin of the Vargas museum exhibit her ex had dragged her to, and which she had, to her own amused surprise, unabashedly enjoyed, in spite of its obvious absurdity. But, then, maybe the obviously absurd were among the few things you could enjoy unabashedly.

Still . . . sex fantasies with a mammalian lizard?

Never mind, in terms of sex fantasies, everyone lives in a glass house. Besides, wouldn't you prefer someone like Hastings Dervish was keeping himself busy with a snake with breasts, rather than running around bothering people like you? As far as Konstantin was concerned, that closed the subject of *Pornography—Threat or Menace?* Permanently.

She tracked the pin-up reptile to a tall, muscular, blond valet waiting with her clothes over his arm. Definitely not Dervish in another guise, according to the Characteristic Identifier program—none of the movements or postural traits matched. The blond guy's recreational tastes were far more exotic than Dervish's as well—he had reserved his billable time to helping the Lounge Lizard dress before submitting himself to be eaten alive. Konstantin panned away with a wince. *Hope the pain was worth the expense, big boy.* That kind of hotsuit wasn't hard to manufacture, but it was outrageously expensive.

Which, when you came right down to it, Konstantin thought with some amusement, was also nothing new.

She shuffled through the various casino cams, stationary and mobile, looking for familiar faces. Hastings Dervish appeared within thirty seconds, enjoying some kind of mutant poker involving eight cards in each hand. She blew the frame up to cover the whole screen. Today he had a taste for bird-people. The two flanking him had a stark sort of beauty, she supposed, all legs and angular wings, but those long sharp beaks looked dangerous. Someone could lose an eye if he wasn't careful.

She let the cam pan around the table and then halted it with a start. Darwin was sitting almost directly across from Dervish, the pile of chips in front of him smaller than Dervish's but respectable. He fanned himself with his two hands of cards alternately while his digital eye displayed what looked like sound oscillations.

Aren't we traveling in rarefied company these days? She sent the camera around twice more to make sure that her Japanese friend hadn't decided to sit in too, making everything immensely convenient. Not today—or at least, not right now. The day, like all days in a lowdown casino, was ageless, as old or young as you needed it to be.

So she would drop in and see what kind of stakes Darwin was playing for, perhaps thank him for making himself so useful. Assuming that was the real him.

Transition from gallery to lowdown Hong Kong participant today required her to step out of the enormous anteroom and into an equally enormous bullet-train station, all glass and UFO architecture. *And all for a single bullet train*, she marveled as she moved along the platform surrounded by humanoid place-holders, all heading for the open boarding doors. She knew she was encoded as a humanoid placeholder as well, although she appeared normal from her own perspective. Either the casinos or the mound had decided it was necessary to camouflage the incoming numbers, for reasons Konstantin wasn't sure she should even bother imagining. It could be something as trivial as a sudden desire on the part of the casino simply to make things look even more mysterious and exotic for the paying custom, or as serious as a census dodge on the hosting network, inflating or deflating access numbers for the sake of prestige or money. Or it could be something completely different, and irrelevant to anything that mattered. When you went into AR, you had to assume you were going to have your head played with in some way you hadn't counted on.

The bullet-train interior might have been drawn from someone's idea of what an old movie about the future might have looked like—essence of Jules Verne crossed with impressions of Andy Warhol. Konstantin liked it: there was something about it that she could only describe as witty. Not the usual adjective for bullet-train interior design, but the only one that fitted.

It wasn't until she felt the train move that she realized it was also a sealed train. She clutched the end of the curtain she had pulled back from what she'd thought was a window, and stared at the unbroken wall of stamped metal, squares debossed with alternating images of a rocket ship and an antique food can.

Her seat was a singleton in what must have been a re-creation of old-time first-class travel. Very comfortable velvety cushions, not your standard paddy-wagon furnishings, and no featureless golden androids patrolling the aisle, demanding tickets or papers. The other passengers were still ciphers, however. She might have been the only real passenger, or one of a million.

"*Taliaferro?*"

The question went out encrypted as an enquiry about her online account; nothing came back except a non-echo. The feeling of acceleration intensified, catching Konstantin off-guard and off-balance, virtually as well as figuratively. Vertigo swept over her; the back of a chair was pressing hard against her back, but which chair—the virtual plush first-class seat, or the dentist's chair in her cubicle?

Before she could start to think about what to do next, a rectangular area on the back of the seat in front of her lit up: 3-D fireworks exploded silently, the twinkling flames cascading into beautiful letters:

SPECIAL INFORMATION ALL TRAVELERS
SHOULD KNOW FOR A SAFE AND
DISEASE-FREE EXCURSION IN HONG KONG MOUND!

Konstantin started to laugh and then suppressed it as a serious-faced young woman began to explain to her, with earnest sincerity, why she should be careful not to bring in rogue batches of dirty data—anything in a visitor's catalog that had been obtained in other areas of AR had to be presented for inspection and clearance at the port of entry. It was also vital that travelers did not accept any encrypted items from strangers asking them to deliver said items to people or addresses within HK mound.

And even if you don't think what you're holding is encrypted—the nice young woman's voice took on an almost grating quality—*or if you're not sure, notify port-of-entry officers at once. You will lose no value and very little time. In return, we can guarantee that HK mound will remain uncorrupted and unadulterated on every level*—

Konstantin shook her head in amazement, wondering how many people would actually fall for that one. Maybe enough to make it worth the effort of funneling everyone through a single entry portal, using valuable time to scan catalogs for *stuff*. Illegal copies of everything from designs to programs would be all over HK in seconds, the prices jacked up to five or six times what you could get for the real thing elsewhere. And meanwhile, they'd be careful to filter out anything that might get sick and rot in duplication.

She sat back, awash with a type of ennui she only felt when she was on the job, or rather, on this part of the job, in AR— when she would find herself suddenly fed up and impatient with tired routines and clichéd scenarios full of stereotyped situations that would no doubt yield bad dialogue from old movies that should have been left on flammable media instead of being preserved on disks and chips.

Wordlessly, she nudged Taliaferro's tap again.

His reply came encrypted as filler music. *Got it. It's an intelligence test. They're looking to hit up all the first-time marks, kind of a* Welcome to Hong Kong *fleecing, you might say. Instead of leaving by any of the exits in your carriage, walk through the train to the last car, open the* Staff Only *door at the very end—you won't see the handle, but if you reach for it where it should be, you'll feel it—and step out. You'll be in the casino.*

Good old Taliaferro. The only thing he'd failed to mention was that she'd have to stand in line to get out that way. She took a little comfort in the fact that no one could actually tell she'd needed Taliaferro to tip her off, so she could look as if she were as crafty as anyone to have figured it out.

She entered the casino by way of a stall in what passed for a lavatory. The stall was there to provide privacy for personal acts unique to AR—persona changes, ordering new items from General Stores, calling up hints or cheat codes or possibly a hot link.

Not to mention the discreet entrance, Konstantin thought, as she stepped out of the stall to find herself amid a group of people that was just slightly too large for the lounge area, with its mirrored walls, overdone thronelike chairs, and brocade wall-coverings. She slipped between the ornamented, the decorated, and the well upholstered, heading for the exit. There seemed to be a forest—or maybe an orchard—of raised hands and arms, signaling, waving, adjusting glittery bits on satiny parts, or possibly just demanding attention from someone, everyone, anyone.

Konstantin pushed her way through them, batting hands away from her as if they were moths. Before she had time to wonder if she were in the middle of a calculated effect, she found she had fetched up beside a giant puce velour sofa of the sort usually found in an adolescent's vision of a bordello. This lurid purple monster, overstuffed and vivid as it was, had been completely upstaged by the coffee table in front of it, which was a naked man on all fours.

Konstantin rolled her eyes. The biggest problem with the war of the sexes, she thought, was that there was too much war and not enough sex. Not to mention all the juvenile displays of sexual one-upmanship. She supposed it was too much to expect to find a lavatory of the neutrally mixed persuasion. On the other hand, she reminded herself, what else would be the point of a lavatory in AR?

Another mammalian lizard of a different variety—Konstantin was fairly sure it was a Gila monster—pushed her way to the center of the sofa and plumped down, putting her feet up on the coffee table heels first. Konstantin saw the flesh on the coffee table shudder and break into goosebumps. She made her way around to the head and squatted down to have a closer look at the artifact.

The coffee table raised his head and looked into her eyes. "Can I help you?"

Konstantin shook her head. A discreet pop-up said there was a ninety-nine percent probability that the coffee table was inhabited. "What's your story—did you lose a bet?"

"What kind of a question is that?" said the man, frowning at her. He was dark-haired and grey-eyed, with forgettable features except for his very soft-looking pink lips. "Or are you trying to find a new way to humiliate me?"

"Hardly," Konstantin said, defensive.

"Good," said the man, "because I like the old traditional ways of humiliation best. Go ahead, put your feet on me. Sit on my head. Do you want me to clean something for you? I have an extensible tongue—"

Konstantin flinched and fell backwards as his tongue unrolled in slow motion and undulated like a snake. Grinning, the man maneuvered the tip up to his forehead and gave each of his eyebrows a lick before retracting it.

"I know, it's an old gag, but it's still a pretty good one," he said.

"Why?" Konstantin asked him, getting to her knees.

"Why *what*? Why *this*?" The man laughed. "Why do you think? Or can't you imagine?"

Konstantin pushed herself to her feet and looked around, suddenly feeling self-conscious. No one seemed to be paying any attention to her, not even the bosomy lizard resting her high heels on the man's back. But that didn't necessarily mean anything.

"What's the matter?" called the man, twisting his neck alarmingly to look up at her. "You afraid someone's gonna catch you talkin' to a coffee table?"

The lizard on the puce sofa suddenly gave him a sharp jab

with one of her heels. "Shut up, jizzbag. Nobody said you could talk to *real* people."

"What if I *want* to talk to him?" Konstantin asked in spite of herself.

The lizard dug her other heel into the coffee table's flank. "Talking's extra."

Konstantin stared at her. "You mean I have to pay extra to talk to him?"

"No, *he* has to pay extra to talk to *you*, or anyone else here," the lizard said, sounding disgusted either with Konstantin's ignorance or with the idea that the coffee table wanted to talk, or possibly both.

"So if I talk to him, it costs him money?"

The lizard gave her an exquisite tortured-by-boredom look. Her eyes were enormous faceted topazes. "No, you can talk to him all you want. It doesn't cost him anything unless he answers you." She kicked him. "Right, jizzbag? Sure." The topazes swiveled back to Konstantin. "Why anyone would choose to talk to a piece of furniture, however, is the question not worth asking. If you're looking for conversation and/or diversion, there's a casino on the other side of that door. Wit and games of chance abound."

Konstantin winced; she'd all but forgotten why she had decided to come in to begin with. She looked down at the coffee table; he was hanging his head, possibly in humiliation, more likely to take the pressure off his neck.

"You still here?" said the lizard. "What is it now, you want a meaningful relationship with the sofa, too? Well, sorry, but it's taken. Find your own furniture."

"You really ought to hiss," Konstantin told her.

"Hiss?" The lizard stared. "Why, for God's sake?"

"It's a very reptilian kind of thing to do."

"Says *who*?"

"Reptiles," Konstantin said, and turned away, heading for the exit.

Darwin seemed to have hit a winning streak. Konstantin wondered if that was why Dervish and his bird-people had moved on. His place was now occupied by a Chinese cyborg that seemed to have been built more for heavy labor than hanging out in casinos. Konstantin could hear the gears and hydraulics as she moved to pick up her cards or put them down. The brushed-metal shoulders must have been three feet across, or close to it. But then, they would have to be, to support that kind of cleavage. *You can take the mammal out of reality*, Konstantin thought, *but you'll never take the mammal away from anything else.*

Konstantin found an empty chair at a nearby table and dragged it over next to Darwin. "I see you survived," she said as he looked over his fan of cards. The game had gone back to one-handed something-or-other.

"No thanks to you," he said airily, rearranging the cards in an order Konstantin couldn't figure out.

"Not just survived but thrived. What do you get when you cash in your chips here—coupons for free travel? Data-lottery tickets? Free admission to the hottest club of the moment?" She reached over to pick up one of the large yellow poker chips from the stack nearest to her. Darwin slapped her hand away without looking up, and went about rearranging his cards again.

"Get your own stake," he said. "This one's mine and I gambled my ass off for it."

Konstantin looked down. Naked metal hip joints dug into the chair cushion; the position of his thigh concealed his groin area, much to her relief. "Looks like you've won enough to buy a better one. What happened to Mr. Dervish?"

There was a smooth whine of gears as the cyborg across the table leaned forward. "Who wants to know?" she asked in a lusty whisper.

Konstantin looked at her. "I do."

The cyborg showed perfect ivory teeth in a smile that, to Konstantin's surprise, was not without a certain amount of charm. Her face had been beautifully designed, complete flesh without even minor metal accents. The long, snow-white hair looked like nylon, though. "Dervish is having a tune-up. He'll be back later."

"Where does he go for these tune-ups?" Konstantin asked.

The other players around the table suddenly came into sharp focus; either that, or she was just now noticing them. "You don't get something for nothing in this joint," said a Moulin Rouge type showgirl. "Put up or shut up."

Konstantin frowned, looking at Darwin for a hint.

The white-haired cyborg across the table leaned forward again. "She means, get yourself some chips and we'll deal you in. Win a hand, and find out what you want to know."

Konstantin was trying to think of a way around it when Taliaferro chimed her. "Put a riverboat gambler suit in the lav for you, with cribs for all the games. Just don't waste any more time with that damned coffee table."

Konstantin nodded at everyone around the table. "Be right back," she said. "Save me a seat."

"That's extra," Darwin called after her without looking up.

8

Gambling for information, Konstantin found, was one of those things that could become as addictive as gambling for money. Thanks to the casino's system, the stakes were whatever you made them. You bought the chips; whatever you cashed them in for was your own business. Unless, as Konstantin discovered, you decided to buy specific kinds of chips, something it was better not to do. It was like trying to play with a currency different from everyone else's, and an unstable one at that.

The strangest part about it for Konstantin, however, was discovering the potential of getting addicted to something she didn't like. Gambling had never interested her—at least, not this type of gambling. Life was risky enough, she thought; introducing elements of chance into the leisure-time aspects of existence was overkill. Or maybe her ex had been right about her not wanting to play unless she was sure she could win. Konstantin preferred to believe winning wasn't always the point of playing, but that might have been more or less the same thing.

The card games themselves would have been incomprehensible without Taliaferro's crib notes and, from time to time, active coaching. Even then, she wasn't always sure of what she was doing, which made her feel especially silly all tricked out as a riverboat gambler, or what General Stores thought a riverboat gambler looked like. At least the illusory hat had no weight to it, though the brim was wide enough for her to touch convincingly. The string tie, the brocade coat and the satin pants all had a cheesiness that seemed to contaminate her surroundings for her, giving the glitter of wealth the flat shiny quality of cheap gold paint and nylon.

She had had three modest wins before she realized that the cheesiness she perceived had to do with the level she was now on, which was somehow connected both to the game itself and to the riverboat gambler outfit she was wearing. The change had occurred so subtly and/or gradually that even Taliaferro had not distinguished it right away. Now it was coming through even as part of the transmission. The colors on his monitor, he told her, had gone garish, with overdone contrast; was she getting anything similar?

"Trust me, even the expensive cyborgs look like baking foil," she told him, trying to remember what to do with the seven cards in her hand. "I think it has something to do with this outfit I'm wearing. Maybe there's a filter on it we didn't notice."

Taliaferro was silent while she took a win from some sort of furred creature in a jeweled tuxedo. Its sex was ambiguous, but she was pretty sure that it was based on some sort of vermin. The Moulin Rouge showgirl kept eyeing it as if she were imagining what sort of coat the fur might make. On the other side of the white-haired cyborg, the ghost of a platinum-blonde sex goddess Konstantin didn't recognize, but knew she was supposed to, pouted with genuine displeasure as she looked around the table. Her gaze stopped on Konstantin.

"What?" she asked the sex goddess finally.

"Are you the one doing it?" the goddess asked.

"Doing what?"

"Lowering the property values."

Taliaferro chimed. "Yes, you are. Don't admit or deny it," he added quickly as Konstantin opened her mouth to say something. "I've just figured it out—Dervish put a curse on you. You're out of phase with the rest of the casino. If you sit there any longer, you're going to end up on the lowest level of lowdown mound."

"How did he know who to curse?" Konstantin asked him.

"He didn't." Taliaferro laughed a little. "He left a curse that would stick to the first person who talked about him specifically."

"Clever little bastard," Konstantin said with reluctant admiration. "How do I counteract this?"

"I'm still working on that part."

"Maybe I should leave the game." Konstantin folded her cards and pushed back from the table.

"So," said the furry creature, "it *is* you."

"We don't know that," Konstantin said. "I'm running a diagnostic. Maybe it's you. You're the one who showed up here as a rat."

"I was a chinchilla when I started out," the vermin said huffily.

"Weren't we all," said the showgirl, giving the sex goddess a significant look.

The white-haired cyborg put her elbows on the table; the discreet machinery sound had become a mechanical clunking. "You're going to have to buy our way back up to the old level. It's only fair. We didn't ask to come down here with you." She looked pointedly at the chips sitting in front of Konstantin.

Konstantin sighed. "How did I know?"

"Maybe you're just starting to get smart," Darwin said boredly. He swept all her chips into his pile and Konstantin smacked his arm, wincing at the contact. It may have looked like aluminum foil but it felt like boilerplate.

Taliaferro chimed again. "They'll try to get all your chips. You actually only need to give one to the Chinese cyborg."

"Too late," said Konstantin.

"Just get out. Make a full exit. We'll get you back in another way."

"Can you put a tracer on Dervish?" Konstantin asked.

"If he existed, yes. But he doesn't. Don't ask now, just leave."

Konstantin nodded as if to herself, pushed back from the table, and stood up. "He's got your re-entry fare," she told the people around the table, gesturing at Darwin. "Meanwhile, I'll be off now—"

The exit prompt seemed to have disappeared. Annoyed, she transported to the first place she could think of, which happened to be General Stores. The area was more crowded than usual, and far more disorganized than she had ever seen it, with avatars milling around like movie actors on coffee break. A walking red machine that looked like a cross between a toy robot and a motorized mailbox marched up and spat a small fluorescent yellow square at her. The square ballooned up to the size of a window in front of her face; there was a number printed on it in dead-serious black type: 107. It hung there for a second before shrinking to the size of a postage stamp and sticking itself to her cuff.

"Hey," she said to the machine, which had started to march away. She tapped one finger on its top, hard, and winced at the feeling. "What's that about?"

"Several software systems are down," the machine told her in a child's voice. "We've had to institute sequential waiting. Like, take a number and wait. If you don't know that one, say yes and you'll get a brochure detailing the process."

"So they figure no one's going to smash up a subroutine out of frustration if it has a child's voice?" Konstantin said sourly.

"Don't ask me," said the machine. "I just work here."

"Taliaferro, tell me you're there."

She heard him give a short laugh. "I'm *here*, but why are you *there*? I told you to exit."

"I couldn't find the prompt."

"Why not?"

"I got flustered, I guess."

A man carrying the upper half of a cyborg body moved past her, squeezing behind what looked like a party of gargoyles. "Excuse me, I think I'm next," he said. "Is this true shite? I've never seen it this bad."

"Are you still flustered?" Taliaferro demanded.

She felt someone else pass closely behind her, but when she turned around there was no one there. "I don't know what I am," she muttered.

"Me, neither," said a featureless placeholder with a musical female voice.

"I did that by accident once," Konstantin said, gesturing at the placeholder body.

"How tragic. Did you get a credit for the mistake?"

Konstantin shrugged.

"Was it another one of these absurd brown-outs?"

"This is a brown-out?"

"I don't know what else you'd call it. Bunch of systems go down, stranding everyone in some transition."

"*Everyone?*"

The placeholder gestured at the crowd around them. "Everyone here, anyway. But why do you think you aren't getting sole, immediate attention from GS? Brown-out, most likely. Or someone's stupid idea of a joke, disabling the programs so we all end up in a waiting room together."

"Konstantin," Taliaferro said patiently, "what are you doing?"

"Investigating," she told him. "I'm an investigator." She paused, looking around the edge of her screen area for the exit prompt. "Still can't see my exit sign. Is there something wrong with my 'suit?"

There was a pause. "I've got your pov on my screen," Taliaferro said slowly, "and *I* can see your exit prompt."

"Where?" Konstantin demanded.

"Call it four o'clock, about."

Konstantin stared hard at the spot, pulling her video back a step so she could see the entire frame of the headmounted monitor screen. "I still don't see it. Are you sure?"

"You lose somethin', lady?"

She turned to find a dirty face grinning up at her from the level of her shoulder. Her Japanese friend, in one of his kid outfits. Of course, who else? "Nothing you can help me with. Go away. Adults only here." She turned away from him. "Taliaferro, does this have anything to do with the curse Dervish put on me? Obscuring my exit prompt, I mean."

"I don't see how," Taliaferro said.

"Looking for somethin' that oughta be there and ain't?" said the Japanese guy, running around to stand in front of her.

"What would *you* know about it?" Konstantin asked suspiciously.

"How about you come over to our place and we trade some information?"

Konstantin hesitated. "Will I actually learn anything?"

"Go ahead," said Taliaferro. "I'm curious as hell myself."

Her Japanese friend was apparently lousy with instant-transport coupons. He took her first to a platform at the top of the Empire State Building in post-Apocalyptic Noo Yawk Sitty, where a giant woman in an evening gown was climbing up the side with a toy monkey under her arm. On the ground, a multitude of people shouted encouragement at her.

"Corny," said the Japanese guy, "but the tourists never get tired of it."

"Those are all tourists down there?" Konstantin asked.

"Actually, a lot of them are undercover cops, or they're playing undercover cops, hoping to meet a real one. We can tell the difference."

"How?"

"Sorry, can't tell you *that*." The kid face smirked at her. He had golden eyes now. "Trade secret."

"Oh, another one of those software packages that measures statistical characteristics," Konstantin said knowingly. "We use those, too, but you have to be careful. Some of those compilers don't screen their sample groups very well. I can tell you which ones to avoid, if you're interested."

The kid face went from smug to defiant, and the look was so authentically childish that Konstantin wondered if her Japanese friend weren't one of those people who was powerless to keep from assuming the identity of whatever mask he put on. Suave James Bond gambler, bratty delinquent—compulsive acting born of a dissatisfaction with one's own identity, perhaps? Or just a good undercover man trying not to get caught out. One more subject for her parabola to approach on its way to zero, she thought. "Anything we use is custom, and all our samples are—" He caught himself and gave her a look she knew she was supposed to wither under.

"Sorry, but I have a hard time taking anyone under the age of thirty-five seriously," Konstantin said, not bothering to suppress her laughter.

Now her friend looked shocked. "Is that true?"

"No. Just in here." Konstantin leaned over the safety rail. The giant woman was getting closer. She was a perfect reproduction of a 1930s movie star, but her expression suggested she wasn't having a good time for real. "We should go, if we're going."

They walked around the platform to a vending machine that sold cigarettes. Konstantin made a face as the kid fed some coins into a slot and yanked one of the knobs.

"Is this artifice absolutely necessary?" she asked as he made a business out of removing the cellophane from the top of the pack and shaking out a cigarette.

"Nah," he said, holding the cigarette between two fingers as it lit itself. "I just do it." He offered her the pack. "Want one? Oh, sorry, I forgot—you don't have the right kind of software." He blew a stream of smoke over her head and then they were standing in a conference room.

Right away, she knew she'd lost Taliaferro. She wasn't sure exactly how she knew, except that the absence of his surveillance was suddenly more palpable to her than his presence had been. Like the loss of a tooth, or—

Her Japanese friend had reverted to James Bond type, complete with tuxedo. "Missing something?" he asked her.

Konstantin sighed. "My back-up. As a cop, you should be able to relate to that. Let me call my partner."

"Tell me where he is and I'll send someone out to get him."

"He's not in here like we are."

"No? Why not?"

"He's not much for indoor sports."

"But he likes spectator sports. Paul Taliaferro, detective and sometimes treatable claustrophobe." He looked smug again, but now that Konstantin had seen that smug expression on a nine-year-old face, it was hard to take it seriously. Either that, or she was just as insufferably smug herself. She knew which way her ex would have voted. "You have to remember, I called you at his place last night. He was up on the roof, right? I mean, since you were sleeping alone."

"Some people sleep alone because they want to,' Konstantin

said, smiling at his obvious attempt to bait her. He had to be very young, she thought suddenly. Very, very young and maybe nowhere near as sure of himself as he liked to project. (On the other hand, she thought, who really was?) "If you want, I'll give you the full story on my sleeping habits right after you tell me why you're so interested in me and what sort of investigation you're conducting that you're so worried about. 'Maybe the first of its kind,' that was the description, wasn't it?"

" 'Certainly the largest,' " he added, nodding.

"I remember that part, too, Goku," Konstantin said casually, looking around the conference room. It was nothing special. They could have been anywhere.

"So, you got that much. Is that my first or last name?" he asked.

"Oh, please," Konstantin said wearily. "All the intrigue is giving me gas. I am a police detective, but not a very important police detective, at least if my boss's constant references to how disposable I am are any indication. But I *am* the only fool the department could force into becoming the AR TechnoCrime division, although lately I've been able to force two subordinate fools into working for me, as well as talking my old partner into working *with* me. So far, I mostly chase patent thieves, copyright infringers, and product counterfeiters around. But I also take complaints from any cranks smart enough to word their complaints well enough to get them past the crank filter, so I occasionally end up listening to people insist that some evil empire is brainwashing people, or that they're being stalked by psychos who have traded places with an intelligent program and become digital. I'm working on one of those right now. Some guy named Hastings Dervish became digital. The Digital Dervish. Now, does it get any better than that, I ask you?"

Her Japanese friend blew smoke over the middle of the

9

"There have been complaints about lowdown Hong Kong raping people's heads for a long time," said the older Japanese man in the cloud-monitor still floating over the center of the conference table. He was Chief Inspector Kozo Yoshida, and her friend Goku had supposedly zapped a lot of verifiable information about him to Taliaferro, who would be able (they said) to have it all verified by the time he caught up with her or before they finished briefing her, whichever came first. She hoped it was the former.

Not that she was in any real, physical danger, she kept reminding herself. There was no such thing as real, physical danger in AR, unless you had a bad heart or a seizure disorder. They could scare you, but they couldn't kill you. For some reason, however, this knowledge was no protection against being spooked, and at the moment she was more spooked than she could ever remember being at any other time in AR or, for that matter, outside of it.

Maybe it was because Goku had dropped the I'm-*so*-cool act, as if someone had cut off his testosterone drip. The older man in the cloud-monitor was supposedly his superior—was very probably Goku's superior, she corrected herself. Considering that Goku had found her outside of AR, and that the DA had obviously had some communication from these people concerning the investigation that they were going to tell her about, she had very little reason left to keep on doubting everything. Except, perhaps, the force of habit. Once you started doubting things, it was hard to stop. No matter how compelling the evidence might be, the compulsion to doubt it was stronger. And maybe *that* was just because she liked being contrary. *Question authority. Sez who?*

"With no legally enforceable contracts possible in AR," Yoshida went on, "you have to find other ways to get to people. It wasn't long before someone figured out that the total immersion in AR was handy for persuading people to believe just about anything. Ever gone to a religious service in here?"

"*No,*" Konstantin said.

Yoshida nodded gravely. "Probably best. Those who have gone maintain that you can feel the presence of God, whether you believe or not ... regardless of the denomination. Most legitimate churches don't sanction AR services."

"Well, I always said that if I wanted to feel the presence of God, I'd die. It's the only way to be sure." Konstantin glanced at Goku; she was somewhat satisfied to see that he looked uneasy now rather than smug.

"Can I ask you a personal question?" he said after a moment.

Konstantin shrugged.

"Do you think you're dreaming?"

She didn't answer, thinking that he was probably as delighted over the uneasy expression on her face now as she had been at his a moment before.

"That's a new question," she said after a bit. "I have to say no one's ever asked me that one before. But what it is— I think—is this sensation of everything being not quite real. Or not real enough, anyway."

Goku traded looks with Yoshida. "This is something you have to beware of," the older man said. "You think it's being skeptical, but it's not. It's more along the lines of dissociation.

Anything can happen to you in a dissociative state, most of it bad. If you do not have a strong sense of what is real to you, you are without a rudder—"

"What's real to me," Konstantin said impatiently, "is being traced to the mattress I'm sleeping on and interrogated in the middle of the night, like George Orwell's favorite nightmare. I want to know who authorized that invasion of privacy and what it was for." She looked from the cloud-monitor to Goku and back again. "Now, do I get some *real* answers or are we going to talk in circles about rudders and moral compasses until our ears bleed?"

"The *real* answer—one of them—is, I was watching and waiting for the right time to engage casino security, when you and your wannabe cyborg friend came stomping into the middle of everything and got yourselves busted," said Goku.

"Just ask me," Konstantin said. "I'll tell you all about it."

"Tell me about what—how you escaped from a paddy wagon and left the cyborg behind?" Goku shrugged. "Don't bother, *I* can tell you all about that. I was prepared to go all the way, take the whole ride from start to finish. I had a whole carton of cigarettes and a dead man's switch with a black box, and I was ready to go. And then you and Mr. Machine stole my ride."

"Sorry," said Konstantin. "I was investigating a complaint from the guy about the casino, something about brainwashing. When he claimed we wouldn't be able to get out of the paddy wagon, I figured he was just a sore loser who'd spent himself broke."

"That was your first visit to lowdown Hong Kong casino?" asked Yoshida.

"Yes," Goku said, before she could answer.

Konstantin nodded at him. "OK, I'm impressed already."

"I know because you were able to find your exit prompt,"

he went on, as if she hadn't spoken. "The first visit to lowdown Hong Kong is always a normal experience. Your second visit, they've got your data and they can play with you all they want, play little tricks on you. Or big ones."

"Like what?" Konstantin asked.

"Like hiding your exit prompt."

Konstantin was silent for a moment. "And if you come back as somebody else?"

"If you come back often enough, it doesn't matter," Goku said. "Most people—all of them who show up at lowdown, anyway—don't really change identity when they come as someone else. They might act a little different for the sake of whatever persona they're wearing, but they aren't different people. The same information keeps adding up, pretty soon the casino knows what you're going to do even before you do."

Konstantin shook her head. "We've got similar kinds of identification programs but that sounds pretty farfetched."

"That's because you're not in this just for the sake of it," Goku said, leaning toward her slightly. "You always come in here as a cop on a case. This isn't your idea of fun. *You* don't wish it was all for real."

"Oh, I don't know," Konstantin said. "Maybe I've just never found the one set-up I could really dig into. Not that I'm hoping I will."

"Let me know if you ever decide to go on a quest," said Goku. "The task force needs the data."

Konstantin felt a surge of apprehension. "*What* task force?"

"We're a loose body of law-enforcement officers from different parts of the world where substantial percentages of the population use AR for recreation, or other purposes."

"And what laws are you all enforcing?" Konstantin asked, even more suspicious.

"We're not, yet." Goku produced his cigarette case and slipped out a long, white cigarette, twirling it through five fingers before placing it in his mouth. As usual, it lit itself. "We're still trying to figure out if attempting to protect the average AR citizen is worth the effort."

"Good question. Kind of offensive, but good. Don't blow smoke in my face, I'm warning you. Is this task force the same as East/West Precinct?"

"East/West has membership."

"And who has leadership?"

Nobody said anything. Konstantin looked from Goku to the cloud-monitor. "Is that one of those members-only secrets?"

Goku shrugged, blowing a stream of smoke into the air.

"Or don't *you* know?" Konstantin added impulsively.

Now her Japanese friend gave her a look. She burst out laughing.

"You don't, do you?" She looked at the older guy in the monitor, but he wasn't giving anything away. "You don't, because this is all one more stupid AR charade. What is it— training program? Final exam? Teamwork-building exercise? Or just general intelligence gathering, seeing how much *real* shit you can get people to tell you online?" She got up. "Nice try, *vatos*, but, like they used to say in Compton, I gots to go. If that slang doesn't register on the East/West meter, just check your email. It's probably in there between *The Communist Manifesto* and *The Cyberpunk Manifesto*."

Her exit prompt flickered into visibility and disappeared again. She stared at the place where it should have been and activated the confirmation subroutine. The subroutine appeared to remain inert, but she could feel it execute. A heartbeat later, she was in the exit hall among the rest of the ghosts. Another instance, she thought with some amusement, of the triumph of faith over mere empiricism. Like the man said, you just gotta believe.

"I can appreciate your desire for complete security," Taliaferro said, "and I concur completely. But I think you're also really beginning to go rooftop. You have to admit, there's something about it." He waved one hand at the broad, flat expanse. There was surprisingly little wind. "If you want, I'll put an extra chaise up on my home roof tonight, so you can try out the sleeping part."

"I'll think about it," Konstantin said. "But right now I want to see what you got on surveillance."

"All right, but you're not going to like this." Konstantin watched herself go through everything again from an ever changing series of angles, as Taliaferro's tap switched vantage points at random. It was like watching a movie directed by a student who had been overexposed to late-twentieth-century music video—a bit dizzying but not disastrous, and almost good.

The change came after she and Goku left the Empire State Building. She could only sit and stare at the screen, unsure whether to be shocked or merely embarrassed. Next to her, Taliaferro was very pointedly not looking at the screen.

"I wouldn't put a tattoo there," she said after a bit. "But if I did, it wouldn't be that one."

Taliaferro shrugged. "I didn't watch it all the way through the first time, so I don't know what you're referring to."

"Thanks," she said, letting out a deep sigh of relief. "I appreciate that lie more than I can say."

Dervish had some very slick software. He had grabbed her image during their phone call, no doubt. He had not only cleaned up the resolution but also retouched it to make it more flattering, before slipping into the footage with the other people, which offended her even more. "Maybe I should file it, in case I ever need an alibi," she said. "Zap a copy to someone so they can dissect it. DiPietro's probably the best expert we've got in video toasting."

"It looks to me like they put it through a regular television filter before sending it on," said Taliaferro. "DiPietro wouldn't find that much in the way of moving parts." Pause. "So I see no reason to put yourself through that kind of embarrassment."

Konstantin nodded absently. "Are you sure I shouldn't look for an even better excuse?"

"Only if you really want to make work for yourself." Without looking, he reached over and blanked the screen. "He's a show-off, with a very nasty sense of humor."

A cartoon icon of an old-fashioned cellphone appeared on Taliaferro's screen and played the opening bars of Bach's Toccata and Fugue in D Minor. Taliaferro looked at her questioningly.

"Yeah, go ahead and answer it," Konstantin said. "Maybe it's Phase 3 Interpol with a lucrative job offer."

The angry virtual face of Susannah Ell appeared on the screen instead. She was calling from her online studio, which was littered with ripped cloth and what seemed to be the broken bodies of her assistants. "Do you have any idea," Ell fumed, "how much billable time it's going to cost me to rebuild my business?"

Konstantin cleared her throat. "When did this happen?"

"Sometime within the last hour, thank you very much for your concern, I'm so sure." Ell's hair coiled menacingly on her shoulders. "He just popped right up like he was supposed to be here. My software certainly thought so. I was on a snipe hunt in Hong Kong. As soon as I realized it was a snipe hunt, I parachuted back here, but it was too late. They went crazy and tore the place up before killing each other."

"What kind of snipe hunt in Hong Kong?" Konstantin asked her.

"Some casino sent for my portfolio and then invited me to an interview. I knew I shouldn't have gone. I hadn't thought I should go at the time, but I was curious and they wouldn't give me any details unless I logged in personally. When I got there, someone gave me a password and I walked in on something that—well. It didn't have anything to do with the kind of designing I do. I didn't know anyone there *except* one rather familiar face. I had the presence of mind to grab a screen before I left. Would you like to see it?"

Before Konstantin could answer, Ell was replaced by a still from the footage she had just been looking at on Taliaferro's machine. The perspective zoomed in on a face in the center. Konstantin was tempted to tell her they'd both been set up, but that wouldn't have enhanced Ell's confidence in the Techno-Crime squad.

"Why are you calling me?" Konstantin asked abruptly. "I thought you were going to throw your lot in with Phase 3 Interpol?"

Ell hesitated. "I couldn't afford to buy a low number on the waiting list."

Billable time, billable justice; it made a sense of its own, Konstantin thought.

"And I figured that if you had so much time that you could play in Hong Kong with your own face on, your caseload must not be overwhelming," Ell went on, acid creeping back into her tone. "Or—don't tell me—you do all your *undercover* work *bare*faced?"

"Sometimes," Konstantin said. "There's a quarantine on your dominion now?"

"It's automatic in the case of vandalism, in case it's a viral infection."

"We'll replace the domain provider's with a police cordon, and then we'll do a complete crime-scene on it," Konstantin told her. "Have you altered anything?"

Ell sighed. "I tried picking up a few swatches."

"Put them back, and don't touch anything else. It would be better if you watched everything on TV for now."

"Perfect." Ell's sour expression deepened. "When someone asks me where the summer line is, I'll just tell them I was watching TV and I got so caught up in a mini-series that I forgot to work." She broke the connection.

Konstantin sat back and looked at Taliaferro. "Did you manage to grab that still from the casino she showed us?"

Taliaferro put it on the screen for her. The face-matching program was already running on it. "You go have a look at Ell's damage," he said. "I'll let you know who else was there."

Ogada caught up with her as she was walking through the squad room to 'suit up. "Someone sent me a screen capture of you," he told her. "Extremely flattering, but unmistakably you. You want to explain it?"

"No," she told him and walked faster.

10

"Bitpicking," Celestine said, not bothering to cover her disgust. "I *hate* bitpicking. This is for Geekforce, not *real* cops. Please, can I go to auto-theft?"

Konstantin ignored her. They were standing at the designated boundary of Susannah Ell's ruined studio, facing in from the spot where the standard entry-point had been. DiPietro was finishing a walk-around of the perimeter to make sure that the area had not grown or shrunk in size, and that no voyeur cams had managed to insinuate themselves. The program he was using manifested as a bloodhound, which Konstantin thought was unnecessarily whimsical. DiPietro had explained to her, at some length, that studies had proved that people worked better with programs that mimicked living creatures. "You can develop a relationship with a dog," he'd said, scratching the program behind the ears. "Maybe you could develop a relationship with a metal detector, but then you'd probably be too weird to use it right." Left unsaid had been the fact that the police department's supplier made bloodhound programs and not mechanical programs. Konstantin had waved him off before he could give her the bloodhound's complete pedigree.

Maybe it would have been a bit less irritating if the bloodhound had not designated each area as conforming to original coordinates by lifting its leg. Not just irritating but discomfiting—the program seemed even more canine than a real dog. But DiPietro had volunteered to use it and he was more than happy with it, so she supposed it shouldn't have mattered. And, given the fact that Ell's assistants had been governed by a dog AI, perhaps it was only appropriate.

The assistants themselves were still scattered over the floor. Spilling out of their torn and broken forms were not blood and gore but springs, gears, cogs, and ball bearings. More whimsy—Ell had confirmed that these were the standard innards for this model of assistant. She found it easier to make any program adjustments via analog mechanicals than by trying to manipulate software. "As a couture engineer," she'd said, "I do almost all of my work with my hands. Or a reasonable facsimile."

Artists, thought Konstantin.

DiPietro finished his circuit of the studio with the bloodhound, and came over to where Konstantin was waiting with Celestine. To her bemusement, it chose her foot to lie down on; barely half a second later, she was looking at a pop-up with the studio data profile. DiPietro looked at her questioningly.

"Yes, it's *very* efficient," Konstantin said, "but I think it begs the question of why anyone would feel the need to have a relationship with a program."

"Studies show—"

"So you told me. I'm just not that much of an animist." She turned to Celestine. "*Now* you can call Geekforce and have them dust the place. They can bitpick, you can supervise. There weren't going to be any exciting stolen-car chases today, anyway," she added as Celestine started to protest. She frowned down at the program, which was still lying on her foot and was looking up at her in perfect bloodhound mournfulness. "I'm going to see if I can get an audience with the elusive Hastings Dervish."

"You know he probably won't see you," Celestine said.

"Oh, I know he won't," Konstantin said. "So he can just see

someone else." She slid her foot out from under the dog. "Excuse me."

"Sure," said the dog, and put his head down on his paws.

In keeping with its exorbitant prices, You (Not You) had an access that remained invisible to all users below a certain credit rating, which made it moot for close to ninety-five percent of the people using AR at any time. Not that this stopped anyone from claiming to have seen it. Common wisdom held that anyone who claimed to have seen it probably hadn't, while anyone who had certainly wasn't going to tell you where to find it.

Konstantin had originally classified it as another rest-stop along the P. T. Barnum Highway of Life, but that had been before the advent of characteristic identifier software. You (Not You) claimed to produce custom-made personas impervious to any identifier software of any type, by massive and exotic encryption of the wearer's output. You (Not You)—"The name says it all," the sales representative had explained when Konstantin had first contacted them months earlier, suspecting some kind of fraud. She had had to send the prospectus they'd given her out to the Geekforce people with a careful note: *Can they do what they claim, and are they actually doing it?* The Geekforcers, whose dedicated concentration on data—and only data—put them on the level of a cloistered religious order, had responded that most people could not afford any program sophisticated enough to break the encryption. Konstantin was pretty sure that this stipulation didn't apply to lowdown Hong Kong. On the other hand she was willing to gamble that, with so many other suckers to fleece, Hong Kong mound might accept her persona at face value, especially if she did nothing out of the ordinary.

And if she could have figured out exactly what that might have entailed, it would have been a perfect plan. Still, even as an imperfect plan, it had merit.

She waited in the entry hall while Taliaferro contacted You (Not You) offline in an official capacity. It wasn't long before he got back to her with the access code. "They're delighted to help us," he said, "at their going rate."

"Ogada will kill me."

"Not if it works."

"I didn't say I was worried, I was just noting it for the record." She fed the access code into her address-finder.

A second later, she was standing on a skyscraper rooftop in a high wind that was almost authentic enough to make her want to blink. More rooftops, she thought. No wonder Taliaferro thought she was starting to feel at home. Or maybe AR was actually full of latent claustrophobes—

"Detective Konstantin?"

The voice behind her was not loud but it cut through the sound of the wind and other ambient noise without problem. Konstantin turned; the man who had spoken was wearing a sort of frock-coat—morning coat? What *were* those things called? He was exactly as tall as she was and had short, thick black hair of the sort that refused combing. Something about the shape of his face reminded her a lot of one of her uncles, though she couldn't have said which. Before she could answer him, he nodded and took a step to the left.

"This way."

He gestured at a single, isolated elevator car waiting with its door open, looking like an oddly misplaced closet or booth. It was all old polished brass and wood paneling, high-class antique—not a mere reproduction but the real thing recreated bit by bit, byte by byte, actual size to pixel, resolution so complete that if you put your nose to the paneling, you could see the exact texture of the grain, and if you touched your finger to it, you would see your fingerprint in the shine.

"It's perfectly safe," he added.

"I was just admiring it," she said and stepped inside. He followed, pulling the outer door closed and then the folding metal gate. Unable to help herself, she put her face as close to the wood paneling as she dared and saw she'd been right. The floor gave a small, genteel lurch to indicate they were ascending. "This is perfect, isn't it?"

"It certainly is." The man carefully moved a black-handled lever and Konstantin felt the elevator accelerate a bit. "Hand-scanned and hand-corrected, built up in layers from wire frame with no dithering or fiddling. We are part of the World Within project."

Shouldn't that be "we (not we)"? she wanted to say, and somehow managed not to. "Very ambitious undertaking," she said after a moment. "Do you really think it's possible?"

"Don't you?"

"I don't know. I can't imagine trying to reproduce—"

"*Recreate.*"

"—*recreate*, yes, sorry—I can't imagine trying to recreate every human artifact still extant."

The man smiled. His eyes crinkled very slightly at the corners. "If you're thinking in terms of a group of college students armed with scanners and notebooks for extra credit, yes, that's impossible. When you get, say, whole towns to agree to scan all of their favorite items for you—including buildings, bridges, landmarks—then it becomes something more conceivable."

"Except for the storage space," Konstantin said good-naturedly. "I can't conceive of that much storage space."

"Most people can't. Fortunately, we have machines to do

it." He moved the handle again and the elevator came to a gradual stop. "We're here."

He pulled back the doors for her, and she stepped out into a strangely bare room with grey carpeting, large windows curtained in translucent white, and two smallish but very overstuffed chairs facing a dais.

"Our showroom and fitting room," the man said, gesturing for her to sit in one of the chairs.

"Thank you," Konstantin said, feeling awkward. "Tell me, are you always so formal, or is it just because I'm the police?"

"We are always this formal," he said. "This is the way it's done. This is what people expect when they pay the kind of money we charge them. Bespoke items demand a certain kind of attitude and ritual, whether it's a Hong Kong suit or a Hong Kong persona."

Konstantin hoped her smile looked as formal as his. "I see my partner's briefed you."

"We need to know as much as possible in order to produce something that meets your needs. At the moment, your partner is transmitting any footage available, along with a complete profile of your vitals and any other pertinent output data. We have to encrypt your vitals so that identifier software can't get onto you by way of a simple lie detector."

Konstantin gave the outfit points for lateral thinking. "Our own identifier software can work that way."

"Then we look at mannerisms, vocal tics, posture, and anything else that might register as a statistic." The man paused and looked at his watch. "Ah, they're done with your vitals."

"They're done collecting them?"

"No, they're done encrypting them. The Mannerism Workshop says you sigh a lot."

Konstantin considered that. "Figures."

"And you blink."

She blinked several times before the comment registered. "I do? Oh. Well, yeah, that too. Is that going to be a problem?"

"Oh, no," the man said expansively, spreading both perfect hands. "They just like to make the client aware of what they have to work with."

"How many people do you have in this workshop?"

Now he looked satisfied. "Oh, no people—none at all. It's one hundred percent AI staffed." He hesitated. "*I'm* an AI, actually."

"Naturally," Konstantin agreed, covering her surprise, although she was hard put to say why she should have been surprised. The guy had been acting like an AI all along, so why should she have been surprised to find that it had been no act?

He consulted his watch again. "We'll have your persona coming up on the dais now, momentarily—"

The light shimmered and a form began to coalesce under the lights. At first, Konstantin couldn't say a word. Then she turned to the AI man without bothering to disguise her anger. If he'd been a person, she might have hit him, or even tried to think of a reason to arrest him.

"You can send that abomination right back to the drawing board," she said, "and you can tell your one hundred percent AI-staffed workshop that—"

"I see I should have told them to warn you." Taliaferro's image insty-screened itself between their chairs.

Konstantin looked from him to the twelve-year-old girl on the dais and back again. "*You're* in on this?"

"I'm sorry, it was the best and most obvious solution."

"You're *sorry*?" Konstantin glanced at the AI man; he was staring into space as if he were completely unaware of her or Taliaferro. She would have appreciated the courtesy if she hadn't been so angry. "*I* can't wear *that*. You *know* how I feel—"

"Which is why it's the best persona they can come up with. With the vitals encryption, the mannerism redirection, and your known dislike of child-masquers, it'll keep *everybody* off your track, including Goku Mura and the East/West gang. *And* their task force, whoever they are. I'm trying to track them down now, but it's pretty much an impossible job from out here." Taliaferro looked pained. "I know it's awful. I knew you'd hate it as soon as I saw the calculations, and I should have told them to go a little slower with you instead of just throwing it in your face like that."

Konstantin was silent. After a while, she got up and went over to the dais.

The girl was an ethnic mix, predominantly Mongolian, the sort of look that would not attract any attention in lowdown Hong Kong.

In the lowdown Hong Kong AR, Konstantin corrected herself. Looking at the child persona made her feel it was very important to remind herself, by way of emphasis of the fact that it was all happening in AR. So *technically*, ever so *technically*, it was all *un*-real. Or *non*-real, as she'd heard Celestine—or was it DiPietro?—say once. Other than real. Simulated. Be anyone, do anything. When anything can happen, nothing matters. Does it?

"Doré," Taliaferro said.

"I'm not talking to you," she said. "So, um—" She pointed at the AI man, who came alert and stood up, looking at her expectantly.

"So do I need any special help putting this on?" she asked him.

"You'll find it all very familiar to put on, but we do have a private area for you to use to get acclimated. You're going to have to get used to feeling like it's alternately sluggish and anticipating you."

She nodded. "Show me what to do."

"If I could say something?" The AI man's expression was still the standard friendly, helpful concern, but the concern seemed a bit more predominant than before.

"All right," Konstantin said after a moment.

"This is not the first project of this kind that we've done here," he said. "Most clients have hated the results."

"What about those who didn't?" she asked. "Did they just not care?"

"Oh, no, they cared." The concern in the AI man's face deepened even more. "They fell in love."

Konstantin winced. "*Disgusting.*"

"Doré," Taliaferro said again.

"I'm *still* not talking to you."

That it felt nothing like being a twelve-year-old girl was no consolation to Konstantin; she still felt like a pervert, and occasionally a parasite as well. The persona, who called herself the New Blue Rose of Chiba City for no reason Konstantin could discern, was an assassin, a popular occupation among lowdown children, but at least not a gang member or a whore. She came supplied with a mythical record of pops (lowdown assassin-speak for *kills*) and a special cat that would have the casual observer believing she was a regular on the assassination circuit. Her specialties were blades, wires, and improvised weapons, and she always worked close up because she liked the personal touch.

The good thing about functioning behind so many layers of encryption, Konstantin thought, was not having to worry about keeping a straight face. She wondered what her ex would have made of that, and then wished she hadn't. This had been the longest time she'd gone without sparing a thought for her ex; it was a shame to break a winning streak.

The AI man had been right about the persona feeling sluggish and intuitively anticipatory by turns. The trick was keeping track of which areas had the greatest amounts of encryption and remembering the slight variations in response times. It was more like trying to execute a tricky dance routine than merely wearing a disguise, even a disguise she hated. As she sidled through a wet, heavily littered back alley leading to one of the casino's service entrances, she wondered if Goku Mura felt anything similar when he was tricked out in his kid-face.

Or maybe he didn't need as much encryption as she did. Maybe he found it easy to fall into new patterns of movement and behavior, or at least different ones. Some people did, the AI man had told her; the workshop AIs at You (Not You) maintained a massive catalog of behavioral decision-trees modeled on observation of volunteers, and added to it regularly. Konstantin couldn't imagine who would volunteer for such a thing. Maybe all of them were like Goku Mura.

The most unsettling part of her new persona, however, was how *small* it made her feel—not in character but from within the character. The kid-face felt like an oversized machine around her, even when she was perfectly in synch with it. *It's a long way from here to the wall*, she thought, taking what felt like giant steps up a concrete stairwell and listening to the tanky echo of her footsteps. *Think ahead, and don't fall down.*

But would it be so out of character if she did, she wondered suddenly, finding the staff entrance to the casino and standing on tiptoe to push her index finger against the entry button, and waiting for the discreet click that would mean the door had unlocked for her. She was twelve—not exactly the age of completely reliable coordination. They'd made her a nailbiter, she saw—not so bad that her fingertips had turned to misshapen bulbs, but serious enough for her ridged nails to show no white, with lots of torn skin around the cuticles. The detail was painfully authentic—the sort of thing the customers would pay and overpay for, in the name of something or other. Verisimilitude? Better-than-average kayfabe? Or just attention to detail. Whatever it is, customize it. Customize until your ears bleed.

Maybe hers were already bleeding so much she hadn't heard the door unlock. She tried the handle; when it didn't budge, she pressed the entry button again.

"Hey, *you*. Fuck-ass lemongrass."

Konstantin jumped and turned around. The hair had been shaved and the new stubble bleached white, but she recognized the nine-year-old boy. Did he know who she was? She searched the sullen face with its crude little tattoos over the eyebrows and on the bridge of the nose—ideograms that were probably supposed to indicate what an incredibly dangerous little shit he was—but couldn't tell one way or another.

He shuffled a couple of steps closer and in spite of the fact that she was taller, she flattened against the door behind her. "Whaddaya mean, lookin' down at me like that, you know how fuck-ass foul that is?"

"I can't help it," Konstantin said, annoyed but feeling as uneasy as she knew he wanted her to, which annoyed her even more. "You're short."

"Not me, big bitch, I'm normal. You're too fuck-ass big. What're you gonna do about it?"

"What *can* I do about it? I'm—"

"Kneel down is what you can do about it. So get right down

there, just like you're gonna pray." He shuffled a tiny bit closer. "Come on, big bitch, you fuck-ass deaf?"

Konstantin started to bend her knees and then suddenly leaned forward and shoved him as hard as she could with both hands.

"*Hey—*"

She caught a glimpse of him flying backwards toward the stairway leading down before she whirled, bashed the entry button with a knuckle, and then yanked as hard as she could on the door. The click sounded like a rifle being cocked and she staggered briefly before scrambling across the threshold and pulling the door shut behind her.

"*Fuck-ass, I swear you die—!*"

She held the door for a moment and then pelted down the hall to her left, swinging around a left turn and pelting along another hallway. This one was lined with open doors; private games, she saw as she went by, mahjong and dominoes, regular and mutant versions. The dominoes rooms were especially energetic, the tiles clacking and clattering as men in shirtsleeves threw them down with great force and announced something she couldn't understand—their scores, maybe, or just a variant on the standard gamer war cry. Showrooms, for the discerning player looking for something a bit more sophisticated than mere jeweled tables and fiery opal lakes.

She skidded to a sudden stop in front of a doorway and hesitated, wondering if she should go in and hide. This room was a private card game with an unusual group of players—one astoundingly beautiful woman in full Dragon Lady get-up, including cigarette in a holder, among a table of almost equally handsome young men who were in various states of undress. Before she could decide to keep running, one of the young men looked up from his cards and saw her.

The muscles in his dark brown arms made her think of

large pythons crammed into a tight sack. He had a roughly triangular face with a fighter's nose and very large almond-shaped eyes that tilted up at the outer corners. The eyes narrowed suspiciously as he lowered his cards to the table. He was barechested, his shirt draped over the back his chair. So he'd lost his shirt already, Konstantin thought, wanting to giggle at the silliness of it all. The Dragon Lady must have been pleased about that, as he had an impressive bodybuilder's physique, broad chest and wasp waist exaggerated just enough to be eye-catching without tipping over into absurdity—a rare show of minor restraint in AR.

The rest of the players noticed him staring and turned to see what had captured his interest. The Dragon Lady raised her drawn-on eyebrows in perfect world-weary surprise and then turned back to the table.

"All right," she said in a low, threatening voice, "who sent out for chicken?"

"Help me," Konstantin said. The voice came out little-girl-lost desperate. "He's gonna kill me."

"Then you better keep running, Chicken Little," said the Dragon Lady airily, waving one hand over her head dismissively.

The shirtless bodybuilder jerked a thumb to his right. "Hurry now."

More annoyed than ever, Konstantin ran down to the end of the hall, turned another corner, and jumped into a large empty elevator just before the doors came together. She wasn't actually afraid that Goku was going to kill her—she had just wanted to see if she could get some help. Apparently not; from the disgusted sound of the Dragon Lady's voice, Konstantin thought the woman probably felt the same about kid-face in AR as she did. *Just my luck.*

The elevator gave a jerk and Konstantin felt it start to move backwards and down at a slight angle instead of straight up or down. As it began to pick up speed, the doors suddenly turned transparent, and she saw that she was moving through a long tunnel on oily-looking rails; she could see Goku in silhouette at the far end growing smaller and smaller, one hand pounding on what she figured must be the call button. Then he raised the same hand and pointed it at her, holding his wrist steady with the other. Konstantin saw his head drop slightly; she threw herself down on the floor just as something hit the back wall, crackled, and blew a hole in it about the size of her head. The doors hadn't gone transparent—they'd disappeared.

What the hell *kind of a thing was that?* Furious, she elbowed Taliaferro's connection.

"He used a demolecularizer." From his casual tone, he might have been talking about something she had in her kitchen drawer.

"A *what*?"

"Something he pulled out of his catalog. Nice bit of premium stuff. Reusable." Taliaferro sounded amused. "If he'd hit you, all of that expensive encrypted face would have gone *kablooie*, leaving you in your virtual underwear with your identity hanging out."

Konstantin rolled over and sat up with some difficulty. The elevator dipped and swayed as it kept accelerating. "You think he knows who I am?"

"No, but he seems to know what kind of face you've got on and he wants to strip it off you."

"What do you mean?" The elevator hit a bump and dropped almost straight down for two seconds, giving her an all-too-realistic sensation of freefall.

"He recognizes the expensive get-up. He might even know You (Not You)'s work. He probably thinks you're the advance for a new kid gang out to take his turf." Pause. "Of course, I'm just guessing."

"OK. Next question: what is this thing and where am I going?"

"It's only a carnival ride," Taliaferro told her. "A little roller-coaster interlude to break up the monotony of everyone chasing around trying to kill each other."

"How long does it last?" Konstantin asked, starting to feel breathless. She closed her eyes and the feeling of acceleration was gone, although the elevator was still rocking from side to side and tilting up and down. The incipient vertigo vanished and she sighed with relief.

"About another minute. Then you get dumped outside in the alley. Look alive, because Goku's going to be waiting there for you."

"Is there any way to get out before that?"

"Only if you have a Lucky Escape coupon in your cat."

The coupon materialized in Konstantin's small hand, which at that moment actually looked oversized to her, but still like a child's. The elevator slid to a halt, and a trap door in the ceiling fell open.

"Wow," Konstantin said, staring up at it. "Talk about your *deus ex machina*. Doesn't it know the doors've already been shot off this thing?"

"The trap door comes with the Lucky Escape, not the elevator," Taliaferro told her serenely. "I suggest you not waste it, however."

Konstantin sighed and got to her feet. "I know. There's no putting the bastard back in the cat once it's out, and if you waste it, it taints anything else you use." She managed to catch the edge of the opening with both hands on her first jump and hung there for a moment, swaying a little and gathering her will.

For this kind of physical maneuver in AR, it was more a matter of will than physical strength. If she let herself think of her body in a reclining chair, she'd find herself lying flat on her back on the floor of the elevator. What she had to do was sense-remember what the movement felt like for real, which would enable her nerves to provide just enough cues for the hotsuit to provide the proper sensation.

You might think this is the squish-headed part, Tonic had told her. *It's more like learning to use a prosthetic limb, except the limb is actually an auxiliary body. Kind of.*

She managed to get one elbow up on top of the elevator, and then the other. After that, she was surprised to find that getting herself out onto the roof of the elevator car wasn't as hard as she had thought it would be.

Child's body, she thought. *Child's body, but I'm willing it with adult strength. I guess.* It was as good a theory as any. She went to the front of the elevator, clambered down so that she was dangling by her hands again, and then dropped. Tarzan was a girl. Take that.

She found a reusable flashlight in her cat and started to head back the way she had come, before remembering the roller-coaster-style drops. "Taliaferro?"

"Walk straight ahead until you hit an incline. There's a door in it that should lead to one of the casino's many infamous secret passages. Follow *that* in any direction for any period of time and use any exit you care to. You'll end up in the casino. And then look doubly alive, because Goku will have figured out why you didn't appear in the alley, and he'll know where to look for you."

"God, this is all so calculated," she muttered, shining the light ahead of her as she went.

Taliaferro chuckled. "As opposed to real life?"

Konstantin kept between the greasy metal rails, noting that the floor seemed to be unremarkable black parquet. No one had found a good reason yet to colonize the more horizontal parts of the elevator shaft, or tunnel, or whatever it was, something that she might well be able to use to her own advantage in some way. She took a moment to activate the bread-crumber in the cat before continuing.

The incline was at a perfect forty-five-degree angle; the door was set into it like an old storm-cellar. It was chained shut, but she found she could pry an opening just wide enough to slip through. No stairway, just a very steep ramp that she stumbled on, almost sending herself rolling all the way to the bottom, where the floor evened out and became a standard secret passage, complete with peepholes—so many that Konstantin turned off her flashlight. They were all on the left side of the passage, which meant that the other side might be an external wall.

The first half-dozen peepholes were all set too high for her to look through, and she didn't want to spare anything else from the cat. "Taliaferro?"

"All I can get it to tell me is 'secret passage,'" he told her. "I'm not even sure what part of the building you're in, whether you're above- or below-ground. Probably below, but don't quote me. The casino develops uneven terrain when it needs it."

"Don't we all," Konstantin muttered, not even sure what she meant except that it sounded right. She came to a peephole low enough for her to put her eye to, and did so.

She was looking at a woman lying on a bed in a room that was unmistakably someone's idea of what a high-class brothel in the Orient must have looked like in the nineteenth century, except the man standing at the end of the bed was dressed in detail-perfect twentieth-century punk-rocker drag. The woman was slumped against satin pillows, one knee bent so that the split in her black silk dress showed plenty of thigh. The guy unbuckled a studded belt and tossed it on a velvet chair. His hair stuck out from his head in all directions in a myriad of lacquered spikes.

Konstantin shook her head. For some reason, people thought that anachronism equaled imagination and simultaneously canceled out cliché. But at least in AR you never had to worry about messing up your hair spikes. She moved on to the next peephole she could reach.

A seven-foot man dressed entirely in red except for the black hood over his head was holding an enormous sword in two hands while another man knelt down and put his head on a well-used chopping block. Behind the second man was a long line that extended beyond the entrance: men, women, lizard-people, bird-people, and a few other creatures she couldn't identify, all waiting patiently to be executed.

A moment later, she realized that the swordsman was actually nude. She flinched and moved on quickly. At the next peephole, she hesitated; did she really want to see any more of lowdown Hong Kong's non-gambling attractions? No, of course not, but it was her job. She stood on tiptoe and put her eye to the opening.

An eyeball stared back at her. She yelled and jumped back, hit the opposite wall, and then just stuck there.

Sharp, thin lines of very bright light appeared slowly around the peephole. The lines held for a moment before exploding outward, blinding her. Konstantin struggled, trying to free herself. Two big hands took hold of her wrists and peeled her arms slowly away from the wall with a practiced motion before pulling her hands up over her head and stripping the rest of her body away from whatever she was stuck to. Her feet dangled as she was carried through the doorway and casually tossed down, the child body tumbling backwards easily in natural acrobatics. She was on her feet again almost before she knew it, with a vicious little serrated blade in her left hand. Only in AR, she thought, looking up at the muscular, shirtless man she'd seen gambling in the private room with the Dragon Lady and the others, would anyone think that a junior Swiss Army steak knife could stand up to a man nearly seven feet tall. From the look on his face, Konstantin surmised he was thinking something similar.

"What're you gonna do that with that little toad-sticker—cut me?" He stood with his legs apart, hands on his wasp waist. "I don't think so, *little girl*." Contempt twisted up his mouth. "You've come around the wrong person, you pervert. Some of us know how to deal with your kind, we don't all fall for your little baby-whore routine. That surprise you?"

He took a step toward her and she jumped back. She tried brandishing the knife, but she felt as if she were threatening him with a nail file. *Come any closer and I'll give you a manicure, you big bully.*

"You filthy-minded creatures come in here thinking you're gonna exploit a lot of weak-minded degenerates that can't help themselves. But I got a little news for you, you pervert. I know some tricks, too. I know how to grab your arm just so that it makes your muscles knot up in such a bad cramp, you sprain it for real." He bent down and put his big hands on his knees. "Give you some bad muscle spasms, maybe you'll think twice about coming back in here lookin' like a *kid*, you unmitigated pervert."

"Why don't you just mind your own business, big fella?" Konstantin winced, not just at the childish, pouty sound of her voice but at her words. What she had actually tried to say was, *Leave me alone, I'm an employee working undercover.* "Taliaferro, doesn't this thing have an override?"

"How should I know?" came the reply faintly. "*You're* the one wearing it."

"Look at the schematic for me."

"Hey, fuckhead, I'm *talkin'* to you."

"So what?" Konstantin's bratty voice said.

"I *said*, if you *want* a beatin', I can help you out."

"Gotta catch me first."

He lunged for her and she dived between his legs, the persona taking over again. Great reflexes, she thought as she rolled over once, sprang to her feet and kept going out the door to the secret passage without missing a beat, while her would-be captor was still in the process of turning around. Still, she thought as her legs carried her along, a persona with pre-programmed responses was hard to get used to. It was like being inside a hotsuit that had suddenly developed a mind and an agenda of its own.

She reached the end of the hallway and took a left. Or rather, the persona took a left—she'd have gone the other way if she'd had any control, but she was just along for the ride now. New Blue Rose apparently knew plenty Konstantin didn't. She gasped as she felt herself leap forward suddenly in the dark hallway, her feet kicking nothing but air. She landed heavily on all fours at the bottom of a short flight of stairs, staggered sideways, and found a railing bolted to the wall. There was just enough room for her to plant her butt on it and slide the rest of the way down, before tumbling off and rolling over and over again, recovering her feet in front of a pair of swinging doors. Momentum carried her through them, and then she was in the middle of a room full of bored-looking casino croupiers and dealers, some of them sitting at small round tables, others sprawled in easy chairs or on the one sofa, and one who looked like a werewolf standing at a table off to the side, demonstrating something with an oversized deck of cards. Next to the table was a door open just wide enough to show that it was an entrance to the main casino.

Konstantin sprinted for it, managing to grab a card out of

the werewolf's hand without stopping. Then she was skidding into yet another overly mammalian reptile-woman, this one a gilded cobra.

"Brat," the cobra-woman said mildly, and tapped Konstantin lightly on the top of her head with a fan. Konstantin grabbed for it but the woman held it high up out of her reach. "Now, now, don't let's get any ideas above ourselves, shall we?" She grabbed Konstantin by one skinny bicep.

Konstantin howled in surprise and pain. She could feel each of the woman's fingers digging into her arm.

"Oh, what a performance," said the cobra-woman and bent her head as if to strike. Konstantin jumped to one side and the fingers dug in so hard she yelled. "Hold still, you little brat. Do you know what most people would pay for—?"

There was a new hand gripping Konstantin's wrist; one by one, the cobra-woman's fingers were pried off her arm. "I believe this one's for me."

"You *believe*?" The cobra-woman batted her eyes at the man who had spoken. Considering her eyelids rose up from below lizard-style, it was about the strangest thing Konstantin had ever seen in her life, if also the least important. "And what's made you into such a believer?"

"O ye of little faith." The hand gripping Konstantin's wrist lifted her up, and she found herself nearly nose-to-nose with Hastings Dervish. An enormous smile spread slowly over his heavily painted face. "Yes, this *does* have my name on it. Or rather, it will when I get done with it."

Konstantin had time only to think about pushing her panic button for a quick disconnect.

11

"I see you've never had the experience of being jammed before."

The voice seemed to be coming through water, something that gave it a kind of auditory shimmer. Or maybe it was her brain shimmering and shaking in her head like jelly.

"You *are* conscious, by the way. It's just taking a little while for the words to make sense, because of the jamming."

Must be jelly, 'cause jamming don't shake like that . . .

"It's a little surprising that you didn't think of this long ago. It tends to make a subject so tractable. But then, this really isn't your medium, is it?"

Konstantin could see nothing. *I'm blind,* she thought. *Not what I imagined blindness would be: seeing nothing. It's not dark and it's not light . . . it's* nothing. But she didn't panic until she realized she couldn't feel her body at all.

"There, there, *child*. Quiet now. You don't want to give yourself a heart attack, do you?"

Child? Images flashed through her mind, all out of order, elements misplaced—an elevator leading to a fitting room, with a Dragon Lady—no, a cobra—and a big man, shirtless but wearing a suit.

"A shame you can't feel anything. This would calm you." Pause. "Maybe. Or it might, um, stimulate you." The nothing around Konstantin shook with laughter. "After all, that's what you *kids* come in here like this for, isn't it, all those thrills. You little perverts." More laughter. Konstantin tried to concentrate on being able to feel herself breathe. Breathe and the world breathes with you, stop and you die alone—

Except you couldn't die in Artificial Reality. Not for *real*.

"Oh, but what if this *is* an alternative reality, rather than something fake the way so many people seem to think? What happens then? If you were to die for real, but you weren't in your *home* reality, so to speak, would you be just as dead?"

If she shut everything out, the voice, the nothingness, even the sensation of nothingness, she thought, maybe she would be able to feel her lungs inflating and deflating. If she could feel that, she should be able to feel her chest rising and falling, even just very shallowly.

"Now, don't clam up on me, we were communicating so well. Some people would say it doesn't count if you don't know you're talking out loud, but I say communication justifies the means. Life isn't fair, so why should we be?"

The voice didn't fall silent so much as *grey out*; it was the only description Konstantin could think of for the gradually increasing onslaught of nothingness. This must be what it was like to be a ghost, she thought—to be disembodied. The old out-of-body experience reinvented by technology.

No. She thought the word as hard as she could, trying to will substance into it. *Not out-of-body. If you can think, then you have something to think with. I think; therefore—*

"You are—"

in a small room in police headquarters, wearing a hotsuit with transcutaneous nerve

"—stimulation. Do you find this stimulating?"

Someone was holding her hands and stroking them. She willed herself not to flinch or pull away, but to let the return of sensation spread to her wrists and up her arms. No hurry, just let it happen, she told herself. Let it—

Her eyes were closed, the lids very heavy, but she made herself open them.

Dervish's face filled her vision. His own; he was a barefaced liar. That figured, though. His ego would insist on his wearing his own face. At this angle he was distorted, a grotesque, stylized clown-gargoyle.

"A child is an acquired taste." He let one of her hands fall and held the other up so she could see him lace his fingers through hers. "You'd be surprised at how many acquire it in here. People it would never have occurred to out there in meat world—in here, their desires become more rarified. Because, you see, they've done everything they can do in here, and that's *everything*." He began to move his fingers up and down in the spaces between hers. The sensation was too smooth, practically greasy. "Intelligent, sentient creatures, when presented with the complete range of experience, graduate from testing what is possible to testing what they're capable of."

Konstantin could feel her body again but she still couldn't move anything. It was as if she were trying to flex a muscle that wasn't actually there.

"People—humans—are capable of . . . so much. There are things that are technically forbidden even here. But what if they happen and no one—no human—knows, outside of the one who indulged in it?"

Dervish bent her hand back and let his fingers dance on her palm, a sensation that was even more revolting.

"It's the feeling, isn't it. It's the feeling that makes the experience." He leaned over and blew on her open hand, his eyes watching her reaction. "Right, I'm *not* supposed to be able to do that. But in this world, there's no *supposed to*. There is only what is possible, and what I'm capable of. What *I'm* capable of."

He licked his lips. Konstantin would have thought he'd have indulged in something long and pointy and too red, but it was just a normal tongue sliding around very human, very normal lips. "By now you must realize I'm capable of things that they would call . . . outré . . . even in here. Outré, and very, *very* big. And that ain't you, little girl. Never broke a sweat even in the act of jamming you."

The heavy, paralyzed feeling lifted as he pulled back from her, dropping her hand. Konstantin looked around. She was sitting on the floor in what looked like a warehouse full of shelving and boxes, none of which was quite distinct enough for her to see. But then, Dervish wouldn't have wanted her looking at anything but him anyway.

"Now, take this sad, ill-fitting rig back to the hack shack you got it from." Dervish stood over her, bent at the waist with his arms folded. "Tell them to give you a refund. Because it's pointless to try to put one over on me, Officer Konstantin. I'll know you no matter what you show up in. And I can do whatever I like with you." He reached down and put his hands on her shoulders. "And I will."

He pushed her over backwards. Instead of hitting the floor with her back, she found herself on her feet in the exit hall, among the usual crowd of ghosts. None of them was on her frequency.

"Don't take *my* word for it," Taliaferro said, gesturing at the monitor without looking at it.

"I don't want to take your machine's word for it, either," Konstantin told him snappishly. "And I wouldn't, except Celestine's got the same data." She slid her fingers into her hair and massaged her scalp. "So does my 'suit log. For all I know, so does every TV channel in the hemisphere."

"Only the dedicated porn channels. They're the only ones who keep cams in the offline sex clubs. Look on the bright side." Taliaferro patted her shoulder with one big, gentle hand. "You've uncovered a potentially criminal piece of software detectable out here as well as in AR. If it gets into circulation, service providers could face losses in the skintillions from falsified records of billable time. When you clamp Hastings Dervish for this one, you'll be a hero."

"That'll be swell," Konstantin agreed. The wind on the roof picked up slightly, blowing a piece of grit into her eye. Sometimes, she reflected, holding her lower eyelid down while Taliaferro dabbed at her with the corner of a tissue, even the little things went against you. "All I have to do is prove that Dervish's jamming program was created with intent to defraud by fooling the AR interface into registering the user as being *off*line while actually still being *on*line. Maybe that will draw attention away from my new alleged hobby of frequenting sex clubs in and out of AR. Ow," she added.

"Nothing," Taliaferro said, showing her the tissue. "I think it's gone."

"Well, it feels like it's still there." She pulled on her upper lid and thought of the cobra-woman. "The other problem is that, as used, the jamming program doesn't allow the user to continue interacting, you should pardon the expression, in the usual way. It causes disorientation and vertigo."

"Possible disabling weapon, then," Taliaferro said cheerfully. "And maybe Dervish just didn't use the continue feature when he used it on you. Since he wanted you disoriented."

"Maybe," Konstantin said, "but I'm betting there isn't any way to jam all evidence of billable time and still move around to enjoy it."

Taliaferro looked surprised. "Why not?"

"Because if there were, Dervish himself would be using it."

She raised her eyebrows at his skeptical expression. "Well, doesn't that make sense?"

"He could be choosing *not* to use it." There was a pause. "Come on, ask me why. You know you want to."

"Just tell me anyway," Konstantin said. "You know you want to."

Taliaferro shrugged good-naturedly. "Maybe he needs solid evidence of where he is, so you won't suspect he's where he *isn't*."

"And if he were digital," Konstantin said, mostly to herself, "he could be anywhere. Or at least he could prove it."

There was a sharp buzz from Taliaferro's console. "That's gotta be for you," Taliaferro said, pushing back in his chair so she could reach the answer button. "Ogada never wants to talk to me."

Ogada was unhappy, and at great length.

"I hate to admit it but it's quite a good likeness," she said, jerking a thumb at the screen on his desk. "Even *I'd* swear it was me, if I didn't know where I was at the time. But I *don't* have a tattoo there. And I don't smoke herb, or anything else."

Ogada tapped the bottom of the screen. The footage of Konstantin in the sex-club lounge shrank to make room for a box with her hotsuit log. "So whoever toasted up *this* recording has also found a way to falsify the inhouse-insuit record of usage to make it *appear* as if you logged out and spent the afternoon smoking dope and . . . doing *that*."

Onscreen, Konstantin's image continued to embarrass her until she reached over and blanked the screen.

"I'll pee in a cup for you right now," Konstantin said. "Call medical. I was in AR, right here. Check our own surveillance cams. You know that's not me."

Keeping his gaze on her, Ogada reached over and tapped the screen on again. The sex-club playback was replaced by a time-and-date-stamped image of Konstantin coming out of the AR booth and walking quickly through the office. Another cam picked her up in an elevator; still another showed her leaving the building. The angle on the last one was overhead and somewhat strained, but the woman in the recording was unmistakable.

"I'm . . ." Konstantin shook her her head, stunned, ". . . impressed, is all I can think of."

The lines in Ogada's face deepened. "You expect me to believe you." It wasn't a question.

"Well, I did upload the details of the case for you." Konstantin forced herself not to look away from him.

"And I did look them over." There was a long pause. "And the truth is, I *am* inclined to believe you. The most persuasive argument in your favor is that it is completely out of character for you to behave that stupidly." Ogada paused and took a long breath. He took another and Konstantin wanted to hit him. This was worse than the little charade she and the arms dealer had played out. He knew he was going to go on and tell her what the persuasive argument *against* her credibility was, and he knew *she* knew. Why did he insist on playing this like a police drama? Why couldn't he just *talk*?

She sighed. "And the argument against is the fact that this is such an enormous job of detailed toasted footage that it's virtually impossible for even a very rich end-user like Hastings Dervish to have found a way to hack into not only a sex club but also to falsify in-house police-recording and surveillance devices."

To her surprise, Ogada looked pleased rather than annoyed. "Either way, you've got twenty-seven wagonfuls of trouble. If you went out and did that on the clock, that's bad. If our security has been breached to the degree that we can't depend on what we see with our own eyes—" Ogada gestured at the screen "—that's worse. *You're* the head of the technocrime unit. It's *your* job to keep that from happening."

"We *didn't* see that with our own eyes," Konstantin said, reaching over and blanking the screen again angrily. "We're looking at something that was seen *for* us. *Big* difference. But I get it. Who wants me off the job?"

"Nobody," Ogada said. "Nobody gives a shit about you. All the political stuff where heads roll, that starts at *my* level. Does somebody want *me* off *my* job? Absolutely. Except it's nothing personal. They don't so much want to get rid of me as they want simply to be where I am. It's all ambition and getting promoted and building an empire. Middle-management office politics—it would be funny if it were a joke. Nobody actually cares who might take the rap for allowing such an egregious security breach, as long as it isn't them. Do you get that, too?"

Konstantin nodded. "I should solve this one as fast as possible because nobody cares about me."

Ogada's expression became pained. "You're getting that unreal feeling again, aren't you?"

12

"Why should I?" said Darwin. "What did you ever do for me?"

"You didn't *really* get brainwashed, did you?" Konstantin asked him.

He shrugged. "How would I know?"

They were sitting in the observer's gallery overlooking the gaming tables in the casino. The design was simple—a 360-degree panorama screen with a running line of basic information along the top and bottom, giving the number of different tables and players, the current population, and a search-directory access number. The view wasn't great unless you paid extra for zoom, but it was one way to get a look at lowdown Hong Kong without lowdown Hong Kong looking back. Konstantin hoped.

"Do you feel any different?" she asked him.

"Yeah." He produced a piece of chamois and began to shine each of his fingers. "It so happens that I do."

"How?"

Darwin shrugged. "Well, I don't ever want to come out, for one thing."

"Did you ever feel that way before?"

The cyborg shrugged again. "I used to be more curious about what was happening on the ground floor. Now I'm not even vaguely interested."

"How long have you been in, this time?"

"I don't know. A day, I guess, maybe a little longer."

"If that's true, someone must be taking care of you out there—physically. And how are you paying for so much online time? Are you a multi-millionaire and you just forgot to tell me?"

"I won free online-time gambling. Every time I use it up, I win some more." He finished his fingers and went to work on his chest area.

"That doesn't answer my other question about who's taking care of you. *Is* someone taking care of you?"

"Well . . . actually, if you want to know the truth," Darwin said, managing to sound both sheepish and smug at the same time, "I don't really know what my body is doing. I set it free."

Konstantin sighed. "I think I know this one: it's something my grandmother used to say. Something about setting something free, and if it comes back, that's nice, and if it doesn't, hunt it down and kill it. *Her* mother was a hippie in the Summer of Love. You can't set your body free, Darwin, unless you die."

"You're wrong. This is almost as good as the Out door. And if enough people set their bodies free, it probably *will* be the Out door."

"OK, OK," Konstantin said. "I'll ride along for a minute. What happens to your body when you set it free? I know you don't know exactly *what* it's doing, but *how* is it doing anything?"

"That's the part I don't really understand," Darwin said. "The 'how' part. It's just on its own with a new guidance system installed."

"Where did *that* come from?" asked Konstantin, forcing herself to sound patient.

"Here, of course. Where else?"

Are you getting this? Konstantin asked Taliaferro. He popped up a yes for her. "Why don't you tell me who you really are,"

Konstantin said to Darwin after a bit, "and I can check on your body and make sure that everything's all right."

Darwin looked down on her. "*Sure* you will." He gave a short, humorless laugh. "They warned me about this—how people, usually some kind of authority like the police, will offer to *make sure* my body's all right. Then the next thing you know, my body disappears completely, turned into a government zombie slave or broken up and sold for parts. Well, you can just go find some other body to snatch, you're not getting mine. We're *both* free now, me and my body, and we're not going to let you or anyone else control us." Darwin stood up and began to back away from her. "And don't come near me again with your low requests to do your dirty work for you. I'm not your personal ghost. You want to clamp Hastings Dervish, do it yourself."

"We don't normally get customers claiming they've spent *more* time in AR than what's on our billing records," said the pleasant-faced AI in Konstantin's virtual office. Its appearance was nondescript male human, but something in the softly rendered brown-gold features reminded her of Celestine. She fought the inclination to feel kindly toward it.

"You know," Konstantin said, "if the department's service provider *really* felt this was a matter important enough to interrupt me while I'm in AR on police business, I'm surprised they didn't send a *real* person to talk to me."

"All of our real people are currently busy with other customers at the moment," the AI said smoothly. "A customer base the size of ours means there's never a lull in the action. And, of course, every paying customer thinks he or she is the *only* paying customer who needs immediate help. Half of them could be served quite adequately by an AI representative within a time period not longer than eight minutes, and half of those in the thirty seconds it would take to tell them they have a hardware problem that has to be addressed by the hotsuit vendor or manufacturer. However, our dedication to the customer demands that—"

"I read the brochure," Konstantin said irritably. "I've read *all* the brochures. Did you—did anyone read my report?"

The AI seemed to think it over briefly. "Yes."

"Who?"

"I did."

"Just now."

"Yes. But it's in the inbox in Technical Assistance: Anomalies and Miscellaneous, to be read as soon as possible. They're all real people there."

"Good. Have a real person from Technical Etceteras call me when one of them has read it. Now, I'm in the middle of—"

"Oh, someone most definitely will. I'm just here to get preliminary information about the incident."

Konstantin tried moving quickly around her virtual desk to stand too closely in front of the thing, hoping that would cause it to back up toward the exit. "If you really did read my report just now, you should have all the preliminary information you nee—"

"What the company wants to know at this point," said the AI, adjusting its close-up vision without otherwise moving, "is how you would rate your AR experience up to the point of the anomaly."

"Rate?"

A slate appeared in its open right hand. "Were there any other minor glitches prior to the anomaly you're reporting, any dips in resolution, slowing of response times—?"

Konstantin put her hands on its shoulders and shoved it

backwards. "Look up the logs," she said angrily. "Any information like that will be in there!"

"There's no need to get abusive," the AI said patiently. "We know about the logs. We're asking *you* about your *personal* perceptions. Did *you* perceive any dips in resolution, slowing of response times—"

Konstantin gave it another shove.

"—sudden, unprompted shifts toward either end of the color—"

Konstantin shoved again.

"—spectrum, any persistent sounds or noises—"

She was sure her next shove should have knocked it over but all it did was take another step back.

"—that did not seem to fit the ambient soundscape, inappropriate light levels—"

It hit the exit and hung there, refusing to fall through even when Konstantin eliminated the barrier of the virtual door itself.

"If you don't log out of here right now," Konstantin said, "I'm going to file charges against the service provider for harassment of a police officer, obstructing justice, interfering with an ongoing investigation, aggravated mopery and dopery, conspiracy, terrorism, insider trading, and unlawful congress with a network."

The AI hesitated half a second. "There's no need for that kind of innuendo. If you stop to think about this for a few moments, it will occur to you that my behavior is all programmed—and by real people, I might add—from decision trees covering every eventuality and response. On receiving a report like yours, the first thing TechAssistAnomMisc would do would be to investigate your subjective impressions prior to the incident, during the incident, and after the incident."

"Why?" asked Konstantin, genuinely curious now.

"Because the situation you describe is impossible."

Konstantin nodded. "I might have known. Being an AI, you're completely stumped by anything original. You AIs think that if something has never happened before, it's impossible. Or that if you've never encountered it before—"

"No one said we had never encountered this before," said the AI. "My statement to you was that *normally* we don't get customers claiming they've spent more time in AR than what's on our billing records. At no time did I ever state that you were the first."

"People have reported this before?" Konstantin yanked the AI back toward her desk and shoved it down into a chair. "Why didn't you tell me that?"

"You mean before now? Since obviously you've just been informed?"

"What did your TechAss do about *those* reports?"

"Those were all handled by AIs."

"You?" Konstantin wanted to know.

"In a sense. It's all one AI where we are, but different manifesta—"

Konstantin bent down and got in the thing's face. She noticed for the first time that it wasn't breathing. Whoever had programmed the thing's appearance had cut a corner, probably in the name of budget. Detail animation like that added up. Konstantin found herself even angrier over the skimping. It was one of those subliminal things that could drive you mad, like dripping water or an itch you couldn't quite reach. You didn't notice people's breathing when it was there—only when it wasn't. No wonder she hated the thing so much. "So what did you, the AI, do about them?" she asked it.

"I sent a notice instructing the customers to correct their records, as they had all obviously made mistakes."

"You didn't turn *any* of them over to your TechAss?"

"In the case of an alleged customer-billing error, Tech-AssistAnomMisc does not step in unless the customer requests it on a follow-up. When they have, each and every instance has been proven to be an error on the part of the customer. With a one hundred percent success rating in that area, it is wasteful to pass tasks on to humans that AI can accomplish just as easily—unless specifically and formally requested to by the customer in a follow-up call."

Konstantin straightened up. Of course, she realized. Any time customers had claimed to spend less time in AR than what appeared on their bills, customer service always proved them wrong. But if an AR access provider told you your bill was *smaller* than it should have been—

Well, the conscientiously honest would report the mistake. But if the company insisted they were right and you were wrong, in this case, the customer would give up right away. Tried to do the right thing, they didn't listen. Q.E.D., and thank you for calling.

"Get out," Konstantin said, turning away. "Don't come back unless you're a real person."

"You ought to get over the idea that a real person is the only solution to your problems," the AI said.

Konstantin froze for a moment and then sighed. "I'm going to turn around, and there's not going to be anyone there," she said. "Right, Taliaferro?"

"Right," he said.

"And you didn't manage to tag it or anything, did you?"

"Nope." Pause. "Would you like to know why not?"

Konstantin sighed. "Is there a special reason?"

"It's because there was nothing there in the first place."

"That's even more special than I would have imagined." She put Taliaferro's face up on the monitor wall. "You have a record of me hanging around here talking to myself?"

"At least this time I have a record of you," Taliaferro said genially. "I've put in a requisition for better hardware and software."

"By the time you get it, we'll both have retired," Konstantin said.

"Optimist."

"It's all right," she told him. "I have another source in mind. I'm disconnecting for real again. Got to make a phone call, and I don't want to do it from here."

The arms dealer's real name was Ross—one name, official— and she was not amused. Konstantin had to admit to herself that she wouldn't have been, either, if the detective who had arrested her for counterfeiting had called to demand favors while all of her worldly possessions were being inventoried and evaluated for payment of fines. But neither did the woman hang up on her, and that was probably good, Konstantin thought.

"I design—designed—weapons," the arms dealer said. Like many people, she had chosen an AR face that was an idealized version of herself. Over the telephone screen, she appeared a bit rougher and larger, with a hint of a double chin, short bristly hair, and smaller, sadder eyes. Still, Konstantin could see the resemblance. "I'm not much for doodling software for its own sake. Besides, I thought you were such a *whiz*, canoodling being your métier, or whatever it was you told me. Big code freak, I think it was? Crooked cop."

"We've got a lot more latitude in AR," Konstantin said, "though I'd bet that'll change before the year is out."

"Until then, I'm sure you'll put it to good use," the arms dealer said. "Against dangerous criminals like me."

"Starting over won't be easy under any circumstances,"

Konstantin said. "But it can be less hard if someone means well for you, especially if it's someone who arrested you."

"So you said." The arms dealer nodded. "But then you keep saying you can't promise anything, and I don't see why I should try to help you out when there's no guarantee."

"That's exactly what will work in your favor," Konstantin told her. "That you helped me out knowing I couldn't guarantee anything."

"Yeah, I'm sure that the D.A. will melt under the knowledge that I've actually got this out-of-the-goodness-of-my-heart template. No one would believe, for one moment, that I helped you out in the desperate hope of getting some tit for my tat. After all, it's not like this is some stupid AR set-up scenario, is it."

Konstantin put her elbow on her desk and rested her chin on her fist. "OK. I'll promise you something."

The arms dealer's smile was sour. "Thought so."

"While I'd like to promise that things could get easier for you, the only thing I can actually guarantee is that nothing will get any harder than it has to be. There's still a certain amount of latitude out here in the real world for things like leniency, and it's better to have a cop owe you a favor rather than vice versa."

The woman's sour expression deepened. "Things can get rougher, too, can't they? As well as easier."

"Well, sometimes things get rougher simply by just staying the same, don't they?" Konstantin said, not unkindly.

Now the arms dealer's face was stony. "I find it hard to believe that someone like you would *really* like Renaissance Festivals."

"The best part about not being in AR," Konstantin said evenly, "is that you *don't* have to stay in character."

The arms dealer surprised her by bursting into hearty laughter. "Oh, don't you?"

13

"How many ways do I have to say it?" asked Susannah Ell impatiently. "Dervish is digital. Digital Dervish."

Her new virtual studio was smaller, and there were fewer assistants buzzing around her. Konstantin could tell they weren't from the same template as her previous set. These looked less finished in some way, lacking a lot of the smaller details—freckles, slightly uneven skin tones, irregular fingers—that had made the other ones look true-to-life. Or truer-to-life anyway.

"If you really believe that," Konstantin said, "I'm surprised that you would deliberately ignore what we told you, and open up another studio in AR."

Ell stood back from the dressmaker's dummy she had been pinning cloth to, considered for a moment, and then shook her head. "Wipe it," she said, and the material vanished. "Yeah, some studio." She gestured vaguely as she went over to Konstantin, who was standing near a table piled high with bolts and remnants. She had been surreptitiously feeling the various materials between her fingers and marveling at how authentic the textures were. "It's a cookie-cutter space in a cookie-cutter brownstone, and I don't like to think what I'm paying for it. I had it made before: rent-controlled loft downtown, all my assistants broken in the way I like them. This set—I don't know how they get away with renting out this paper-doll crap. But it functions, and that is the acceptable minimum, because the people who contracted for my summer line don't care what happened to me. They *can't* care. They can't afford to. There has to be a line of clothing, or I'm just out. And once you're out in this business, officer, you never get back in. I'd end up tailoring smocks for theme-park employees. That's not what I had in mind for my life."

"But if Dervish is, uh, digital," Konstantin said, frowning, "he can just destroy everything again, can't he?"

"I'm insured this time," Ell told her. "It's all fractally contained. That's why everything's so cramped. If Dervish blows me up again, I can simply pick up where I left off, with the next level of regress. It's not perfect, of course, because you have to go in and dither for any fine detail that gets lost, but it should get me through this season. After that, I hope you will have caught him, or stopped him, or erased him, or—"

"Please." Konstantin put up her hands. "Look, I know that you're an educated person, and I know that you must have a certain amount of perception, so I don't think I'm telling you anything when I say that I just don't believe that Hastings Dervish has transmogrified, or however you want to put it, into a digital . . ." she floundered briefly ". . . entity."

Ell stared at her blankly.

"Right?" prompted Konstantin. "You know I don't believe that's what's happened here. And you must also know that I don't really understand how *you* can believe that."

Ell's blank expression began to harden slowly into one of hostility. "I didn't think this came down to a matter of what *you* believe."

Konstantin managed not to groan out loud. "What I mean is that the situation you describe is impossible."

"You saw the ruins of my studio. Are you telling me that didn't really happen because it's impossible?"

"No, no, no," Konstantin said quickly. "The destruction of

your studio happened; of course it did. I mean Hastings Dervish cannot possibly have *become* a—a program. A digital being."

"What do you want to call it?" Ell asked her, gathering her hair around herself for comfort. Even the hair wasn't as long and thick as before, nor as active. "I'm just an end-user, I don't get intimate with data. But let me ask you this: if *you* don't believe Dervish is digital, and *I* don't believe Dervish is digital, what does it mean if *Dervish* believes it?"

"You should come out of there," Taliaferro told her as she boarded the sub-oceanic bullet train for lowdown Hong Kong.

"I've been in and out so many times already today that I've got serious reality-lag," Konstantin said, handing a coupon to the elfin steward waiting just inside the car. This train was mid-twentieth-century Space Age rather than Jules Verne, and there was something melancholy about it. Perhaps it was the fact that the Space Age future had never materialized, and all the shiny-happy looked a bit naive and pathetic from the perspective of the present, AR notwithstanding. Or maybe, Konstantin thought, she just didn't like shiny-happy but she did like Jules Verne.

"All the more reason to come out," Taliaferro said.

"You sound worried." She settled down in a first-class seat and managed not to squirm as it molded itself to accommodate her. No one sat next to her. In AR, no one ever sat next to you in first class unless you asked specifically. But, as in real life, you paid extra for the privilege.

"I am worried. It's a filthy, thankless job but somebody's gotta do it. You're heading right back into Dervish country."

"Heard from our friend the arms dealer yet?" Konstantin flicked on the screen in the arm of her seat and began paging through the special catalog offers. Accessories were big again.

"You're putting an awful lot of faith in a total stranger," Taliaferro said. "I really don't understand why you think she can come up with something to shield you from Dervish's tricks."

"The Smith & Wesson was completely undetectable," Konstantin said. "I had to get her to strip off the modifications just to make sure."

"That was an inanimate object."

"So is a persona, really. In here, it's all data. Varied configurations and permutations, but there's no real difference—digital is digital is digital."

"Then you should wait to see what your arms dealer comes up with. *If* she comes up with anything."

"That's what I'm doing," Konstantin said. "But I'm going to wait in lowdown Hong Kong."

"Why?" Taliaferro sounded appalled. "What if something happens?"

"Then I want it to happen where Goku Mura can see it. Besides," Konstantin added, "what could *actually* happen?"

"I could lose track of you again."

"I'm here in a small room in police headquarters. If things get strange, tell Celestine or DiPietro to pull my plug."

"And what if it looks like you've pulled your own plug?"

"Well, then, send one of the Gold Dust Twins to make sure—in person."

Taliaferro sighed. "You can't be thinking straight."

The feeling of acceleration was slightly too intense to be authentic. Konstantin leaned an elbow on the windowsill and watched the ocean go by. The simulated ocean. "What I'm not doing," she said, resting her head on her hand, "is treating this like a real situation. I won't. I refuse. All of them—Ell, Darwin, Goku Mura, even Hastings Dervish—they're behaving as if we've all agreed nobody violates the kayfabe. All we actually need to do is unplug everyone, cut off a few AR privileges for a while. I'm not playing along any more."

"What Ell told you about Dervish has nothing to do with kayfabe. She doesn't think of this as a scenario."

"I know. She's obviously lost touch with reality, her and Dervish both. *They're* doing a little pas de deux in the land of the lost. *They* need a snootful of anti-psychotic drugs and a year of intensive stability therapy, not me."

Taliaferro's chuckle had no humor in it. "If anyone else overheard that, the department would be open to a lawsuit."

A shark the size of a small boat flew along beside her window, occasionally rolling to one side to show her its slash of mouth. This was a ride you could take for real between the Indian subcontinent and Australia, and presumably the shark had been lifted from actual footage on one of those real rides, though it looked as if someone had smoothed out its appearance in the toaster before turning it loose in AR. Konstantin wondered idly if the enhanced AR experience made the real thing look a bit shabby. *Real life: low-rent and the lines are longer.*

"Maybe," she said after a bit, "but right now, I don't get the feeling anyone's going to do anything more elaborate than twitch some nerves in a hotsuit."

Sitting through twenty minutes of commercials was considered, by the average AR end-user, a small price to pay for forty extra minutes at no charge. Konstantin used the time to walk from one end of the train to the other and back again, looking at her fellow travelers. None showed much interest in her; they were mostly couples. Of those, however, over half were paired with an AI rather than another person. Computer dating was back. Konstantin wasn't sure what to make of it. Were there really that many people who couldn't find a partner? Or just that many who couldn't find a partner willing to pretend to take a sub-oceanic bullet train to lowdown Hong Kong?

Or was the precious kayfabe, that all-important consensual reality, easier to preserve when you worked it with an AI who never got bored or upset, or otherwise behaved in an unpredictable manner?

Konstantin had a sudden vision of walking into the casino to find that everyone in it was an AI.

Then she laughed at herself. As if the job would ever get *that* easy.

Celestine buzzed her as soon as she was through the entry channel and out in the square in front of the train station.

"Your friendly arms dealer wants to have a sit-down with you," she said. "In there, of course. I'm bringing her through."

"No," Konstantin said firmly. "Wait. I'll come out—"

"Too late, we're already in and on the way."

Konstantin groaned. "Do you have a place where we can meet?" She paused in front of a noodle and seafood bar, where tourists jockeyed for elbow room with a full spectrum of Oriental customers. You could tell who was real and who wasn't by who was eating. The real people were openly leering at the plates, at the busy chopsticks, the mouths in motion. They looked as if they were watching porn. Maybe they were. Food porn? Maybe in AR, porn had different parameters: any natural act that, in AR, becomes impossible and therefore unnatural.

"There's a British Empire nostalgia joint just off the square where you are right now," Celestine told her. "Nobody of any consequence ever goes there, but the ambience is unreal."

"Is that so?" Konstantin said, wondering if Celestine ever listened to herself.

"Well, *I* don't actually know first-hand. This is just what your friendly arms dealer says. You can practically smell the Boodles gin."

Konstantin smiled to herself. Every so often, it was uplifting to be reminded that smell-o-vision was the one thing they'd been spared thus far.

The plaque embedded in the glass-topped table, where Konstantin sat waiting for Celestine and the arms dealer, assured her that all the rattan in the place had been hand-rendered, hand-corrected, and hand-colored by people who were authorities on period furniture. There was almost nothing *but* rattan in the place; she wondered how many people had gone mad doing the detail work.

Or maybe if she'd cared to look more closely, she'd have found that there was actually just a relatively small area of original, painstakingly hand-rendered, hand-corrected, and hand-colored weave, which had then been exploded fractally and variegated randomly via software. Thank God she didn't have to police claims of authenticity, she thought.

Across the bar, which was probably bigger than any real Hong Kong bar had ever been, she saw the arms dealer stroll through a beaded curtain, followed by Celestine in her cyborg drag. She had replaced her steel arms with what looked like brass. Each time she moved, little puffs of smoke erupted from various moving parts. No, not smoke, Konstantin realized; steam. As they got closer, she could hear an airy, rather pleasant wheezing and whooshing coming from the gears or hydraulics or whatever they were.

"I see you're admiring my new arms," Celestine said, flexing them as the arms dealer sat down across from Konstantin.

"Not there.' Konstantin tapped the chair beside her. "Over here. Back to the wall."

The arms dealer smiled with half her mouth as she changed places. "You think I'll be safer?"

"I just want to know if anyone *you* know comes in," Konstantin told her, and motioned for Celestine to sit where the arms dealer had been. "Brass fittings. Very nice."

Celestine made a muscle with her right arm; steam whooshed from her shoulder and elbow.

"What do you call that?" Konstantin asked her.

"Steampunk."

Konstantin managed not to roll her eyes as she turned back to the arms dealer. She'd chosen to wear the same appearance as when she and Konstantin had met about the Smith & Wesson. "So what was so important that you felt you had to come and talk to me in here?"

"I can get you all the software you want, for anything you want to use it for," the other woman said, eyeing a waiter who went by carrying a martini easily five times the size of the real thing, sporting a green olive the size of a golf ball. "But, ah, in the words of the prophet, it won't mean a thing 'less you got that swing."

"That's illegal."

The arms dealer was disgusted. "What, you think nobody goes in here loaded?"

"I didn't have to take drugs to get you," Konstantin reminded her.

"If you *had* dosed up, you might have picked up a lot more than me." The waiter passed them again, going the other way with an empty martini glass on his tray. It looked even larger than the full one. "Jeez, you can practically smell the Boodles here. Somebody order me a drink."

Kontsantin sniffed. "I don't smell anything. Power of suggestion doesn't work if you don't know what something smells like, I guess."

"You don't know what *gin* smells like?" The arms dealer frowned at her. "Order me a drink. I just want to handle it and look at it and play with the olive. Martinis smell great, but they taste like paint remover."

Celestine's cyborg-face was unmistakably expectant. Konstantin nodded at her and she lifted her arm to signal the waiter with a wheeze of steam.

Stubbornly, the arms dealer refused to go on until she had her giant martini in front of her. This olive was even bigger than a golf ball, and Konstantin felt her mouth suddenly begin to water. Damn it, she thought; when had she last thought to break for lunch?

"If you've got someone breaking in on you," the arms dealer said after a bit, "they're boosted. Nobody's got the natural speed or reflexes to sort through bits looking for a way in."

"Boosting doesn't last all that long," Konstantin said. "When it wears off and the crash comes, they slip and we get them."

"Things can get real funny in here," the arms dealer said, running a fingertip around the broad rim of the glass, and looking far too happy about it. "Ever occur to you that maybe there's something about AR—light waves, frequencies, vibrations, resolution, maybe even subliminal messages—that makes some changes in people's heads, in their brain chemistry. They dose up and it has a different effect. Sometimes maybe it doesn't work as well. But lots of times the boost you get is something else. Because your atoms are dancing to a different drummer, so to speak. Sound and vision and a little something extra. Some people stop coming out; they just stay in and hope that someone's seeing to their getting cleaned and fed, like they were in a coma."

"A coma," Konstantin muttered under her breath.

The arms dealer looked at her sideways. "Ever been jammed?"

"What do you know about that, about jamming?" Konstantin asked her a little too quickly.

"I know that you can't do it to someone who's dosed the same way you are. Or close enough for government work."

"What is it?" Konstantin asked. "How's it done?"

The arms dealer plucked her olive out of the martini and held it up between two fingers, smiling at it. "I don't know. But I might *know* who knows."

"If you're so with it," Konstantin said, "why didn't you use any of that stuff on me?"

"Oh, please. You don't run around firing off your biggest gun all the time." She dropped her olive back into her drink with a small splash. "For one thing, the ammo's real expensive. And, for another, you attract attention that way and—"

A small, dirty hand flashed in front of the arms dealer, grabbing the olive out of the martini and spilling the drink. By the time Konstantin could get out a half-strangled *"Hey!"* the kid was halfway to the door.

Celestine never even turned around; she threw her right arm up and back and there was the metallic whiz of cable unwinding as her forearm and hand zipped through the room and caught the kid at the curtain. Still not turning around, she reeled him in, dragging him across the floor and around the table to Konstantin.

"Hey, fuck-ass," the kid said sullenly, twisting his neck to avoid looking directly at her. The facial tattoos were unmistakable.

Konstantin pried the olive out of his hand and took a close look at it. It didn't seem to be anything except a very faithful if oversized reproduction of an olive. "Hello, Goku."

"Friend of yours?" said the arms dealer. "He owes me a drink."

The kid grabbed the olive out of Konstantin's hand and

popped it into his mouth. Moments later, he spat the pit out hard, making it bounce on the table twice before it hit the floor and rolled away.

"Now he owes me an olive," the arms dealer added.

"He's just showing off," Konstantin said. "Aren't you?" She pushed her face up close to his, trying to make eye contact. He struggled in her grasp and when he finally did meet her gaze, she was shocked to see that the lack of recognition in his eyes was sincere.

She was so surprised, she loosened her hold on him and he broke away from her. Celestine threw her arm at him again, but all she got this time was a scrap of his shirt.

"Can you trace that?" Konstantin asked her as the woman examined the bit of material.

"I'm not sure," Celestine replied. "But I've seen it before. In a studio."

"Little bastard was boosted. You need a boost to catch up," said the arms dealer. "Take a boost. I can get you one. You'll get everything, including the manufacturer's home address."

Konstantin looked at Celestine, who shrugged. Silently, she nudged Taliaferro.

Readings as to whether that was really our friend Goku are inconclusive, he told her. *Not enough coherent interaction.*

If it wasn't Goku, who else would *it be? And why?*

A better question might be, what do you think your best chance is of finding out?

14

"We've been trying to get an appointment with you for about a month," said the narc. His name was Thorpe and he looked like any of the thousands of anonymous young businessmen who populated the commercial canyons of any large city. Konstantin had always thought of them as the contemporary descendants of cliff dwellers, who spent their days clambering around the different levels of skyscrapers and office buildings with briefcases and portfolios full of talismans, fetishes, and shiny beads. The business suit, fundamentally unchanged for close to two centuries, was exclusively theirs for both male and female, much like a judge's black robes or a police uniform, except the skirt as an alternative to trousers had faded away completely.

"You have?" Konstantin made a pained face. "I'm sorry, I've never seen any messages from you or your division."

"No, you wouldn't have," Thorpe said, sitting back and putting his feet up on his desk. He wore vintage wingtips. Copies, undoubtedly, but expensive ones. "We've been trying to go through Ogada."

Konstantin nodded. "Yeah, that explains it. He's never said anything to me."

"Protocols," Thorpe said vaguely. "We probably didn't fill out the reply form properly or something and it bounced out of his mailbox, just like all the follow-up inquiries. And we've had our dance cards pretty full. So, have you finally made a direct connection between an AR property and a drug dealer?"

"I could probably make a very strong case for the possibility," Konstantin said, her half-smile sympathetic. "But a direct connection? Not yet, sorry."

"'Not yet'?" Thorpe pulled his feet off the desk and sat up straight. "Does that mean there's a definite hope?"

Konstantin hesitated. "Actually, I came to see if you could release any material evidence you might be storing."

The narc's expression sagged. "For 'research purposes,' right?"

"As part of an undercover operation proceeding partially in AR," Konstantin said. "Proceeding *mostly* in AR, to tell you the truth."

"Uh-huh." Thorpe put his feet back on his desk and slumped as far down in his chair as he could. "That sounds like one neat trick *and* a hell of a walk on the wild side combined. Pioneering new areas of police work, are you?"

Konstantin leaned forward and put her elbows on his desk. "You sound skeptical."

"You tell me you're conducting an undercover investigation in a place where evidence, even of the hearsay variety, is legally impossible. And what you want, essentially, is for me to function as your dealer, probably so you can track some AR criminal through what someone has probably told you is an area not accessible to anyone who isn't *accelerated*. Do I have that right?"

"I have a material witness in custody."

That got his attention; Konstantin felt vindicated.

"We've been working in AR together. Whatever falls out in the way of controlled substances is all yours. Credit included."

Thorpe's anonymous face looked doubtful. "You have to understand that we have had an operation of our own in place for some time. We've been cultivating sources, informants, suppliers, trying to infiltrate the higher levels so we're not just busting a lot of people who look like this—" he indicated his suit "—who are just desperately trying to get ahead at work or support households. Locking up the consumers doesn't do a thing, they're a constantly self-renewing source. They're the victims of the so-called victimless crime. Putting them away never solves the problem. Half the time, I think the old-skool guys used to do it just to get their hands on someone else's property. You know, zero-tolerance meant that cops could seize all of a suspect's belongings and, even if the suspect was cleared, they didn't always give them back. Those were dark days."

"Sounds like," Konstantin said patiently.

"Sorry. That kind of abuse of power bothers me. I don't know how they could call themselves narcs. Anyway, we do things differently now. Since you have a material witness in custody—local?"

Konstantin shook her head. "She's in custody in her own locale, but that department has ceded the investigation to me. They don't have a TechnoCrime unit, so they're just monitoring. Or, rather, depending on us to monitor for them."

"Yeah, everybody's busy. Anyway, I can release a certain amount of the currently fashionable AR speed for your use, but we'll have to go across town to get it. We're out of everything at the moment."

"You are?" Konstantin frowned, puzzled. "You ran out of evidence?"

"Happens at least once a week," said Thorpe, getting up. He grabbed a keycard out of his top drawer. "You wouldn't believe the demand."

*

"This is a police front?" Konstantin asked. The unlit neon tubes that spelled out WAXX 24 across the front of the blush-pink stucco building would have registered as an illegible tangle of dirty glass if she hadn't known better. The slash letters and numerals that spelled out the club's name were interspersed with more neon tubing that formed the outlines of palm trees, cocktail glasses, musical notes, and a grinning half-moon that blew bubbles.

"Infiltrated," Thorpe said, locking the car with a keycard. "We just completed the deal for the lab space last week." His expression was smug and Konstantin realized she was supposed to be impressed. Perhaps WAXX 24's real-world aspect had become fashionable again. The last she'd heard, it was only the AR version most people were trying to get into. But then, as was usually the way with places like this, ownership had changed hands a few times since her own less-than-pleasant experience there. The name, however, never changed, probably because you just weren't going to get neon that good any more, at least not on that scale.

Thorpe used his keycard on the faux-wood entrance, led her through a dark brass-and-velvet lobby-bar to a door that looked like an airlock.

"Saucer Room," he told her as he took her through a passageway that skirted the large, round dancing area. "It's some old motif from two owners ago or something. We spent a lot of nights dancing around in the Saucer Room, cultivating our presence, making friends. Hardest duty I ever pulled." He grinned over his shoulder at her. "Completely ruined me for nightlife. Still can't figure how people would do this to relax, because for us it was nothing but hard work all night long, having a good time."

They came to an alcove with a skinny elevator door. Thorpe found another keycard for it. They stood self-consciously back-to-back in a space no bigger than an old-fashioned telephone booth, which took them down six floors and opened onto an area that had once been an indoor swimming pool. The pool, tiled and still smelling faintly of chlorine, was filled with long rows of tables where workers in white plastic anti-contamination suits stood pushing around mounds of what looked to Konstantin like brown granulated sugar, using pharmacists' paddles. Konstantin started to ask a question and Thorpe shook his head sharply.

No one looked up at them as she followed Thorpe around the edge of the pool, past a set of bleachers where about a dozen people were having a coffee break, or Konstantin assumed that was what they were doing. They were drinking coffee and a few were eating a sandwich or some other snack, but none of them was talking, not even in whispers. Apparently there wasn't much of a social aspect to this area of the drug trade.

Thorpe took her through another door at the far end of the pool, and up a short flight of stairs to a glassed-in terrace, where a man and an androgyne were sitting on either side of a small table, watching the area below. They looked from her to Thorpe, who shook his head. "One of ours. This is Doré Konstantin, of the fabled TechnoCrime unit."

"TechnoCrime?" The androgyne's smooth, milky-white face took on an amused expression. Every androgyne Konstantin had ever met seemed to have perfect skin. "Do we finally have a solid connection between an AR service provider and a drug supplier that will stand up in court?"

Thorpe made a seesaw motion with one hand. "She says there's hope."

"I take it this means it's all right to talk," Konstantin said.

"Oh, yeah, up here it's fine," Thorpe told her. "It's just a discipline thing. Most of those people down there are day-workers, so they aren't in on it. We found that the kind of people you get for this kind of job, they do best in real structured work environments."

"It's something that wouldn't occur to you right off," added the man, "but when you give it some thought, you know it's the best way to keep order. No talking on the premises means they pay attention to what they're doing and don't screw up the proportions of filler to pharmaceutical, as it were." He smoothed an ebony hand over his white silk shirt, sending moiré rainbows through it. In contrast to Thorpe's American salaryman, he was the picture of wealthy leisure, his leggings either genuine leather or the best substitute Konstantin had ever seen. The androgyne was in one of those monochromatic layered tunic/kimono/pajama/toga combinations that most androgynes favored. Konstantin found herself picturing Celestine in one, even though Celestine wasn't an androgyne, and had never expressed any desire to be one within Konstantin's hearing, muttonchops notwithstanding.

"We also get a little amusement sometimes," said the androgyne. She pointed toward the bleachers, at a skinny man standing up and preparing to throw the remains of his coffee break in a nearby waste bin. "That guy there? He's an investigative journalist. He thinks he's working undercover in a mob operation. Nobody can talk to him except one of us, of course, and only when he's not working the pool, so we feed him all kinds of shit."

"How do you know he's a journalist?" Konstantin asked.

"I got a good memory for faces," the androgyne told her. "A lot better than his."

Konstantin frowned at Thorpe, who shrugged and laughed a little. "Maybe he's actually trying to change careers. Step up to big pay in the drug trade."

The androgyne shook her/his head; the beads woven into

the cream-colored dreadlocks rattled against each other. "Every day when he reports to the pool, we take a look at how the story's shaping up on his archiver. He actually takes it with him and leaves it in his locker. If we really *were* the mob, he'd have been dead before lunch on the first day." S/he chuckled. "Besides, who the *hell* would pose as an investigative journalist?"

"Someone from Internal Affairs," Konstantin said before she could think better of it.

No one said anything for what seemed like half a day and might have been all of half a minute, if that.

"So how can we aid and abet the war on TechnoCrime?" the androgyne asked finally, the stricken expression on his/her face fading only a little.

"Our colleague needs some evidence to use in her investigation," Thorpe said. The other two detectives sagged visibly as the tension went out of both of them.

"Well, all right," said the man, relief large in his voice. "I don't mind that, but I coulda done without the scare."

"We're very superstitious here," said the androgyne solemnly. "There's three things you don't mention around narcs: the nine billionth name of God, and IAD."

"That's only two," said Konstantin.

"IAD counts as two things on the list, so with the you-know-what of God, that makes three. Those things will send your planet spinning out of orbit and into a black hole, or something even worse."

"I don't think I'm clear on this," Konstantin said, looking to Thorpe for help.

He spread his hands. "And I'm afraid you'll have to stay that way. Obviously, there are built-in problems about explaining it better. But I can give you a quick-and-dirty on our operation," he added, before she could insist. "This, as you can see, is where we process the product. Which means we step on it a few times, take out that troublesome potency that causes shrinkage of the profits. Today they're working on the AR addict's best friend, boost. Sometimes we get in psychoactives, occasionally there's a shipment of chill-powder for some niche market. But we've found the demand for boost is bottomless. Probably because these guys—" he indicated his suit "—use it as much, sometimes more, depending on what the stock market looks like."

"Where does it come from?" Konstantin asked.

The three detectives laughed. "We're working on tracing the routes."

"Oh. Well, who buys it?"

The man laughed some more. "What do you mean, who buys it?"

"I meant, who buys it when it first comes in, from wherever it comes from?"

The androgyne and the other man traded looks and then stared at her as if she were crazy. "This is our operation. *We* buy it."

"I thought the drug lords bought it," Konstantin said, confused.

"They do," said Thorpe. "After we buy it and step on it, they buy it from us."

"But you don't know who you're buying it from, or where."

"We have very strong leads," the androgyne said. "Like a lot of people, you don't understand how long it can take to build a case that'll stand up in a court of law, with all the hard evidence and all that."

Konstantin looked down at the pool workers for a moment, but the answer wasn't down there either. "But how do you get the stuff if you don't know who to buy it from, or where?"

"Drug lords use their connections for us. We've just got to

tie the two ends together, and so here we are in the middle, trying to do just that."

"What if you pulled out?" Konstantin asked.

"Pulled out of what?" asked the man. The look on his face said he was sure she was out of her mind.

"Pulled out of the middle. Just quit, told the drug lords to get their own operations going, and then you just followed their connections—"

"Well, first of all," said the androgyne, "that would tip them right away that we were cops, and we'd have to spend the rest of our lives running from one witness-protection program to another. That wouldn't be a very long time, either. But even if they were all stupid and didn't get it, we pull out, it throws everything into chaos and they still come looking for us to kill us in the most painful and slow ways they can think of. Plus, our connections and evidence are all down the drain." The androgyne lowered one eyebrow and raised the other. "I personally cannot imagine what would make you suggest something like that."

"I'm just not a narc, I guess," Konstantin said after a moment.

"I'll go get your evidence for you," said the man, standing up and giving Thorpe a worried look. "Maybe all this makes you uncomfortable, huh? I mean, TechnoCrime and AR, it's not like when you're working there, you're really doing anything. Anything risky, I mean. It's not like you could get killed."

"No," Konstantin said, refusing to sound apologetic. "But I have noticed that wherever drugs are involved, the fatality rate has a tendency to rise. If I can find out something about that by working in AR, maybe someone else won't get killed, either."

She could tell they weren't impressed. Thorpe drove her

back to headquarters, but refused to talk to her. Was he actually put out with her, she wondered, or was it just a discipline thing. At least she'd managed not to blurt out the nine billionth name of God, though she was sure that if she'd stayed there any longer, she might have managed to do that as well.

15

"The only way these guys know you're serious," said the arms dealer, "is if you do the time. You're on the clock or it's all off."

They were sitting in the stern of a classic junk, bobbing up and down as they crossed the bay. Only the two of them; the arms dealer had made it clear that Celestine wasn't invited. Just as well, in Konstantin's view—the arms dealer would now believe they were alone, and Celestine could keep busy tracing the kid's shirt material.

Konstantin kept closing her eyes periodically to fight her incipient seasickness, but the old trick wasn't working as well as it had in the past. The boost she'd gotten from the narcs seemed to have made her credible body even more credible. She probably *would* end up having to have her blood changed, and it wasn't something she was looking forward to. "I don't understand how someone spending more money on billable time is some kind of show of good faith or intent. It's not like you're on their clock—the money goes to the service provider."

The arms dealer folded her hands and rested them on her knees, with the metallic pinky stuck straight out. *Info dump*, Konstantin thought. It was getting so she could always see one coming. Function of AR, perhaps?

"You have to show you're willing to go as far as anyone," the arms dealer said, the patient tone in her voice only slightly exaggerated. "They're on billable time, too. It's not like they get theirs free, but you have to pay. You got to ante up like everybody else. Once they see you're willing to go the distance, there's something to talk about."

Konstantin sighed against her incipient nausea. "But wouldn't they—whoever *they* are—prefer you spent your money with them, instead of giving it to some AR provider service?"

The arms dealer stared into the middle distance thoughtfully for a bit, before turning back to Konstantin. "You're in here," she said, "but you're not really *in here*, are you? It's all the ground floor for you, isn't it?"

"What's *that* supposed to mean?" Konstantin asked, trying not to gulp.

"It's all in the way you think. You think of money as something you *have*. You ever seen any? Outside of a museum, I mean."

"You can still get currency if you want it," said Konstantin disdainfully.

The arms dealer laughed. "There's nothing that would make me believe *you* had a money fetish. You're a good citizen, you don't waste time digging in your pockets for coins." Pause. "Do you? Or are you one of those kindly souls that keep a few coins for the street beggars? Most of the good citizens I know are just as glad not to have anything for the beggars. If you make it impossible to live by begging, people won't beg, right? End of *that* street problem, isn't that what they say?"

Konstantin made a pained face. "I had no idea you were so in line with the current administration."

The arms dealer laughed again. "That's all just ground-floor thinking—OK for those who want to spend their lives on the ground. Some of us have a better idea. *You* can waste time digging in your pockets for coins if you want. I'll just go straight to the good part."

The good *part?* she whispered to Taliaferro.

You're soaking in it, he replied.

Fog was descending on Kowloon. By the time the junk docked, they might have sailed into a cloud. Her heart was starting to beat faster now, the boost taking effect, giving her a strange false feeling of anticipation, mixed with very real anxiety. The fog wasn't helping. Konstantin found, if she looked closely enough, she could distinguish tiny individual beads of moisture floating in the air. That was AR, she thought—extreme in detail, no matter how impossible.

"This here," said the arms dealer, gesturing at the narrow alley they were walking through, "this is all window-dressing for the marks."

"You don't say." The fog had barely penetrated here. Konstantin saw two small children watching her from a fire-escape landing where they sat with their legs dangling over empty space, their faces solemn and composed. Letting the passers-by know they'd been seen. Konstantin nodded at them. *I've seen you, too.* Her mouth was dry and she wished she'd had the foresight to put a stash of hard candy in her headmount.

The arms dealer had followed her gaze and was grinning up at the kids. "What pass for surveillance cameras around these parts. Marks find it unnerving." She gave Konstantin a sly look. "Not marking out and finding it unnerving yourself, are you?"

"Is it still OK to register dislike at an image that doesn't appeal to you, or is all unsimulated emotion uncool now?" Konstantin replied evenly.

The arms dealer's smile was knowing. "What's it to you?"

"Just trying to keep up on the local customs."

Something that looked like a cross between a manhole cover and an airlock was embedded in the pavement just ahead of them. The arms dealer came to a stop beside it and gave the small wheel in the center a nudge with her foot. "Care to do the honors?"

Konstantin didn't move. "Now I have to show I'm willing to get blown up so they'll know I'm sincere?"

"You're really *not* as dumb as you look, are you?" said the arms dealer as she resumed walking.

"I'm not even as dumb as *you* look," Konstantin retorted and felt pleased with herself, while the arms dealer pretended she hadn't heard.

"It wouldn't have actually blown you up," said the arms dealer. "You'd have just gotten lost and then maybe been booted out a side exit to nowhere. And had to start over." She shrugged. "It's like an intelligence test, I guess." She looked back, and then up. Konstantin followed her gaze and saw that the fog was now making its way down the alley as well as descending on them from the narrow band of white sky overhead. The arms dealer hesitated and then walked to the filthy brick wall behind Konstantin. Konstantin followed.

The arms dealer stared steadily at the wall as the mist accumulated around their feet and began to rise, deliberately enveloping the arms dealer in a way that reminded Konstantin of Susannah Ell's hair. It was around Konstantin, too, but in no particular pattern.

After a while, she could see that the mist was following some kind of line from the arms dealer's eyes to the wall, where it began sketching a triangle about the size of a human head, and then filling it in with billowing lines. When the lines had merged into a single roiling mass, the arms dealer beckoned to Konstantin to stand next to her.

It was like looking through a window at restless clouds, either high above or far below.

"And?" Konstantin said finally, turning to the other woman.

"*And* you stick your head through, and you're there. Only room for one head at a time. You want to go first, or you want me to show you the way?"

Irritated, Konstantin grabbed the arms dealer by the back of her neck and pushed her face into the mist. There was no feeling of resistance; plumes of mist blew back and disintegrated. Konstantin wedged her hand into the left side of the triangle and pulled; the wall tore away like layered cardboard. Still holding the arms dealer by her hair, she managed to tramp down a space big enough for both of them to go through.

She was mildly surprised to find the arms dealer staring at her admiringly. "I have to say, for someone with the cops, you sure don't much like playing by the rules, do you?"

Konstantin shrugged, not really wanting the woman to think they were bonding.

"Someone like you could carve out a nice territory in here for herself," the other woman went on, as they stepped through the wall together. "You could be big. The Pope of Dope. Mean Queen of the Mean Scene."

"Empress of Ice Cream," said Konstantin, waving one arm to scatter the remaining mist. They were in the entrance lobby of what they were supposed to believe, or at least not disbelieve, was a very fancy hotel of the art deco persuasion. Original art deco, or perhaps the original first art deco revival, Konstantin wasn't sure. It was a décor that appealed to her, which meant she had to try not to let herself be influenced by any positive feelings she had about it. *This is my life*, she thought as she marched the arms dealer up to the front desk. *Watching other people watch their time pass, and trying not to like anything too much.*

Abruptly, she found herself facing the Dragon Lady on the other side of the polished counter. She was so surprised, she almost let go of the arms dealer. The Dragon Lady showed no sign of recognition, only boredom. "If you got in here, you should know the rules," she said in a low, Dragon Lady voice. "Come back when you're . . . up to it."

"I'm up to it," said the arms dealer. "Or I will be. My friend needs some help."

The Dragon Lady shrugged. "Why tell me?" Today's outfit was pure white silk brocade; her lips were as glossy and unapologetically black as her hair. Konstantin was suddenly possessed by the idea of laminated lips. Now she couldn't stop staring at the Dragon Lady's mouth. *I'm all wrong for this job*, she thought, wishing that this realization alone were enough to quash the urge to laugh.

"Because we seek your advice," said the arms dealer respectfully.

The Dragon Lady leaned her hands on the counter. Her long nails were painted black as well. "Advice is all I can give you here. And any advice I do give is, you understand, all lies."

"We're depending on it," Konstantin said.

The Dragon Lady's expression became a frozen mask of disgust. The arms dealer looked at Konstantin as if she were crazy. Konstantin sighed.

"You can tell the overeager peasant she is too low to be recognized as human, or even a well-trained primate," said the Dragon Lady after a bit. "But she is not too low to be part of the food chain."

"You're too low to be recognized as human," the arms dealer said to Konstantin. "And if you try to talk to her again, we'll never get in."

Konstantin opened her mouth to give the arms dealer a message of her own.

"It would be a mistake to talk at all, at this point," the arms dealer added quickly.

Konstantin nodded and kept her mouth shut.

The Dragon Lady was silent for several moments, either composing herself or trying to make Konstantin squirm; Konstantin suspected the latter.

"Have you prayed?" the woman asked finally. "And ... fasted?"

Konstantin felt herself biting the inside of her lower lip and made herself stop.

"We are doing so now,' said the arms dealer. She reached over and put Konstantin's right hand on the desk, positioning her own beside it. "We offer our vital signs as proof."

The Dragon Lady looked at the arms dealer's hand, and then at Konstantin's, before moving to an old-fashioned pigeonhole unit behind her and pulling a brass key-ring out of a spot near the top. She turned the arms dealer's hand over and put the key-ring on her palm. "Elevators to the left. No loitering," she said, and made elegant shooing motions with her fingers.

909 said the number on the thick, slightly tarnished rectangle of brass. Konstantin took it from the arms dealer and turned it upside-down so that it read 606. The feeling of upward acceleration in the elevator was giving her goosebumps—the way the boost-enhanced sensation was, in Konstantin's mind, too pleasurable not to be followed by something equally unpleasant. It struck her as being a rather fatalistic way to have a good time.

The arms dealer was obviously relishing her own experience. "I don't get to do this often enough," she sighed, stretching one arm and then the other. "But doing it on a pharmaceutical-grade boost sanctioned by the cops gives it that extra bit of perversity to enjoy."

"Perhaps it'll sweeten the crash later," Konstantin suggested.

The arms dealer was unperturbed. "You really got to learn how to live in the moment you're in. Thinking ahead is OK for planning your pension, but that's not what you're doing *now*." Then she frowned at Konstantin. "Oh, wait—maybe you are. My mistake."

Konstantin shrugged, wondering how far up the elevator was going to go.

"Makes me wonder what you guys do to have a good time."

"I'd tell you," Konstantin said, "but—"

"—but then you'd have to kill me. Heard it. I'm serious, though. You ever have a good time, or do you have to go around being a white hat without a break?"

"Maybe I don't see myself that way," Konstantin said.

"What, like a white hat?"

"Like someone who has to avoid doing anything that might be remotely enjoyable." Konstantin let out a put-upon breath. "Why am I having this conversation with you?"

The arms dealer grinned. "Boost makes you want to talk."

The elevator began to slow and Konstantin sighed again, this time with relief. "God, it seems like all I've done in here is ride in elevators. As if I couldn't do that anywhere."

"You don't enjoy carnival rides, either?" The arms dealer shook her head pityingly. "Jesus, warn me if we're about to do anything you *do* like, so I don't faint with shock."

The elevator took such a long time to come to a complete stop that Konstantin's nerves had turned to Holy Rollers by the time the doors slid open. The arms dealer led her through what felt like several city blocks' worth of plush, red-carpeted hallway complete with candle-shaped sconce lighting and flocked red and gold wallpaper, before they came to room 909. Room 606 was right next door.

16

"Whenever you're ready," said the arms dealer after a bit. "Just remember the rule: no loitering."

Konstantin was frowning at the doors. "Funny, I thought it would be something more like 101 and 110." The arms dealer looked at her blankly. "Binary," she clarified.

The arms dealer still looked mystified for a few moments, and then shook her head. "The cyberweenie revival isn't due to hit for another couple of months yet, at least according to the Popular Culture Index," she said. "Come on, pick a room while we're still on the way up."

"Does being on the way up call for a lower number or a higher number?" Konstantin asked.

"Best thing to do is always go with the number you saw first," the arms dealer said. "Did you see 909 or 606?"

Konstantin didn't hesitate. She unlocked the door marked 909 and pushed it open with her foot, holding onto the jamb. The arms dealer crowded up behind her and Konstantin twisted around slightly to give her a look.

"Do you *know* what the word 'loitering' means?" the arms dealer asked her, hair swinging impatiently.

"She knows," said a familiar voice. Konstantin jumped as she felt Darwin's hand close like a steel cuff on her arm. "She just keeps forgetting to take it personally." He yanked her forward and she was overwhelmed with the sensation of either falling or flying, she wasn't sure which. *One more thrill ride,* she told herself firmly as tingles of fear struck sparks in her. *It's just roller-coaster heaven for people who can't face the real thing.*

Something hard and firm smacked the soles of her feet and clung there while she tumbled weightlessly end over end. Then the vertigo was gone and she was standing on the surface of the lake of fire in the casino.

"Yeah, she's dosed," said Darwin cheerfully. He was on the shore with the arms dealer. Konstantin thought absently that she should have looked out of place in her yacht-club president outfit, especially next to the cyborg, who had upgraded some of his parts., but somehow she didn't. She looked at home.

Taliaferro, start recording this, if you're not already, she whispered to him. *I'm so speedy and disoriented, I can barely find the edge of my screen. I think there's been some kind of side-effect having to do with my eyes, or my pupils, or something, I feel like I'm trying to open my eyes in a dream.*

He didn't answer. It wasn't practical to, she told herself, watching Darwin and the arms dealer on the shore. Two chefs passed over their heads on an air bridge, bearing a giant roast goose on a platter, and she was suddenly filled with the superstitious dread that if she dared to look around she would see herself as she had been when she had first come to lowdown Hong Kong casino, to investigate Darwin's complaints of brainwashing.

Darwin made a throwing motion with his arms; she found them coiled around her waist. He reeled her in, dragging her across the opals without letting her fall. It was like skating bladeless on lumpy ice, not unpleasant but very, very strange. He stood her up next to the arms dealer and then retracted the arms. Little puffs of steam came out of the shoulder and elbow joints in a way that made Konstantin think of punctuation. Or maybe emotion lines in a cartoon might have been closer to the mark.

Closer to the mark? Hell, she *was* the mark. Couldn't get much closer than that.

Her mind was racing. She concentrated, trying to slow it down, but it was already getting away from her again. She couldn't stop staring at Darwin's new arms. If they really were Celestine's, it just meant that he'd stolen some data from her or made an unauthorized copy. It didn't mean anything bad had happened to Celestine. And even if something had, nothing could *really* happen to her. *The idea is to give you the creeps. So have them—they're monitoring your vitals, they want to know it's working. But make your mind remember the truth, even if your gut won't.* She meant to whisper aloud for Taliaferro's benefit as much as her own, but her lips felt strange, almost numb. Speaking aloud at normal volume was no problem but she couldn't feel whether she was whispering for real or not.

Of course, she realized: the fillers that Thorpe and Co. used in their drug processing. But why a dental anesthetic? Just because it was cheap, or did they think it lessened the discomfort of the dry mouth side-effect or—?

She gave herself a long, painful pinch on the side of one thigh to divert her racing thoughts. It didn't matter what or why, not at the moment. Later she could file a consumer complaint, maybe directly to Thorpe's face with her fist if she thought she could get away with it by claiming the crash was—

The arms dealer's face filled her vision. "How much did you take?"

"Enough to keep up with you," Konstantin said defiantly. "So show me something."

"What do you want to see?"

"You know what I want to see." Konstantin pulled her a short distance away. Darwin didn't try to follow, but Konstantin gave him a warning glare anyway. "You agreed to help me obtain the program that would protect me from Hastings

Dervish's jamming. It would also provide hard evidence that Dervish was in possession of and actively using a program meant to defraud AR service providers by supplying false data, which is the only way I can touch him in Key West. If you no longer feel like doing that, we can just log out right now and you'll never see me again. You'll be so busy raising the money for all your fines and legal bills that by the time you can afford to get back into AR, I'll have retired."

"I keep forgetting how irritable the boost can make someone who isn't used to it," said the arms dealer mildly. "Not to mention the paranoia factor. Plus, some people just don't like that speedy feeling. I told you we got to put in the time. Do I also have to remind you about the kayfabe element here? Did you forget you're not in an air strike? You try to rush any of this and you're gonna tip your hand. Now, do you want to do this undercover or do you just want to stage some kind of raid and fuck the whole thing sideways?"

Konstantin thought of the narcs busily working the middle ground between two ends that just couldn't quite get tied together. "How long do you think it'll take?"

"As long as it takes to get it done. Take it or shake it. You afraid someone's gonna accuse you of enjoying yourself in here?" The arms dealer smiled. "Or are you afraid that you *will* enjoy yourself in here?"

Before Konstantin could answer, the arms dealer was moving flirtatiously back to Darwin, skirt swishing behind her, hair swinging in an echo of the same motion. Konstantin wasn't sure if the sight was hypnotic or just making her seasick again. She marched over to the woman, ignoring Darwin's metallic leer.

"Preserve the kayfabe all you want," she said, "but this gearhead knows I'm a cop. He called me in here in the first place.

So if you want to pose for *him*, do it on your own time. *After* you're done working for me."

The arms dealer suddenly looked so thoughtful it was almost shocking. "Really." She looked the cyborg up and down, as if memorizing his appearance. "It's so hard to keep track."

"I'm so sympathetic," Konstantin said. "Now, exactly what constitutes a decent interval to wait before we get something done? At the very least, I'd like to know why I'm back here again when we had to make a big point of taking a junk to Kowloon. Wait, don't tell me—carnival ride."

The arms dealer looked even more troubled. "Consider anger management."

"I'm managing to be angry just fine, thanks," said Konstantin before she could stop herself. *Taliaferro, I really hope you're getting this, I think I'm out of control.* The weird non-numbness was spreading up either side of her face; she wondered idly if the narcs had poisoned her for mentioning IAD in their presence.

"Are you sure?" said Darwin mildly. "You look more like you're in the freak mix."

"A cyborg using the word 'freak,'" Konstantin said. "*Now* I've heard everything. Come on, what happened to the no-loitering rule?"

The arms dealer turned her around and led her to the ladies' room.

The lounge area was as crowded as ever with women and other female creatures jockeying for position in front of the mirrors or each other. The only place that wasn't crowded was the monster puce sofa, which was occupied solely by a hybrid human-tyrannosaur in pink and black striped Capri pants and a pink-sequined tube top. She had her feet up on the coffee table, which was still a naked man on all fours, although Konstantin couldn't have sworn it was the same man. She tried to remember what he had looked like but, disconcertingly, she could only summon up a mental image of Thorpe.

On impulse, Konstantin sat down next to the tyrannosaur-woman and put her feet on the man's back. The tyrannosaur didn't react in any way. Either she was truly unaware of Konstantin or she was too loaded to move. Why anyone would spend billable time too loaded to move was beyond Konstantin's understanding.

"Shall we remove a layer so we can get around more comfortably?" said the arms dealer, close to her ear.

Konstantin was about to ask her what she meant by that when the tyrannosaur beside her vanished, as did about half the number of other people. The ones who remained seemed oblivious to what had just happened. But then, they would be, Konstantin thought, because nothing had actually happened except that the arms dealer had removed their perception of the unboosted masses. *Was I supposed to get hysterical?* Konstantin wondered, gazing calmly at the arms dealer.

"I knew it would be much easier on your sensibilities if I took you in here for that," the other woman said, sounding pleased with herself. "If you see it happen in a space as large as that casino, you can get hysterics. On this scale, it's just a relief." She waved a hand through the emptier space around her. "They're all still there, of course. On *their* level. We could go on perceiving them, but we'd see them slowing down more and more until the sight became completely ridiculous. And intolerable. When you're boosted, you don't want a lot of snails cluttering up your vision-space."

Konstantin looked around, her gaze coming to rest on the coffee table, which was still visible.

"He's furniture," the arms dealer said, gathering her skirt around her and sitting primly on his back. "He stays because we're using him."

Konstantin stared at her unhappily. If the tyrannosaur-woman had still been in sight, her feet would have been in the arms dealer's lap. "I don't understand how two things can occupy the same space at the same time," she said.

"Nothing's occupying space," the arms dealer said. "It's all digital. There's always room between digits."

"909, 606," said Konstantin.

The arms dealer nodded. "That way, too."

A flicker from the mirror caught the edge of Konstantin's peripheral vision, but when she turned to look she only saw a woman zipping herself into a rubber-suit that molded her torso and limbs into elongated pipestem shapes. Konstantin found she wasn't sure what repelled her more—the way the woman herself looked, or the kind of person who would find her appearance arousing. There was no mistaking, from the placement of the zippers, that this was meant to be arousing to someone. Or maybe some*thing*.

The woman's head, still normal, but too large on that narrow elongated neck, swiveled around to regard Konstantin with enormous Cleopatra-style eyes. There was no defiance, no embarrassment, no emotion at all as she took a small black clutch purse from the counter and picked her way over to the door, moving on her spindly limbs like a marionette controlled by an inexpert puppeteer.

"People's imaginations," sighed the arms dealer. "It's amazing what they can think of getting up to in here."

"All that, and boosted too," said Konstantin. "Are we waiting for someone or something in here, or can we go now?"

The door opened and Darwin stuck his head in. He looked at the arms dealer and nodded. Konstantin started to get up and suddenly found herself receding rapidly from the arms dealer, who shrank to nothing and disappeared. But only from her own point of view, Konstantin thought, feeling stupid. Most likely, it had happened the other way around.

She might have been less annoyed and more startled if she hadn't found herself on yet another carnival ride.

17

The whole point of a roller-coaster is the thrill. The thrill is the illusion of falling or being hurled to your death. In AR this has to be accomplished by disorientation.

Had Tonic told her that? Or had she heard that on some popular-culture analysis program?

The key to overcoming disorientation is focus. Dancers executing a long series of fast turns counter dizziness by focusing on one point of the area they are moving toward, turning their heads faster than their bodies to keep it in sight as long as possible. In AR, where there is only the illusion of movement, closing the eyes can sometimes do the trick but not always, because of the high suggestibility of the human mind, especially under the influence. Instead, concentrate on one part of the physical body. The hands are good. She could practically hear the voice but she couldn't identify it. Didn't matter; she concentrated on trying to feel her right hand curl into a fist and then open out again.

Abruptly, she felt her hand close around something live. Startled, she opened her eyes to find herself sitting on the puce sofa in the ladies' room. The arms dealer was holding her hand between both of her own. "Can you hear me?" she asked Konstantin.

"Yeah. What was *that* about?"

"If what I read from your vitals is correct, you're hallucinating. I think you've taken just slightly too much boost for your level of tolerance. Which is zero."

"An overdose?"

"No, just a shade too much. You're going to have those moments where you lose contact with your surroundings. Just ride them out."

Are you getting this, Taliaferro?

No answer. There was no sign of her exit prompt or her panic button, but her eyes still felt funny.

"Where's my software?" she managed after a moment.

"You don't get something for nothing in this joint," said a Moulin Rouge showgirl. There was a pause while Konstantin flew headfirst through a looping tunnel of strobing lights for a few seconds, before she found herself at one of the tables in the casino, sitting next to Darwin and across from the Chinese heavy-labor cyborg. "Put up or shut up."

The chips were already there in front of her. She tossed one into the center pile, as the Moulin Rouge showgirl dealt her in. Konstantin felt less than optimistic. The last time she'd tried gambling for information, it had been a complete failure.

She looked around for the arms dealer but the lights were too bright, or not bright enough, depending on the angle. How the hell was she supposed to see her cards? Not that she would necessarily understand them if she *could* see them. She picked them up anyway. Maybe Taliaferro would come through for her.

A jumble of hearts, spades, diamonds and clubs leaped up at her face and then pulled back again, as if they were on springs. A face card suddenly resolved itself into hard clarity: the Goku of clubs.

Konstantin looked up sharply, squinting in the bad light at the other people around the table. The chinchilla made a twittering noise; it was looking more like a rat already. *Damn, not again*, Konstantin thought. "Something wrong with your cards?"

"There's definitely something wrong with mine," said the sex goddess. "I've got five suits and one of them's tweed. I just can't believe it. I look *hideous* in tweed." The texture of her white halter-top dress changed briefly, just long enough to demonstrate she was right.

"Don't blame *me*," said the Moulin Rouge showgirl. "How I get them is how I deal them."

"*Someone* must have brought some extra cards," said the chinchilla.

Everyone turned to stare at Konstantin. She looked down at her cards again quickly. The Goku of clubs was now the knave of clubs. "Not guilty." *Taliaferro, did you* see *that?*

The arms dealer was leaning over her shoulder. She pulled the knave of clubs up slightly out of the fan of cards, and then slid it down again. Her satisfied smile looked distorted and alien on her face. "Nothing extra. You could use it. Fold."

The Chinese cyborg took the chips in the center of the table, sorted through them and found one marked with a K. "You have to tell me something I want to know."

Konstantin frowned. "That's not how it works. The game isn't over, you don't get that till you cash in your chips."

"You're on a different level now," said the chinchilla. "You're playing boosted. We do things differently up here. This is rare air up here."

The cyborg got up and leaned across the table.

Abruptly, Konstantin was being dragged backwards down a long sharp incline under a sky boiling with angry, purplish clouds. She squeezed her eyes shut. There was a roaring in her ears and a vibration that shook her like a rag doll, and then something behind her released or disintegrated so that she was suddenly in freefall.

She hit the chair sitting upright, and would have fallen except that the arms dealer was there to prop her up. The

Moulin Rouge showgirl was dealing a new hand of cards. Resignedly, Konstantin picked them up without bothering to try to sort them.

This time, she had a Goku of hearts, two Gokus of spades, and a Goku of clubs.

She snapped the fan of cards shut, but not quickly enough. The arms dealer grabbed them out of her hand and spread them on the table. The face cards had all changed back to kings and queens but apparently the arms dealer wasn't fooled.

"*Little bastard!*" she bellowed. The floor of the casino shuddered and began to crack. The table broke into fragments, scattering the other players. Konstantin got to her feet and staggered back. The arms dealer grabbed her by the front of her riverboat-gambler ruffled shirt and shook her. "How did you smuggle him in? I cut everyone off, *everyone*! *No* one can *see* you, *no* one can *hear* you! *How did you do it?*"

"I thought I was hallucinating," Konstantin said honestly.

"Frigging *liar!*" The arms dealer lifted her by her shirt and threw her. Konstantin felt herself rising, and squeezed her eyes shut against the sensation. This was beyond fear or excitement—it was as though she could feel every millimeter of her own skin horripilating so intensely it must have been levitating the hotsuit away from her in every direction.

She flailed her arms, or tried to, hoping she could hit some part of the chair and make the outer world break in on her that way. All of her prompts had disappeared so completely that she couldn't even believe them into working. *Gotta have faith . . .* that, or better, drugs, she thought grimly. She tried to sense how fast her heart was beating but she couldn't muster up any awareness of it beyond a kind of tightness in her chest. *Vitals,* she whispered; nothing.

Maybe I died.

She could almost hear Taliaferro laughing at her. *Don't be looking to get any time off until after you wrap this case.*

Her ascent was slowing; eventually it would come to a stop and she would plummet. The fall wouldn't kill her, but she wasn't sure she could survive the anticipation.

So you're going to let some fifth-rate petty criminal functioning as a mob placeholder—a bookmark, for chrissakes, a paperweight—wipe you out with a little carnival-ride action? He can say that he's got a clear field to defraud, extort, dominate, stalk—whatever the hell he feels like doing—because you had to unplug.

No, of course not. She was tougher than that. It wasn't like she could actually get killed in here, unless the boost gave her a heart attack. Was that what Hastings Dervish was trying to do, induce cardiac arrest?

She felt her rise finally come to an inches-painful halt, and braced herself for the sensation of falling.

Nothing happened.

She waited, and the wait stretched so slowly she was sure that time itself had stopped. And still nothing happened.

She opened her eyes. The moment she did, she fell. Headfirst she accelerated toward a large dark pit with a tiny spark in the middle. It took a long time for the pit to swell in size as she approached. No wind in her face, but it roared in her ears and began to twist her around like a corkscrew. She felt her eyes roll back in her head, so far back and so hard that she wondered if they could pull loose in their sockets.

Concentrate. Even if you're loaded, you still know this is an illusion.

Tell my inner ear, she thought. And then: *Who am I talking to?*

Taliaferro, is that you?

She got her eyes open just in time to see the surface of the pit inches from her face.

And then nothing.

She came to lying on the floor of her cubicle with Ogada bending over her. He must have removed her headmount for her. Not that he looked as if he were in the mood to do her any other favors.

"*You*," he said, "*you* are in such a *pit* of trouble, I don't see how you'll ever dig your way out. If you ever see daylight again, it'll be a miracle."

She didn't attempt to move or respond. A fresh wave of numbness had spread through her mouth, from the back of her throat all the way to her chin so that she was even having trouble swallowing. *Ogada's going to stand over me counting my sins while I drown in my own spit, and he won't even notice*, she thought. *Welcome to the real world.*

"What you've done is against every regulation, everything this department stands for," he went on, while she tried to cough. "You have taken drugs on duty, and performed under the influence, and for no reason that anyone can discern other than your own recreation. Rather than investigating Techno-Crimes, you appear to have used a possibly false complaint by a *very* dubious character passing herself off as a legitimate fashion designer, when what she *really* is is a scam artist well known to several AR service providers who are *still* trying to collect overdue fees from her—" He paused and nodded. "Oh, yeah. You didn't know about that, did you? Of course not. All you'd have had to do was run a credit check on her, something *you* never thought of."

Konstantin finally managed to make a noise and tried to sit up, but Ogada pushed her back down.

"Lie still. You've had some kind of seizure thanks to your drug use. We're waiting for an ambulance. If I'd known that you were just one more AR junkie out to feed her sex and drugs habit at all costs, and damn the torpedoes, I'd have terminated you before I'd have let you go near a hotsuit."

Konstantin glared up at him, fuming. That was just like him, the son of a bitch, to start working on covering his ass, making like the whole TechnoCrime assignment had been her idea and not something he had forced her into. And rather than even asking her for her side of events, he was just assuming she was guilty of every crime in the book. He was as bad as IAD. She tried to sit up again, and he pushed her down even more roughly than before.

"Don't make me cuff you, detective," he said threateningly. "I don't want to send you out of here on a stretcher in handcuffs, but I will if I have to." He thought for a moment. "Maybe I should. Who says you deserve any consideration after the way you've abused your position?"

"*Unreal,*" Konstantin croaked.

Ogada raised an eyebrow at her. "What? What did you just say to me?"

Her numb lips felt gigantic against her face. "Unreal," she managed. "Unreal." Pause. "Feeling."

"I suppose it's too much to ask that you make *any* sense." He looked to his left, toward the door. "Where the hell is that ambulance?"

Konstantin coughed again. The drug was still very strong in her system. If Ogada didn't let her get up soon, she was going to start vibrating like a wire in a high wind, even have another seizure.

"What?" Ogada was glaring down at her again. "Feeling chatty? All speeded up, ready to talk?" He gave a short, humorless laugh. "Forget it, I don't need to hear anything you have to say. I can get the whole story from Taliaferro. He's not gonna cover for you. You'd be surprised how fast partners sell each other out in these cases. Nobody wants to be the one to fall."

The jittery feeling in Konstantin's chest turned to ice. Of all the things that Ogada might do—arrest her, have her hospitalized, hang her out to dry and twist slowly, slowly in the wind—the one thing he would not do was call Taliaferro her partner. That argument had been settled in Ogada's mind, and he didn't know about the tap.

Anyone who did, however, would have assumed, quite naturally, that she and Taliaferro *were* partners.

Stop, she told herself. *Stop thinking. Vitals are up. Stop thinking.*

Ogada smiled a little. "You look kinda scared, Konstantin, you know that?"

He couldn't have put it over on her forever. Maybe not even for very much longer. But how long had he expected to? And, even more important, *why*?

Dervish is digital. How many different ways do I have to say it? Susannah Ell's voice in her mind. Why does a person stalk somebody? Particularly why in AR? Dervish could cost Ell money, ruin her deadlines, destroy her peace of mind but, hell, it wasn't like he could kill her, so what was the big deal? She never even saw him in person. People went into AR for precisely these kinds of thrills. It wasn't Dervish's fault she was delusional, saying he was somehow converted into a digital being. Pure AR fantasy! If Susannah Ell couldn't take the heat, she should stay out of the frying pan. Konstantin could practically hear Dervish's lawyer making the case in court.

And herself? Right, the junkie cop with the penchant for sex clubs. Drugged on the job, couldn't tell the difference between AR and Ground Zero. A software program meant to defraud

AR service providers by falsifying online records? If it please the court, let's call it by its real name—the fruit of the poisoned tree.

Which would mean that Dervish, digital or not, would be free to continue playing his strange, terrible games in AR with anyone he chose, whether they liked it or not. *I can do whatever I like with you. And I will.*

This had all gone through her mind in one zap of gestalt. Her thoughts would not stop racing; if anything, they seemed to be working faster. She felt as if she were trembling. Dervish looked down at her with his Ogada face, enjoying himself. Now that she knew, she couldn't imagine how she had *not* perceived Dervish's essence leering out at her through the Ogada mask.

Or the arms dealer's, she realized.

She could crown herself genius of the year later, she thought. Understanding everything was great, but it didn't help her figure out how to get away from the son of a bitch. He thought he was digital, which, to answer Susannah Ell's all-but-forgotten question from some eternity ago, probably made him psychotic. But he also seemed to command practically unlimited amounts of processing power, almost as if he really *were* digital. How did you fight against something that strong?

Dervish rose slowly from his crouch to stand over her. He looked a hundred feet tall from this angle. She made herself go as limp as she could.

The element of surprise was crude, but still effective. She waited for him to look toward the door again before she sprang up and shoved him as hard as she could through the open doorway. Instead of the squad room, there was nothing but a black void beyond the threshold, and she had managed to surprise him so well that he dropped like a stone immediately, disappearing before she even slammed the door and locked it.

"I thought you'd *never get up*."

She whirled. Goku was standing by the chair, holding her headmount. He lunged at her and slammed it down onto her head.

18

"I know, you don't have to say it," said Konstantin as they sat in the stern of the junk. "We don't have much time." The junk certainly seemed to know it, too. Instead of bobbing up and down, it was cutting through the water as smoothly as a powerboat, heading back to Hong Kong from Kowloon.

Goku laughed. "We don't have *any* time. We're making our own. Or, rather, uncovering it." He reached into his still elegant black tuxedo jacket and came up with his silver cigarette case.

Konstantin sighed. "This is no time for affectations."

Now he stared at her. "Well, thank you so much for that helpful tip." He flipped the case open and helped himself to a pure white cigarette. As usual, it lit itself and he blew the smoke in her face. She started to say something and he shook his head. "I know, you didn't feel that, but it's disrespectful." He took another drag and this time blew the smoke directly at her chest.

Konstantin's white-hot flash of rage was replaced almost immediately by an odd buzz that was spreading upward from her neck to the top of her head. She raised her hand to where she thought her cheek would be and felt her face—or *a* face, anyway—under her fingers. Immediately, she rested her elbows on her knees and put her chin in her hands, deciding not to burden him with the knowledge of how long she had been wanting to do that in AR. It didn't feel quite like the real thing, but it was close enough to be comfortable.

I've got that unreal feeling again, she thought. *Time to log out.*

Taliaferro, are you there yet?

"I'll reconnect you to your partner shortly," Goku said, blowing a cloud of smoke around them. Not exactly a cloud—it seemed to be more like a curtain or a veil with a visible lattice weave in it. Instead of dissipating as it grew, it became thicker, or so it seemed to Konstantin. "As soon as you're capable of communicating at a more normal speed. It all sounds normal to you but it would be unintelligible to your long-suffering partner."

Those weren't lattice patterns in the smoke, she saw; they were fractals. She looked at Goku.

"East/West Precinct is a bit less ... *fussed*, you might say, about its operatives keeping up the appropriate pace."

She winced. "You're Phase 3 Interpol."

"*I* am, yes. Not all of East/West is, however. Yoshida isn't, for example. In any case—"

She tried to interrupt.

"In any case," he repeated, talking over her, "it was me talking to you before, not Taliaferro."

"How did you know what to say to me?"

"You were muttering a mile a minute on Taliaferro's frequency. I could hear you just fine."

Fractals parted before Konstantin's eyes, slid through her peripheral vision, and disappeared just as more appeared. "That was a pretty neat trick with the cards at the casino. How did you manage to get past Dervish's blockade?"

"Trade secret." He shrugged. "Any tech-head at East/West can give you chapter and verse. What *I* need to know right now is what you want to do."

Konstantin frowned at him, confused. What was he asking her for—a date?

"Are you going to log out?" he said patiently.

"I didn't *get* that son of a bitch," Konstantin said. "If I can't prove he's got software capable of defrauding AR service providers, everything he put me through was for nothing."

"Very gung-ho," said Goku, freshening the fractal veil.

"Gung your own ho," Konstantin said irritably, not caring if she made sense. "I've been through it today and I'm not in the mood. That's the only charge anybody's gonna take seriously against this guy. He's got his ex so crazy she thinks he changed into a conscious digital creature that never leaves AR and has unlimited power to make her life miserable. You saw what he did with me, so God knows what he can do to anyone else on a whim. I think he's just getting started. The fact that he can't physically *touch* anybody, let alone kill someone, could have him going in and out of court on a conveyor belt—mostly out, I'd bet. But let it out that someone's developed the AR provider's worst nightmare, the decoy time-sink, and everyone'll be paying attention."

Goku didn't say anything.

"What?" she said finally.

"Dervish gives every sign of being digital," he said. "Or of being so adapted to the digital environment he might as well be."

Konstantin stared at him. "How long have *you* been in? I know a cyborg who's convinced he's set his body free and he's going to spend the rest of his life in AR. Of course, that's easy to check with him—he's local. We've got his name and address because he filed an official complaint, and we can send someone around to check on him." Konstantin thought about it. Maybe she'd go herself, just for a change in routine. Besides, she wanted to see what someone who would choose to look like a cyborg looked like in real life. Someone other than Celestine, anyway.

"If you think Hastings Dervish is digital," she said after a bit, "maybe lowdown Hong Kong's put some weird shit in *your* head."

"Or maybe if you go fast enough long enough, you learn how to outrun your own shadow."

"The stuff of urban legends," Konstantin jeered.

"Prove it."

"Why am I arguing with you about this?" she yelled. "You told me you were looking into complaints that lowdown Hong Kong mound was raping people's minds—*your* term for it. I think Dervish is behind it, with or without Hong Kong mound's complicity. Spend half an hour at high speed with him jerking you in every direction, pushing you onto those carnival rides, you'll believe anything." She paused. "Is that what happened to you when you were the kid?"

He looked at her. "When did you see the kid?"

"I wasn't sure if it was you— you didn't recognize me. You stole an olive out of a martini, ate it and spit out the pit. I thought you were showing off."

"I was being jammed," he said. "I'd been chasing down some lowlife tourist in an expensive pre-fab kiddy-whore get-up. Stupid tourists go get that shit and they don't know what they're asking for. They're sure not ready for what happens to them, and the fuck-ass company that supplies them don't care. They're making too much money. Anyway, this one got away from me."

"Really," said Konstantin, keeping her voice neutral. "What were you going to do to her, or him? Or him/her?"

Goku gave a short laugh. "Just scare the jerk to death. At the time, I was really looking forward to it, too, so maybe it's just as well. You don't want to enjoy that kind of work too much, it makes you into something you'd never want to be. But I was all puffed up with self-righteous anger, and I got careless. I got jammed. I don't know how long it lasted—there's something about the white noise they use that scrambles your sense of time passing. But when I came to, or woke up, my suit had logged me out. But the kid had been busy running errands for someone. Dervish, apparently. He went and got all the information he needed on Ross."

Konstantin blinked. "Ross?"

"The arms dealer," Goku said patiently. "Didn't you know her name?"

"Right, yes, I did, yes. I just always thought of her as 'the arms dealer.'"

"That's another hazard in AR. You start thinking of people as *what* instead of *who*. And they start behaving that way. But that's a tirade for a more convenient time." He blew out another fractal crowd and looked at the cigarette. "I've got maybe two more clouds and then that's it, we're out in the open again. You want to get Dervish for defrauding his AR provider?"

Unbidden, Ogada's story about Al Capone rose up in her mind and, in spite of herself, she smiled. "Well, we sure can't get him on assault, rape, or aggravated mopery and dopery—"

"Yet," put in Goku.

Konstantin hesitated. She wasn't so sure about what disadvantages there would be in a system where they could, but there wasn't time to meditate on it now. "Maybe we can add tax evasion, just to make sure he's tied up for a while."

Goku looked impressed. "When all else fails, call the taxman. I wish I'd thought of that."

"Don't worry, you will."

He gave her a confused look.

"Nothing, nothing, old joke—you had to be there. Did you have a plan for putting Dervish in the money shot, so to speak?"

"It's a tough one," he said.

"One of us gets jammed. Or both of us."

"Both of us only if we're *very* unlucky."

"How does the one who picks the short straw get unjammed?"

Goku shot his cuffs, looking smug. "I've got some software."

"*You* do?" Konstantin gave him a look. "Then why didn't you use it when you got jammed?"

"It didn't work then."

"But it works now."

"It had better."

Konstantin let out a long breath. "You Phase 3 Interpol people are, as they say in post-Apocalyptic Noo Yawk Sitty, crazy motherfuckers."

Goku nodded. "Good thing we're on your side, eh?" He blew out a very thin cloud of smoke and tossed the cigarette over the side into the water. "OK, we're about to be really busy." He stood up and pulled Konstantin to her feet. They were approaching a floating dock several yards from the harbor itself. "The junk won't stop completely, so we'll have to jump for it. Be ready to move fast as soon as we hit." He frowned. "I mean *really* fast. You're going to have to turbo-charge the boost. The software should help, but a good part of it is sheer will."

Konstantin remembered her climb out of the elevator. "Spirit is willing," she said. She felt something funny spreading upward from the bottom of her jaw, and thought that another dose of numbing filler was kicking in. Then she realized that she was actually feeling wind on her face.

"Software," said Goku, watching her expression. "Better transcutaneous stimulation, more thorough. It associates more nerves so eventually your face gets tuned in. There's a lag sometimes between what you perceive and what you feel, but for the most part it's a lot better than nothing."

Before she could respond, he put his arm around her waist

and they were vaulting from the edge of the stern onto the dock. The landing was stiff enough to give her knee a twinge. She rolled over, stood up, and found herself standing outside Room 606 with the key in her hand.

To Konstantin's surprise, Room 606 was a regular hotel room of the utilitarian sort meant for business travelers who didn't stay anywhere for very long. Instead of a window, however, it had a smaller version of the multi-screen wall in her virtual office. Goku perched on the edge of the king-sized bed that took up most of the space, and picked up a remote. All of the screens went on at once; he scanned them quickly and then pointed the remote at the lower right-hand corner.

Konstantin watched herself entering room 909 from the hallway. The arms dealer crowded up behind her, as she remembered, but when she was suddenly yanked into the room, the arms dealer flew backwards, hit the opposite wall, and then fell through it and disappeared.

"The old switch-ola," Konstantin said, more to herself. "The real one. Where Dervish switched himself for the original."

The screen split into upper and lower halves, the latter containing a long, complicated read-out of figures Konstantin didn't understand. She looked questioningly at Goku.

"East/West's analysis says that program is neither fully human nor fully AI," he said.

"What program?"

"The one running the arms dealer. It would seem to be part Dervish and part AI."

"That's—" Konstantin bit down on the word *impossible*.

Goku gave her a half-smile. "That's . . . *interesting*, right?"

"Among other things. Where is she now, really?"

"Data says she's offline. Since she's in police custody, that's probably true." He aimed the remote at a screen in the left-hand corner. "Not the case with your friend Darwin. Data says he's offline now, and he's been offline for about twelve hours. The truth is, he hasn't been out of AR since I started watching him."

The image on the screen was a fetus about a month away from full-term. "Are you sure that isn't a decoy?" Konstantin asked, repelled.

"As sure as you can be about anything in here. He doesn't know he's a fetus. He doesn't know anything at the moment, because he's completely jammed. Every so often, Dervish unjams him and lets him frolic in his cyborg drag in AR, but he mostly keeps him in limbo. Whoever he is, he's not especially strong-willed and he's highly suggestible, so it didn't take long for Dervish to brainwash him."

"Jesus," Konstantin whispered.

"You were next," Goku told her.

"Me? Why me?"

"Because his ex-wife sicced you on him"—Goku shrugged—"probably. Also, the idea of doing a cop appealed to him as much as anything. Hastings Dervish really hasn't been out of AR for—well, I don't know how long. He's got some kind of intensive-care style set-up in Key West, mostly automated: intravenous feeding, catheters."

Konstantin made a disgusted noise. "How did you figure that out?"

"I'd like to tell you I calculated it all from watching his vital signs over a long period of time, but the truth is, I've got an old buddy who works on the island, and she pointed me at a service employee who was open to financial encouragement to talk."

Konstantin made an even more disgusted noise. "I think I know her. She wouldn't do that for *me*."

"She wouldn't have done it for me, either, if I'd asked her in the capacity of a law-enforcement officer looking for information on Hastings Dervish."

"Did she show you that squirt gun?"

"I'm the one she took it from. Anyway, Dervish doesn't bother trying to tinker with his own online time data. He just stays plugged in and, because it's Key West, he can go to hell in his own way. Which, of course, he would."

Konstantin took a long, thoughtful breath. "What if he isn't actually conscious?"

"You mean a fugue state or a trance?"

"Or he's been brainwashed, himself. What if he's just a front for a mob operation?"

Goku looked as nauseated as she felt.

"Think about it. How else could he get away with it? He's not some rich family's pampered golden boy; he's a placeholder. Who would allow a *placeholder* to indulge himself like that? Maybe he got the position because he was willing to wire up twenty-four/seven. *And* they told him he could have some fun with his ex on the side." Konstantin stared at the fetus on the screen. "Brainwashing a cop, that would be a good experiment. And if it went wrong, there'd just be Hastings Dervish, the lone gunman. For all we know, he might really believe he *is* a lone gunman." She paused. "Just how was he going to brainwash me, anyway?"

"They started the process after you went into room 909. All those falling intervals in between periods of relatively normal activity. About half a day of that, and most people would be a quivering mess."

"Well, it wouldn't have worked," Konstantin said. "I was getting used to it. If I ever had even a mild fear of falling, it's gone now. When this is over, I'll probably take up skydiving just to relax."

"After that would have come the jamming, while the boost was still in your bloodstream. How well do you think you'd have come out of that?"

Before she could answer, he stood up and aimed the remote at a screen in the center of the wall, which turned into a small window.

"Grace period's over. Dervish found us. Time for the next step."

"Which is?"

He picked her up easily and flipped her over so that she was stretched out over his arms face-down, as if he were going to teach her how to swim. "You dive through the center space."

"And then?" Konstantin asked.

But he had already hurled her forward and she discovered that the window in the center was not actually small but very far away.

19

Konstantin had been prepared for another long flying fall once she finally reached the window. Instead, she found herself back in the secret passage she had first discovered wearing the child persona from You (Not You), staring into a darkness interrupted by pinpricks of light from the many peepholes along the wall. Had Goku meant to put her here specifically, or had she just fallen through the nearest back door?

The back door, she realized. *The* back door for all of the casino, and possibly a good part of lowdown Hong Kong as well. If you were going to make what was essentially a virtual theme park, it made sense to utilize analog versions of certain theme-park maintenance methods. Maybe it was clumsier and slower in some ways, but it was probably a lot easier than stripping everything down to code whenever you needed to—

Her heart gave a sudden irregular flutter in her chest as she realized she wasn't alone.

Come on, she told herself. *You might have had a minor fear of falling, but you've never been that spooked by the dark.*

Something moved, briefly blocking out the light from a number of peepholes; a person, she realized, and closer than she had thought.

It's not the dark—it's what's in the dark. That's not fear, that's being a cop, remember? You were a cop once, before someone got the bright idea to turn you into a cartoon character.

She felt a sudden intense surge of loss and regret. Hell with it. When she was done with this case, she'd let Celestine and DiPietro handle TechnoCrime, and loan herself to auto-theft. She needed something *real*.

Something slightly more substantial than moving air touched her face, sending chills up the back of her neck into her scalp. She held perfectly still, waiting for whatever might come next. The waiting stretched from a few moments into half a minute. Konstantin felt her apprehension turn to annoyance. *God* damn *it*, she thought, *why is everything dragged out until you sweat blood? What is this suspense fetish?*

Something about the darkness changed, and she knew that whatever had been there with her was now gone. She sighed; it was probably nothing more than the venality of billable time at work. Drag everything to the last possible moment, so the mark finds it impossible not to stay in AR to see what happens next.

Never chalk up to conspiracy what can be explained by stupidity or greed or both. Who had said that? In AR it was doubly true, she thought, and started to move along the passageway. Being adult-sized now, she had a much wider choice of peepholes this time. Would there be a much wider choice of sights as well, or just a greater number of kinky rooms? More spiky hair, more slit skirts, more executioners and willing victims. Why on earth would you go into AR simply to stand in line for your own execution? Even if someone could tell her, she doubted that she'd understand.

I'm in the dark and I don't understand much of what's going on. Almost like being in love.

The thought gave her pause and then she kept moving, wondering what she could find here that would be useful in proving her case against Dervish. Probably an exit—

Probably? This was the back door. From here, she could find Dervish's main node, she realized. She wouldn't be able to interfere with the connection between the node and Key West, but she could log his use of the jamming program from the node, and prove it that way.

All she had to do was figure out what his node would look like, and then figure out how to activate a logging program. Or, as her ex used to say, *If we had some eggs, we could have some ham and eggs if we had some ham.* Yeah, that was almost like being in love, too.

No, everything *was* there. She just had to identify it. And this time, she reminded herself, she was on a faster level, with access to more information. Things wouldn't necessarily look the way they had when she'd been here in her kid outfit. She put her eye to the nearest peephole.

And, then again, she thought as she looked at the woman in the slit skirt lying on the bed, she could be wrong about that.

No kid with hair spikes, though; she looked around the room as well as she could, but the woman was the only one there, and she seemed to be asleep. Or comatose. Or, Konstantin thought, after watching to see if her torso would move even a little, non-dead. No breathing—none at all.

Cutting corners? Just a case of just having so many different things to control that certain details got left off? Dervish was digital and digits didn't breathe?

She put a hand on her chest, feeling her own respiration. *You've got to turbo-charge the boost,* Goku had said. But how— by hyperventilating?

No . . . by being quick enough to act between one breath and another.

The image of the fractal clouds Goku had blown around them came to her almost like a cloud itself. Breathing techniques, meditation—not the nap-on-a-pallet-under-the-desk stuff but the mystical control of yogis and fakirs. She knew nothing about any of that.

Then it looks like you'll be getting on-the-job training.

Oh, sure thing—she could simply take up, on the fly, practices it took a lifetime to master, assuming you could even learn them at all, just because she was in AR. Hell, she didn't even know if she was right about—

You're right. You know you're right because it's easy for Dervish and practically impossible for you, and that's how these things usually work. You're right because you have to be faster than you ever have been, and that's as fast as you can *be. And even if you're wrong, it's more right than standing in the dark doing nothing.*

She drew back from the peephole, her hand still pressed against her chest. So how did you even start? Did you first slow down your breathing while you tried to figure out what it meant to exist fast?

Pray, and fast.

She'd thought it was a joke, a bad pun, and it was ... but that wasn't all it was. Pray: concentrate. Fast: abstain. But abstain from what?

Deep inside her mind, she felt a sensation like diving through very deep water, deeper than was usually safe without some kind of protection against the pressure. It was an odd sensation but at the same time there was something familiar about it, as if she were discovering some talent she'd been aware of only on a subconscious level, something she'd been born with but had never used until now. A sense-memory for something she had no conscious memory of?

Come on, boost *yourself up out of that elevator. You're the one who said Tarzan was a girl.*

She was afraid she'd blown it by mixing the idea of lifting herself up with the sensation of diving, but somehow it seemed to be the right thing. Suddenly she felt less confined in some way, as if the limitation of acting between breaths had actually countered the whole idea of limits altogether, canceling it completely.

Contradiction can also mean balance, stability. Come on, Tarzan, let's swing.

There was a fast flash of light, an image that passed just that much too quickly for her to register, followed by another, and then another.

One at a time won't do the job. You can't get a whole picture one pixel at a time.

One room with an executioner. One with an expensive whore. One filled with impossibly fabulous things to eat that no one would ever taste. One where the characters go to rest between demands. One with an eye looking back at you, but this time not fast enough to catch you. And one, and one, and one, and one, and one—

She stood back from the peepholes in the darkness, looking at the constellation they made. Was her vision not big enough, or still too slow?

The wall behind her was soft. Or she was soft. Both, yes. And she was getting ... not *bigger*, exactly, but that was the only word she could think of to describe it.

You know how time is there to keep everything from happening all at once?

Someone, she realized dreamily, was talking to her. Someone she had known once. *Space has its equivalent barrier.*

Definitely coming from outside herself. This was not the sort of thing she ever had on her own mind.

But when you're digital, those boundaries don't exist. Not in the same way.

Konstantin felt the familiar impact of the mental speed bump, but she was going too quickly for it to matter. *What did the Buddha say when he met the hot-dog vendor in the park?*

Make me one with everything.

For once, panic worked *for* her. She leaped the chasm to her next breath, and inhaled.

At the top of her breath, everything slowed again. *No,* she thought and tried to exhale.

You let time pass. Maybe more time than you can afford. Now you'll have to be even faster.

She was about to protest that that was impossible, but she was already doing it. She was faster than her own shadow, faster than her own pixels—they appeared to her now like pebbles. They multiplied, enveloping her so that even the smallest movement on her part had her swimming through them. They struck sparks against each other trying to make a coherent picture for her but she was too fast to see it, too fast for it to catch up with her and hold onto her, nail her down and keep her there.

She reached through the fire opals, into the densest part where they would have appeared to her to be all jammed together if she had been any slower, and found Goku. As soon as she touched him, he was out, and she had something else in her grip.

You can't jam someone who's dosed the same way you are.

Your problem, however, is that old chestnut about how, when you have the bear, the bear also has you.

If she ever saw real daylight again, she was going to swear off metaphors, especially the ones her ex had left lying around with the in-jokes.

You can swear off right now. Dervish is digital. That's no metaphor. He forms, he re-forms. He morphs, he torques, he crawls on his belly like a reptile and *he's both commutative and associative. He can be Dervish-plus, or even Dervish-minus, though Dervish-plus is better.*

He passed through her, their components occupying the same area, but without touching because she was moving as fast as he was.

Oh, come on. Konstantin-plus would be an improvement. You'd like it. You owe it to yourself to try it.

Not Konstantin-plus-Dervish, no thanks.

Afraid you'll like it too *much? You are afraid, aren't you?*

Something somewhere hurt. She wasn't sure whether it was her pain or his, or something else entirely. Maybe it was just some damned metaphor.

It's a different kind of pleasure. Bypass those unreliable body parts, go straight to the good stuff.

This time, the mental speed bump would have rattled Konstantin's teeth, she thought. *That* was it? The whole thing, for Dervish, had been about nothing more than achieving a better method of *gratification*? *That* was the sum total of his ambition?

You know what they say about the banality of evil.

Konstantin willed herself higher, pushing her way up out of the elevator again. There was a new presence, or rather an additional one, and she was almost going fast enough to sense it in full now, *almost . . .*

You have to stop. You can't come here. Or rather, you can, but once you do, there's no going back. Not in the usual way.

It was the same presence she had felt in the dark hallway, she realized. Except it hadn't actually *been* there as much as it had just been looking in on her. Sort of. Now she was almost to where it was—

Where *she* was.

And will remain.

The realization that flooded in on Konstantin brought with it a feeling of new weight, or old weight having returned, a heaviness, a burden that began to slow her down. And something somewhere definitely hurt.

You can come out now, Konstantin told her.

I am out. *Never mind, I'll wait till you get back. And by the way, detective—*

People on the shore of the fire opal lake were shouting something to her, but Konstantin was reasonably sure there was no race involved. At least, she wasn't going very fast.

The opals diminished to sparks, little tiny points of light in the darkness. And then the darkness turned inside out and resolved itself into white with black dots. The black dots were in the ceiling tiles in her cubicle.

Taliaferro was cheering her on. He was yelling anyway. She watched, amazed, as he raised his fist and brought it down hard on her chest.

—you can breathe now.

20

It's too soon, Dervish is digital, Dervish is still *digital,* she kept saying as they did things to her, moving quickly, although nowhere near as quickly as she had been moving before Taliaferro had come in and started punching down on her like a bowl of rising bread dough.

Thought you were off metaphors.

That's a simile.

Dervish is digital, and that's literal.

She kept telling them and telling them. Sometimes she could hear her own voice saying it aloud, so she knew she wasn't talking too quickly to be understood. Or too slowly, for that matter. Her voice was OK. It was everything else that was a shambles. Spatial barriers were back, but they felt funny, as if they'd been rearranged. Time was also in force, keeping everything from happening at once, but things were happening in the wrong order, out of sequence. It was difficult, but she finally managed to make someone understand that. And someone responded by telling her that it would all look better tomorrow morning.

"It does look better," she told Taliaferro. "But it feels a lot worse. You cracked one of my ribs, you big brute."

Taliaferro's face in the monitor next to her hospital bed was solemn. "You got off easy."

"Which makes me luckier than Hastings Dervish, I can tell you that. Call East/West, ask for Goku what's-his-name—"

"Mura," supplied Taliaferro.

"Right, Goku Mura. Mura got him dead bang. Mura had anti-jamming software, we can prove in a court of law that Hastings Dervish did willfully defraud—"

Taliaferro sighed. "You've been saying that in your sleep. Did it, did it already. Got in touch with Mura, everything."

"And?"

Taliaferro sighed again. "I'm going to have Mura call you and give you the whole story. It's just easier that way."

"Oh." She paused. "When I was talking in my sleep, did I happen to thank you for voluntarily entering not only a building but a little tiny room to give me CPR? Even if you did crack my ribs."

"If you're thanking people, thank Goku Mura for contacting me and telling me your vitals were flatline." He smiled, a little sadly she thought. "And it was only one rib. A tap wasn't enough. I had to pound you a few times."

"Thank God you tell lame jokes. It hurts to laugh."

Mura didn't call. He came to see her in person instead.

At first, she thought it was her eyesight. After a few minutes she realized why Goku Mura looked blurry to her in person—real life just didn't have as high a resolution as AR. Perhaps that *was* her eyesight after all, but suffering only in comparison to a standard that had crept up on her without her noticing.

Besides looking a little blurry, he was also paler and gawkier. The easy physicality of his movements and posture had been, apparently, all software. Not that Konstantin felt especially critical. If anything, it was more of a relief to find out the James Bond suave had been left behind in AR. If he'd borne too much of a resemblance to the gambler she'd first seen in the lowdown Hong Kong casino, her resulting inferiority complex might have killed her.

"When your partner called me," he began in his soft voice, "I knew that I would have to come here and talk to you in person."

Konstantin nodded. "Under the circumstances, I think I'd have done the same."

"But perhaps it's not what you were expecting."

"I'm not sure what you mean," Konstantin said after a moment of hesitation. "What am I expecting? I wasn't expecting you to come in person."

"I mean what you're expecting to hear," he said.

"Well, the parts I don't know, I don't know what to expect," Konstantin said, apprehension starting to build in the pit of her stomach. "You can tell me those and I'll tell you how little I expected."

Goku Mura looked pained, and Konstantin's apprehension turned to nausea.

"OK," she said. "Just tell me. Get it over with. We're not going to make a case against Hastings Dervish, are we."

He shook his head.

"Because it's just too . . ." she floundered, trying to find a word, ". . . preposterous?"

"Dervish is not digital," he said gently. "Dervish is dead."

The words fell to the floor of her mind with a thud and lay there. *Dead. Dervish. Dervish is dead.* He sat silently in the chair next to her bed and didn't try to hurry a response out of her, which she appreciated.

"Someone's seen the body, then?" she said after a bit.

He nodded. "There is most definitely a corpse, and it has been positively identified as Hastings Dervish."

"Well, there you go," she said. "The first thing I'm going to do when I get out of here is visit a few narcs and inform them that it is, in fact, possible to get yourself more than slightly dead in AR. I almost did, and Dervish went all the way."

Goku shook his head. "Dervish died while he was logged into AR, but not because he simply stopped breathing, as you did."

"No? What happened?"

"He was murdered."

Konstantin couldn't speak.

"The story from Key West is that a trespasser, an alien looking to enter the United States illegally, happened to fetch up on Hastings Dervish's beachfront. After breaking in and helping herself to some food, she was exploring the rest of the house, looking for valuables, when she came upon Hastings Dervish all done up in his hotsuit and headmount. The sight scared her so much she pulled a gun and shot him."

"Lone gunwoman, huh?" Konstantin said.

Goku smiled slightly. "Exactly. There has been no suggestion that any formally or even informally organized crime group was financing various developments in software and mind-control techniques and had decided the stooge they were using as a front was becoming far too high-profile such that he might have managed to get himself directly connected to a felony crime committed while resident in Key West, thus making him and all his associates vulnerable to an investigation."

Konstantin blinked. "Really. No one's even tossed that out as a theory?"

"Hard to believe, I know."

"Well." She took a breath and let it out, automatically putting a hand on her chest to feel it move. "I realize prosecuting a dead man is one of those . . . difficult cases, but wouldn't your anti-jamming software justify at least confiscating Dervish's set-up, including *his* software?"

There was a short pause. "The anti-jamming software didn't work."

"What do you mean, it didn't work? You got out."

"*You* got me out. You and whoever was helping you. Was that Celestine or DiPietro?"

Konstantin stared past him, unsure what to think. "Neither."

"Oh." Goku looked troubled. "I suggested to your Ogada that he put you and the one helping you in for a commendation."

"*My* Ogada is not even a concept. I don't know what he'll put me in for. Competency tests, maybe." She rubbed her forehead. There was something reassuring about being able to touch your own face, your own head, which you couldn't appreciate until you'd spent too many hours headless in AR. "What are we left with?"

"Nothing."

"That much?"

"Dervish being digital was a flop as an idea."

"But . . ."

"And I'm afraid that the only log anyone has of *your* activities from the time Dervish cut you off from Taliaferro, and any other communication outside lowdown Hong Kong, would be suitable only for the kinkiest of adult networks."

Konstantin felt the blood draining out of her face.

"So I've been told," he added quickly. "I didn't see it."

"Even if you did, lie to me and tell me you didn't," Konstantin said darkly.

"It is generally acknowledged by all concerned as a clever fake."

"Has it been destroyed?" Konstantin asked skeptically.

Goku didn't answer.

"All right, I can look into that myself when I get sprung

from here." She gave a short laugh. "What about *your* log? Are you a porn star too?"

He shook his head. "My log is one long blank. Mechanical failure or something."

"Never mind. I still have a report to make. I can raise some questions—"

"They're going to claim that you stopped breathing because of an allergic reaction to one of the fillers in the boost you ingested."

Konstantin groaned and looked at the ceiling. There were no answers up there. "I'll kill those narcs." She paused. "Maybe *they* really *were* trying to kill *me*."

"Why would they do that?" Goku asked, looking sincerely confused.

"Never mind. It's too preposterous, even for AR." She wiped her hands over her face. "I can't believe this. I'm sitting here in a hospital bed after having nearly died in an investigation, and I've come away with *nothing*."

"Your Ogada—I mean, your boss Ogada seems to anticipate a fight from you about that."

"At least he's right about that. I wasn't the only one involved besides you. There's a cyborg named Darwin who got brainwashed, and a fashion designer named Susannah Ell who would swear to anyone that Dervish was digital, she being the one who told me in the first place." She looked at Goku. "They aren't . . . dead or something, are they?"

"No," said Goku. "But you seem to have forgotten that everything people say in AR is a lie."

Konstantin looked at the ceiling again, but the answers still weren't up there. "Why?"

"Because anything unexplainable is unacceptable? Because the only thing that *really* happened in the real world was someone shooting Hastings Dervish? Because too much depends on the testimony of a cop who was under the influence of an illegal drug at the time? Because the faked porn footage of said cop would be too devastating to the department's image and credibility, even if it were proved to be fake? And how fake is it really, since she already admits to being on drugs?" Goku shrugged. "Or because AR service providers and certain parties with addresses on Key West pooled their resources to pay to have the whole investigation paved over, each for their own excellent reasons?"

Konstantin shook her head. "Which?" she said.

"Take your pick," Goku said. "Whatever the reasons might be, they all come down to one thing—four out of five, or five out of six, or eighteen out of nineteen people directly affected by this investigation believe justice is best served by explaining everything away and closing the file."

"Eighteen out of nineteen?" Konstantin said. "Or eighteen out of twenty?"

"That's nine out of ten, actually."

"Yeah. I know."

After another long and very awkward silence, Goku stood up. "I shall come and see you again tomorrow. It's no trouble." He frowned thoughtfully. "I want to thank you for being able to unjam me when the software failed."

Konstantin shrugged.

"I would not have stopped breathing as you did," he went on, "but it was a very unpleasant experience. It has triggered a depression in me that will take some time to . . ." His voice trailed off and he spread his hands.

"Come back tomorrow morning," Konstantin said. "Taliaferro can send us over some blueberry pancakes for breakfast. I've been told it helps."

Goku nodded. "I accept." He started to leave and then paused at the door. "P3I is hiring."

"I'll keep that in mind," said Konstantin.

Some weeks later, Konstantin paid a visit to the maintenance facility where the Japanese woman slept on. She was sorry to see that the woman's body had started a more definite curl toward the fetal position. Perhaps it was only inevitable that everything should look explainable . . . kayfabe.

She considered whispering something in the woman's ear but, in light of everything that had happened, she found herself at a loss for words.

All for the best, she reflected. A lifetime ago, Featherstone-haugh had warned her against admitting to anything outside of AR. All things considered, it was probably the best advice she was going to get, in this life or any other.